Praise for *The Ti*

"Will Leitch has written anot[...] novel that I could not put down. What [...] amazing writer is his keen eye for what makes us human, all the seemingly invisible threads that connect us and those shocking moments when we're pulled together and forced to reckon with the world. Leitch is as empathetic a writer as they come, and I trust him to guide me through any danger, any story, and know I'll come out of it with something special."

—Kevin Wilson, *New York Times* bestselling author of
Now Is Not the Time to Panic

"With kindness, empathy, and the generosity of spirit that is the hallmark of his work, Will Leitch takes seven very different characters and brings them vividly to life, skillfully weaving their fates in a story that is taut, surprising, and ultimately speaks to the character of America itself."

—Jenny Jackson, author of *Pineapple Street*

"Leitch touches on issues of historical concern as well as current social ills as the suspense builds toward Tina's misguided, violent attempt at settling scores in a game she may not totally understand. Humor and empathy propel Leitch's characters toward their fates."

—*Kirkus Reviews*

"Leitch's panoramic narrative hopscotches back and forth between the viewpoints of his characters as they go about their daily routines, oblivious to their impending fates. Leitch brings a Chekhovian economy to the storytelling—Tina's guns are mentioned in the first act, and they indeed go off before it's all over—but his emphasis is on the humanity of all involved. It's an all-too-plausible slice of life."

—*Publishers Weekly*

THE TIME HAS COME

A NOVEL

WILL LEITCH

HARPER ● PERENNIAL

NEW YORK ● LONDON ● TORONTO ● SYDNEY ● NEW DELHI ● AUCKLAND

HARPER PERENNIAL

A hardcover edition of this book was published in 2023 by Harper, an imprint of HarperCollins Publishers.

HarperCollins books may be purchased for educational, business, or sales promotional use. For information, please email the Special Markets Department at SPsales@harpercollins.com.

FIRST HARPER PERENNIAL EDITION PUBLISHED 2024.

Library of Congress Cataloging-in-Publication Data has been applied for.

ISBN 978-0-06-323852-7 (pbk.)

24 25 26 27 28 LBC 5 4 3 2 1

TO WILLIAM AND WYNN

THERE WAS THIS FUNNY THING OF ANYTHING COULD HAPPEN
NOW THAT WE REALIZED EVERYTHING HAD.

—Raymond Carver

THE TIME HAS COME

10. THE FINAL MISSIVE

Today's the day. This is what I've been building up to—this is what *all this* was always pointing toward. Part of me cannot believe the day has come. Part of me cannot believe I made it.

It is important, here at the end, that you understand that I am of sound mind. I come to you clearheaded, sober, with all my faculties intact. Know that I stand here before you, on the cusp of this, entirely aware of what I'm about to do, the ramifications of it, all that you will all say, all the motivations you will ascribe to me. You will claim that I am crazy, that I am delusional, that I was "disturbed."

You'll be right on that last one: I am disturbed. Aren't you disturbed? How can you look around at everything and not be disturbed by . . . all of it? Disturbed is putting it *lightly*. We are all disturbed. It's a disturbing world right now. To be disturbed is to be human.

It is my hope that there will be people who understand. Perhaps not at first. It'll be shocking at first. I'd be shocked by it, if I were coming across it on the news, if I were just hearing about it for the first time. But when people get past the initial shock, when they take a step back and realize what was going on, what I was trying to do, what he and his family were doing, what I was trying to *stop*, I do believe there will be people who understand, who will be able to put themselves in my shoes and say that they would have done the same thing. Though it doesn't really matter. As long as I stop it, as long as I expose it, I've done what I set out to do. I will have made a difference. Whether *you* understand is beside the point. I'm just trying to help. That's all I can do, all any of us can do: I can just try to help.

It is sad that it came to this. It hurts just to say any of this out loud. This is the end for me, one way or another. Nothing will be the same after this—Every decision I've made, everything that's ever happened to me, every person I've ever known. This will not only be the defining moment of my life, it will be the defining moment of everyone else's. Mom's, the neighbors, the teachers I used to work with, my ex-boyfriends, those weird distant relatives out in Alabama, everybody. They will all be asked what it was like to know me, if they ever could have seen something like this coming, and, you know, I'm not that sure I would like it if my cousin Ethel in Tuscaloosa said, "Oh, yes, I always assumed Tina would storm into a place, guns blazing, at some point." I hope she'll be surprised. I am sort of surprised myself.

I've had to make peace with the fact that I'm about to lose much of what I love. I know they'll never let me see Mom again. Even if I make it out of this, they'll never let me back in her facility, and they're certainly not going to wheel her to wherever I'm locked up. And I've made my last trip to Sue's grave. I went by today. I placed a couple of the little peonies I've been growing on the front porch on her stone. I took the two prettiest ones. The others are going to wither and die without me.

I'll miss so many of the little things. I've eaten my last chicken salad sandwich from Marti's at Midday. I've watched my final episode of *Game of Thrones*. I won't get to sit at the dog park again, just reading a book and being delighted by every puppy, so happy they finally get to run run *run*. You know what I'll miss? Movie theaters. I love to sit in the second row, right in the middle, and just lean my head back and get lost in whatever place the movie takes me. For two hours, sitting in the darkness, I am someplace else, someone else, just traveling through space and time.

I've seen my last movie. I know that. I am not pretending otherwise.

But I have already lost so much. What more can be taken?

It must be done. He, and that family, must be exposed. I have been planning for this for too long, with so much at stake, to back out now. Who am I if I cannot do this? That place, that building, those people, that *family*, they have gone too long without answering for their crimes. They have hurt so many people, they have gotten away with so much, they have grown wealthy from the suffering of others. No one has ever stood up to them. Not the leaders of this town, not those they've hurt, certainly not my mother or anyone else whose lives they ruined.

But I can. I can stand up to them. I can help. I can stop them. I can let people know about them. I can end this.

I am scared. I am very, very scared. But know that I do this for you, for them, for her, for all of us. *I have to help.*

Whoever reads this, then, please get these details correct:

My name is Christina Elizabeth Lamm. I go by Tina, though my students all called me Miss Lamm, or my nickname, Mommy Mario.

I am thirty-nine years old and live in Athens, Georgia.

I am the Tina Lamm who served as a fourth-grade teacher at Fox Mountain Elementary School in Watkinsville and Murray Elementary School in Athens.

I am of sound mind and body.

I am the one who entered Lindbergh's the evening of June 24.

The weapon I was carrying was bought legally. You will find my license among my important papers, in the briefcase containing my passport, the title to my home, and my last will and testament.

No one else was involved in this plan. I acted alone. I am the only person who should be held responsible.

There is nothing anyone could have done to have kept me from doing this, short of stepping up and stopping what was happening at Lindbergh's themselves.

There is a stray neighborhood cat here in Five Points named Piggy that I feed every morning. Please make sure this cat is cared for.

I love my mother. I miss my sister. I wish all of this had turned out differently.

So: the time has come. I wish you well. I hope you all understand.

June 24

THEO

6:14 a.m.

Even when he was a kid, Theo had never thought the drawing looked anything like him. There surely hadn't been a single day in his life when he had not seen the drawing in one way or another. Maybe it was on a T-shirt worn by a Lindbergh's employee, or on one of the old lunch boxes that Athens children had carted to school every day for decades, or of course on the bright fluorescent sign above Lindbergh's, which got a fresh upgrade every five years or so but never once dared to deviate from that signature logo. Everywhere he had been, everywhere he was, everywhere he would ever go, that sign felt like it was shining above him, little Theo locked in forever as a smiling five-year-old with a lollipop and a pet terrier sitting eagerly at his feet. In real life, his parents never even let him have a dog.

The drawing was the work of Jack Davis, the most famous cartoonist in Georgia, which for most of Theo's life might as well have meant that he was the most famous cartoonist in the world. Everybody has seen Jack Davis's work, even if they don't realize it. He is most well known for being one of the founding cartoonists for *MAD* magazine, creating grotesque yet weirdly accurate satirical drawings of celebrities. He once said that he learned to draw by listening to Bob Hope and trying to draw what his voice sounded like; everyone in his drawings had big oval heads and skinny little legs and looked like they were deeply amused by a joke only they understood. (He's the guy who did the poster for the movie *The Bad News Bears*.) Davis had gone to the University of Georgia on the GI Bill, and even though he became a national celebrity as a cartoonist, as much as anyone can become a national celebrity as a cartoonist, he was a Dawg at heart. After he'd made his name in New York City he moved back to Athens, where he split time between there and St. Simons Island, where all the old rich white people ended up who wanted New England, but in Georgia. Davis died in 2016 but remains such an icon in the state that when you walk through Hartsfield-Jackson Airport in Atlanta, all the TSA advisory signs—COVER YOUR MOUTH WHEN YOU SNEEZE or PLEASE EXIT THE TRAM TO YOUR LEFT—feature his drawings with them.

And Davis *loved* Lindbergh's. He was old college buddies with Buddy Lindbergh, Theo's grandfather, and they spent every Sunday golfing and fishing together. Buddy was Athens royalty as much as Jack Davis was. He had been a football star at Athens High, flown bombers in World War II, and returned home after we won the war to marry his high school sweetheart Marie, who'd been waiting for him. Buddy said he got the idea for Lindbergh's because he was looking for a place where all his old friends could just gather and have coffee and cigarettes together, and when Marie told him she wouldn't let him own a tavern, he decided on a drugstore. Lindbergh's Apothecary was founded in 1948 as a true mom-and-pop soda-fountain pharmacy, with a griddle and milkshake machine and countertop and spinning booth chairs that gleamed in the sunlight but still creaked when you turned around, even back then, when they were brand-new. In the early days Lindbergh's had everything, including a little barbershop in the back, but more than anything else, it was truly that gathering spot that Buddy had imagined. Old men would sit and smoke all day, college kids would come in for root beer floats, ladies would shop for beauty products in the back, children would scamper through the front door after school. Your whole life was there. Your parents bought your diapers there. You got your shots for mumps and polio there. You stole your first condoms there. You picked up all your prescriptions there, at the pharmacy in the back, behind Buddy's favorite private joke, a black metal door fashioned out of metal he'd saved from a plane one of the members of his squadron had shot down over the Pacific Ocean. Every time you went in, the same men would be sitting on stools at the soda countertop, a little older each time, but always there.

Buddy sat behind his counter and door and watched it all happen. He and Marie had only one son, named Jack, after his old college buddy, and Buddy started training Jack to take over Lindbergh's for him essentially the day he was born. Jack did what was expected of him: he went to school at Athens High and college at UGA, and he was working for Buddy the first Monday after graduation. Jack spent a few years enjoying being a handsome young man in a college town before meeting Theo's mother, Betty, who had just moved to Athens for graduate school in economics, the only woman in her class, not that she ever mentioned it, or allowed anyone else to. After she graduated, they married, and all she got to use her degree for was to balance Lindbergh's books while Jack worked alongside Buddy, wiping down the soda counter, filling prescriptions, grousing about how the Dawgs couldn't win the big one. Eventually Theo came along.

Jack Davis did the drawing when Theo was five. This was in the early nineties, when little drugstores like Lindbergh's were starting to feel the pressure from chains like CVS and Walgreens, and Jack and Buddy, who was starting to think about retiring anyway, decided they needed to double down on the local neighborhood aspect of Lindbergh's—the pharmacy with familiar faces that you and your family have known for generations, the place where a grilled cheese with bacon still costs a buck seventy-five, the place where you can get the medicine and treatments you need with discretion.

So: the drawing. Davis happily volunteered to do it. Lindbergh's represented everything he cared about in Athens, and Georgia, and really, America. (Besides, they made a chocolate malt that made him fall out of his chair.) So he made Buddy, Jack, and little Theo sit down for about an hour as he sketched them, and three days later he delivered the illustration. The counter, Lindbergh's famous counter, black door and all, sat at the center of the frame, and the three Lindbergh men stood in front of it. Buddy is on the left, grinning, smoking a pipe. Jack is in the middle, wearing a pharmacist's smock but holding a piping hot Styrofoam cup of coffee. And then there is the fake dog, and tiny Theo, looking less like a boy and more like a Little Rascals character, the lovable scamp you can't help but want to tousle the hair of. He even had freckles. Theo had never had freckles.

This was Theo, then, today and forever: That little kid, etched in the immortal stylings of Athens' beloved Jack Davis, representing all that Athens was and all the change it would soon be fighting against, the next generation of Lindberghs, the avatar for a future that, here at Lindbergh's, we assure you, will look just like the past.

Theo's life was locked in for him at that exact moment, no matter how he'd tried to fight it. He would try to leave, to make his own way. To study abroad. To hike the Appalachian Trail after graduation. To actually move away and try to open a hipster restaurant in Atlanta with fancy cocktails that he'd hand-picked all the cucumbers for. To push for a life outside the one destined for him by his last name. None of it was ever going to make a difference.

He realized that now. He knew he probably should have realized it long before.

As he jiggled through his pockets to find the key for the front door of one of the only family businesses still holding on in Five Points on a pleasant, cool, lovely Athens morning in June, he wondered why he'd tried to fight it so hard, and for so many years—how much trouble he could have saved himself, how much time he could have saved. Who was he trying to kid? This was who he was. He was a Lindbergh. He was the kid on that sign. He always would be.

He opened the door, walked his bike inside, and turned on the lights of Lindbergh's. He looked out onto Lumpkin Street, his street, and glanced up at the sign as he had done every morning that he could remember at this point. This was his life. Right up there. The least they could have done is let him have a real damn dog.

THE CALL HAD COME FROM BETTY—HE'D ALWAYS CALLED HER BETTY, NOT Mom; no one in the family, including him, was sure why—just before Christmas 2019. Theo had wrapped up his shift at Empire State South, the Atlanta restaurant he'd been filling in at after Dinner Party—the South Asian fusion restaurant everyone told him was a bad idea, but he was going to make it work, goddammit—closed down the previous August. The place had survived exactly five months, which was two months longer than Jack had said it would, a fact that gave Theo more satisfaction than it probably should have.

Dinner Party had never really gotten off the ground. Theo wanted to rent out a space in the prime location of the Ponce City Market, where all the Atlanta yuppies and buppies gathered and looked fabulous, but he didn't quite have the capital (he was outbid by a Jamba Juice), so instead he made a bet on downtown, hoping the recent upturn in the area, thanks largely to the new Falcons stadium, would allow him to get in on the ground floor. But it was obvious now to Theo, as it had been to his friends and his father, that downtown Atlanta was not ready for a South Asian fusion restaurant, whatever that meant anyway (Theo had never even been to Asia, south or north), with intricately mixed cocktails, a jazz-club-inspired decor, and waitstaff that all dressed like fifties bobby-soxers. Theo's vision for the place was always a little hazy, even to himself: he told his girlfriend at the time that he wanted to "shake people out of their dining complacency," but she said that was bullshit, and he knew she was right. He just wanted something that was his, and only his, even if that meant a decor and menu that felt randomly spackled together, as if created by a Mad Lib. Anything that wasn't aggressively *different* felt derivative to Theo.

Theo had to have his own thing. But what did that mean, exactly? What did *his* truly mean? In his more honest moments, Theo had to admit he wasn't sure. (He wasn't even certain that he *liked* South Asian food.) And who in the world names a South Asian restaurant *Dinner Party*?

All told, though: it was the phone thing that did Dinner Party in. Why had he insisted on the phone thing?

Theo had once gone to see Dave Chappelle at the Fox Theater, and as he went through security, he discovered that Chappelle's policy was to confiscate all cell phones. They didn't *take* your cell phone. They made you place it in a pouch that, once the phone was in there, locked shut. You could take it into the show with you, but you couldn't open it; the pouch could only be unlocked by security once you left the theater. Chappelle had instituted this policy because his shows were being taped and posted to YouTube within minutes of him completing them, but what was most astounding to Theo was how, suddenly, *free* he felt without his phone. He found himself instantly alert—present. Chappelle's jokes were funnier. The crowd was more engaged. For the first time that he could remember, he felt connected to the strangers around him, and they felt connected to him. At one point, during intermission, he just struck up a conversation with a random guy while waiting for a drink at the bar, and they talked about the show, and their lives, and sports scores, and chitchatty normalities. Who cares what they talked about? What mattered was that they *talked* to each other. When was the last time that had happened? When Theo exited the venue, and security went to unlock his phone and give it back to him, he gave a big mock frown. "Aw, do you *have* to?"

So this was his big idea for Dinner Party: *No phones*. Dinner would not be two people occasionally looking up from Instagramming their plate, not at Dinner Party. You could sit across from your date, or with a group of old friends, and for once actually *be there*. Be present, be aware, be alert, be connected. It would be communal, a thoroughly engaged, even transcendent dining experience. This was Theo's big innovation. This was what he'd be remembered for, what would be uniquely *his*. People would be grateful. People would never forget how he'd reminded them what it meant to be alive.

The policy lasted precisely two nights. Everyone indulged him on opening night, because everybody there was invited and therefore knew and liked him. But when the place brought in actual customers, Theo discovered that explaining the phone policy— "You'll be present! You'll feel legitimate human connection!"— was roughly analogous to slapping them in the face the minute they walked in the door. The first four couples, once they understood what Theo was saying, turned right back around and left the restaurant. One woman threatened to call the police on him: "This man's trying to steal my phone!" They had a total of eleven customers that night. Nine of them interrupted their meals to ask for their phones back. Devastated, Theo reversed the policy on day three, but by then it didn't matter. From that point on, Dinner Party was the Restaurant That Took Your Phone. You should have seen the Yelp reviews.

After the restaurant imploded—and it had gotten so dire at the very end that Theo changed the name from Dinner Party to Lindy's, an obvious and desperate attempt to salvage his failed restaurant by leaning on the goodwill of his family name, which was of course the exact opposite of why he'd opened the restaurant in the first place—and left Theo owing more money than he thought possible, he bartended at Empire State South, whose owner was an old family friend from Athens who liked Theo and wanted to cut him a break. Theo wasn't cut out to be a bartender, though. He enjoyed the early part of the evening, when there were couples out on dates, groups of friends gossiping and catching up, but the end of the night, when the place got packed and became more of a social event space, that part had too much chaos for Theo. All those gorgeous kids, waving their dad's credit cards at you, rolling their eyes when you take too long, handing their drinks back to you with sour lips, *this isn't right*, and acting like you, personally, are standing in the way of their otherwise perfect night. Bartending felt like answering customer service phone calls, except everyone was right in his face, all of them drunk, mocking him with their perfect youth and their whole lives in front of them, constantly reminding him that everything he was doing was wrong and probably always had been. He appreciated the work during a period of his life that could be fairly classified as "transitional." But it was terrible, and it ate him alive. He'd started sneaking drinks himself just to make it all the way through his shift. First it was just for the final hour. Then it was halfway through. By December, he was doing shots before the dinner crowd got there.

That night, the night of Betty's call, Theo had sat on the sofa bed in the middle of his apartment, pouring himself a screwdriver and idly watching a West Coast basketball game. He had stopped going out after his shifts—he just went to work and went home and drank—and he hadn't seen most of his friends in several weeks. He and his girlfriend had broken up not long after the restaurant went under, and if she ever came by—of course she never would—she would find the apartment in the exact state she had left it. Theo hadn't even thrown away her toothbrush.

This was what Theo's life was in December 2019, and he always tries to remember this, to remember that as much as his life was upended by Betty's phone call, there really wasn't that much of a life to upend at all.

His mom's face lit up his phone. It was 1:45 a.m. Even in his haze he snapped to attention: 1:45 a.m. phone calls from your parents were never good news.

"Hey. Is everything OK?"

He heard Betty take a deep but hurried breath. He could tell she was trying to slow herself down. She did this when she was upset. His mother was upset a lot.

"It's your father," she said. "He said he wasn't feeling well when we went to bed, and when I got up to use the bathroom, I noticed . . ." She paused. She'd started talking too fast again. ". . . I saw he wasn't breathing. I tried to help him, but . . . oh, Theo, he's gone, Theo, he's gone, I'm so sorry." Theo would find out later that Jack had suffered a brain hemorrhage, out of nowhere; no doctor and certainly not Betty could have seen it coming. Something in his brain had just popped, and that was that. Jack had seemed indestructible to Theo, and really everyone who knew him. But he wasn't.

It was complicated, *it was very complicated*, but Theo loved his father, he thought, probably. He didn't feel any grief, though, not yet. He just wanted his mother to be all right. If he could calm her down, if he could make her less upset, if he could make her stop crying before the phone call was over, it would all work out, he would deal with whatever happened when she hung up the phone after she hung up the phone. He settled her, made sure she'd called 911, told her to have Martha down the street come by and sit with her until the paramedics got there. He said he'd be there in two hours, as quickly as Atlanta traffic in the middle of the night would let him. Then he went into the bathroom, splashed water on his face, brushed his teeth, packed a backpack with a week's full of T-shirts, underwear, and socks, grabbed his laptop, and drove back home to Athens.

He only went back to the Atlanta apartment one more time, a month later, for his television, to grab some bills and to return the keys to the landlord. There were no discussions about whether or not he would take over Lindbergh's. The morning after the funeral, Betty simply handed him the keys to the front door and said, "We'll be ready to open back up on Tuesday. You know your father's system. It should still work just fine for you."

And it had. The system had held up. Lindbergh's, when Theo took it over, was about to go through the most challenging year of its existence, from shutdown to fights about reopening to kids doing their remote learning at the tabletop to mask mandates to, eventually, Theo, who was not in fact a pharmacist and frankly had no business doing so, injecting some of his late father's closest friends with a life-saving vaccine. Theo had been there for every step of it, he'd been in charge of it, and he did it, to his surprise, effortlessly, like he'd been training his entire life for it, like it was all he'd ever wanted to do. He did it because he had to, he did it because no one else could, he did it because people needed him, and no one had ever really needed him before. This place, this Lindbergh's, it didn't feel like his, not by a long stretch. This was still Buddy's place, still Jack's place. Theo felt more like the care-taker at an old lighthouse, just making sure the beacon was still on, making sure no one crashed a boat into the place. He was good at it. But he'd navigated the storm. He was proud of the work he was doing here.

Was this it? Was this his destiny? He didn't think about that all that much anymore. It was all about just putting one foot in front of the other, every day, until you did it again tomorrow, and next thing you knew a week was over, and a month, then another. You get up at 5:15, shower, ride your bike to the store, unlock the door, look up at the sign, lament the dog, turn on all the lights, and head back to the pharmacy in the back to set up all the protocols for the day before Sandy shows up to take her spot at the register and Emily puts on her hairnet and fires up the grill. He loved to be here before anybody else. A little world, his little world, the lighthouse keeper, keeping all the various trains running on time.

Theo took a deep breath and poured himself a cup of coffee. He walked to his desk and pulled open the drawer to the safe he kept in the lower-right-hand cabinet. He put in the combination, 23-44-022, and took out a small ceramic case, one he'd made for his mother in middle school crafting class, with drawings of donkeys on it.

The case contained, in three neat rows of fifteen each, forty-five pills labeled OPANA, the brand name for oxymorphone. They'd stopped giving out Opana years before, when the FDA took it off the market after the opiate crisis exploded, and no doctor had prescribed it in years. But when Theo took over, more than eighteen months ago now, he found fifty full boxes of Opana just sitting on a shelf behind some old tax forms.

Theo, still a bit dazed back then, had opened a box and just popped one of them then and there. Lately, most mornings, he took two. He loved to be here before anybody else.

DOROTHY

6:21 a.m.

Dennis had always loved to have sex in the morning.

Dorothy giggled a little bit when the thought popped into her mind. How inappropriate! Here she was, still in her nightgown, in her front yard in East Athens, picking up the *Athens Banner-Herald*, feeding the neighborhood cat, watering plants, that poinsettia looks *fantastic*, an old lady doing old lady things. It surprised her how much she had aged in the last year or so. She supposed that's how it happened. You just keep stacking days together, and each one of them just feels like you being you, and next thing you know, you're old. Dorothy was in her thirties, and then her forties, and then her fifties, and she was always still herself. She drank a little bit too much wine with dinner, she'd sneak a joint when she went on her yearly trips to St. Simons with her friend Gwen, she was a little too judgmental of the neckline that one woman at the club was sporting, her husband would turn her over on Sunday mornings before they were really awake yet and you could hear the birds starting to stir and chirp and they would do it like when they were twenty-five and they were forty-five and they were sixty-five.

Sure, they didn't come home from parties or dinner all drunk and sweaty and engorged like they did when they were kids, but after a full night's sleep, Dennis was always ready and so was she. Maybe that's where the "old" part came in, feeling your most rowdy and randy in the mornings rather than at night. But he could still do it at seventy the same way he did when they first met. And so could she. Nothing old about either one of them in the morning after a full night's sleep.

She found herself grateful when these memories of Dennis arose. Those years had started to fade lately. That was happening too quickly, Dorothy thought. Dennis had only been gone about fifteen months, and even accounting for Dorothy's memory not quite being what it used to be, fifteen months shouldn't be enough time for any part of him to vanish. Was there a conversion rate? X years of marriage to y months of him being gone? Even if one year with him got away from her, say, each month, she'd have more than four years before he was gone entirely. Had she lost fifteen years already? It was possible. She didn't remember much of the nineties, now that she thought about it. Both of their children went to college then, she knew that part, but other than that, not much jumped out at her from that decade. Dennis just kept going back into court, as always, and she kept tending the garden and playing cards at the club and going to all the Dawgs games, as always. Maybe those were the parts that went first: the parts that weren't all that memorable in the first place. She found herself wanting to revisit them—not relive them, exactly, but maybe just having an old newsreel of the highlights run on a projector in the kitchen, fast-forwarding through the slow parts.

They were gone, though. Whatever happened, it no longer mattered. It was over.

She would hang on to those mornings while she could.

DENNIS WAS NEVER GOING TO RETIRE. BEING A JUDGE WAS ALL HE'D EVER wanted to do. He once told Dorothy that when he was a kid watching courtroom scenes in movies, he always paid more attention to the judges than the lawyers or the witnesses. ("Everyone's always trying to earn their approval," he told her. "You should try it sometime.") Every move he'd made in his life was resolutely focused on that goal, though when she met him while he was in law school at UGA, she didn't know that. He was just a guy who was going places. She'd been a waitress at the Grill in downtown Athens, idling, really, a little too old to be serving drunk frat boys but too young and indecisive to commit to anything that would limit her options moving forward, whatever those options might be.

He'd come in every weekday at 5:30 p.m. and order a black coffee and two eggs, sunny-side up. She was instantly smitten. He was so cute in his light-blue shirt that he kept buttoned all the way up to the top. He was the only Black student at the law school back then. There was something so casually precise about him. He spoke like an actor who had spent decades doing the same play and grown into the role so comfortably that every word felt coated in apple butter. His clothes were perfectly fitted, but he was so skinny they seemed to hang off him anyway. She'd never seen a person so clearly relaxed in his own skin, and so certain of the mark he was about to make on the world.

The first week he came in, he said nothing other than "Thank you" and "Have a nice day, ma'am," but the second week, she noticed he had started drawing pictures of little dogs on the checks he handed to her. Each one was a bit more complicated. Tuesday there was a litter, Wednesday there was a kennel, and by Friday the dogs were running their own society, with a solemn basset hound serving as mayor and an incorrigible beagle who kept robbing all the banks.

"Hey, so what's with all these dogs you keep drawing on my checks?" she said, flirting just the right amount.

"Thank God you finally noticed," he said. "I've been trying to get your attention all week. I figured dogs might help. Everybody loves dogs." He smiled. "Would you like to have dinner with me?" Oh, would she ever. They were married three months and six days later. It happened like that back then. Dorothy believed people would be a lot happier, and their lives a lot more pleasant and simple and easier to manage, if it still happened like that now.

She was also not wrong: Dennis was going places. He graduated near the top of his law class and immediately went to work for the district attorney's office in Clarke County. He was such an obvious star there that he ran for the top job and won it, at the age of thirty-five. By then he and Dorothy had their sons, William and Wynn, two years apart, and she quit her substitute teaching job to stay home with them and work on the garden. She didn't mind. She enjoyed teaching, but she didn't need a school to teach. She enjoyed having this life in front of her, every day a new challenge but one that always made sure you could color within the lines to resolve. Maybe one of the boys got in a fight in school, maybe one of them was worried about a big baseball game coming up, maybe one of the neighbors had fallen ill and needed her help. They were normal issues, and she dealt with them in normal ways. Dorothy had been raised to be strong, to make her mark in the world, and this was her way, she thought: by supporting Dennis, by making sure those boys were strong and proud, and by trying to be helpful to anyone who needed her. Life didn't need big dramatic moments because it was nothing *but* big dramatic moments, if you knew where to look for them. This was her purpose, just like that garden. Go out there and make everything a little bit better than it was the day before. Not perfect. Not transcendent. Just better.

The boys left for college, William to Yale, Wynn to Georgia Tech, quietly breaking their father's Dawgs-fan heart, the same year Dennis finally got the call: President Clinton nominated him as a US district court judge for the Northern District of Georgia.

And from then on that was just their life: Judge Johnson, his wife Dorothy, the garden, Dawgs games, important men coming over to shake her husband's hand, their wives whispering to

Dorothy how awful those men were in private, Dorothy trying to be empathetic but so grateful that wasn't her life. Then weddings for the boys, then grandchildren, those beautiful little girls, finally some girls in her life, and a new addition to the house, and a fortieth-anniversary trip to Kauai, looking over those cliffs and feeling like the world had spread out before her just exactly right, how lucky she was, what a break she'd caught. She'd never really made any plans and wasn't sure what she was going to do in the world, and then this handsome man in his button-up shirt showed up at her diner and drew her little dogs, and now here she was, in a place so gorgeous it felt like another planet, and she was holding the hand of the man she loved, who was doing exactly what he'd always wanted, and their boys were wonderful and their girls were wonderful, and sure the world was tough and scary sometimes but if you just stayed the course and just kept putting one foot in front of the other and were always kind to people and tried to be helpful, it would all work out, it would all end up fitting exactly right.

She remembered turning to Dennis, as the sun set over Poipu Beach, and taking his face in her hands.

"Thank you for this," she said.

Dennis chuckled. He was so good at deflecting all the nice things other people said about him, even though you knew he knew it was all probably true. "Lady, you're the only reason I do anything," he said. "There's no point otherwise." They went back to the resort, had a nightcap in a coconut, and fell asleep at 8:30. They had sex the next morning. They had sex every morning on vacation.

FOUR MONTHS AFTER KAUAI, DENNIS CAME HOME WITH A COUGH. HE'D been in Boston visiting Wynn, who was working for some biotech firm doing something Dorothy didn't understand, but had good benefits. Dennis's first night back in their house was awful; he'd stayed up half the night coughing and sweating. She got up and made him some tea and soup and scolded him for not taking a heavier jacket to Massachusetts in March. He was a little better the next morning, but still wobbly and groggy. Dorothy insisted he rest one more day in bed before heading back into court.

"You'll give them the same thing you've got if you go in there," she said. "They're not going to have to shut down the entire court system of Georgia if you call in sick one day." He groused at her, but his eyes betrayed him. He was too weak and clammy to wear the robe, and he knew it. Dorothy tucked him into bed, gave him some melatonin to help him sleep, and went to meet a friend for lunch. It was a bit of a business lunch, such as it was. The woman worked for the Athens Anti-Discrimination Movement, an organization Dorothy had long supported (as had Dennis, not that he could tell anyone, not in his position), and she was the featured speaker at an upcoming fundraiser. People always reached out to a judge's wife. It was a focused lunch, impressively so, and Dorothy came away feeling strong and useful, like having the sort of power she and Dennis had found themselves having wasn't so bad, wasn't bad at all. She went inside to change into her gardening clothes and found Dennis lying on the floor of their kitchen in his underwear. He had smashed his head against the countertop. There was a shard of glass from his spectacles embedded in his cheek. She could not get him to wake up.

The paramedics told her she could follow in the car behind them. She felt they were driving way too slow on the way to Athens Regional, and at one point she almost passed them before realizing that sort of defeated the point of following an ambulance. They took him to the ICU while she filled out paperwork, and after two agonizing hours, a doctor came out to update her. The doctor was accompanied by a surprisingly large number of people: a nurse she recognized from somewhere, as well as three people wearing suits and ties and looking grave and rattled. She also noticed they were all wearing masks, even the guys in suits.

The doctor told Dorothy that Dennis was "stabilized," but

that he was having serious problems breathing. They were considering putting him on a ventilator.

"Wait, I thought he had a heart attack," Dorothy said. She had assumed it was a heart attack. Dennis had always been healthy and fit, but her father had died suddenly of a heart attack, so anytime something happened out of nowhere, Dorothy immediately jumped to "heart attack."

"No, it's his breathing," the doctor said. She paused and made a confused face. "Well, if I'm being honest, it's a lot of things. Which is why, uh, we've all come out to talk to you." It was Dorothy's turn to make a confused face.

"Has Dennis, um, has he traveled anytime recently?" the doctor asked. "Any overseas trips?"

"He just came back from Boston?" she said. She realized she was saying it like a question even though she did, in fact, know he had just come back from Boston. Why did she do that? "Yes," she said, straightening her blouse and taking a deep breath to reset. "Yes, he just came back from Boston."

"Did you go with him to Boston?" asked one of the suits, a goateed middle-manager sort Dorothy instantly hated.

"No," she said. "Why?"

"I was wondering if you might like to come with us for a second," said the doctor, trying to look soothing under the mask, and failing. "We've got an open room over here."

"Wait, wha—"

"We can't have you in the waiting room," the goateed suit said.

The world went blurry. Dorothy could feel her legs buckle. Next thing she knew, she was sitting in a chair in a hospital room, drinking a glass of water, surrounded by the same people from the waiting room.

The doctor, still masked, was more in her element here, more in control of the situation. "Your husband, Judge Johnson, er, Dennis, he, well, he is very sick," she said. "His oxygen levels are dangerously low." Dorothy noticed that the doctor, while trying

24

to be reassuring, was slowly, almost imperceptibly, moving away from her. Dorothy had heard of the coronavirus, of course: Who hadn't at that point? But it was something in China, or Spain, or maybe even Seattle. It wasn't here. It sure wasn't in her Dennis.

"We need you to wait here while we run your test," the doctor said. "We just got in some test kits, so it should only be a few hours. Is there anyone else that lives in your home?"

"No," Dorothy said. It felt like someone had hit her in the forehead with an ax: there was nothing but light and a blast of cool air piercing the middle of her skull. "Can I see him?"

The doctor frowned and took another small step backward. "No," she said. "Absolutely not."

Dorothy closed her eyes and slumped out of her chair and onto a cot. They'd wake her two hours later. That wasn't a very long time, she'd think later. But it was enough time for Dennis to be gone.

THAT WAS THE WAY IT WAS, IN THE EARLY DAYS: IF YOU LOST SOMEONE IN March 2020, you didn't get to say goodbye, you didn't get to gather with loved ones to mourn, you didn't get to eat baked beans and corn bread the neighbors brought by while you shuffled awkwardly through that nice clean room in the house no one ever is allowed to sit in unless someone dies. You didn't even get to bury them. The best Dorothy got was a FaceTime video of some scared-looking EMTs wheeling Dennis's body out of his room. They told her Dennis was gone, they sent her home. They'd get a system down for this later, whether it was a Zoom-streamed incineration or even an actual funeral in which only the closest to the deceased were allowed to attend. But in March 2020, you got nothing. It was remarkable to Dorothy, when she thought back about it months down the road, that a month later her state's governor— she'd met him plenty of times, nice man, but plenty dim—would open up gyms and hair salons and movie theaters and buffets, and people could get tattoos and their nails done, which meant of course they could (and would) start doing pretty much everything else. In April 2020 you could go *fucking bowling*. But in March 2020 you couldn't even see your husband's dead body. You couldn't see him put in the ground. You just sat at home, alone, mourning, while everyone else who loved him—*my boys*—had to do the same thing. All the things that you're supposed to do when the person who is the center of your entire life dies, Dorothy didn't get to do any of them. They sent her Dennis's ashes in an urn, with a certificate. It sat at the center of the kitchen table for weeks, while flowers and bills piled up around it. She occasionally video chatted with her sons, who for weeks would have the same stunned, mouths-agape looks on their faces as she did. At least she thought they did. It was hard to tell over Zoom.

It was as if God had just simply reached down and plucked Dennis out of Dorothy's world. After years of being chased down by everyone who wanted a piece of Judge Johnson, she wouldn't see anyone other than the neighbors on either side of her home, and only from a safe distance, for months. She finally saw the boys in person for the first time over Christmas. They left the girls back home with their wives. It was still too soon.

And yet today, through it all, here she still was. Dorothy had had a lot of time these last fifteen months to sit in this house, and work on that garden, alone, and try to understand what had happened to her world and her home and this life that felt specifically, *palpably*, like the sun shone solely on her and the people she loved.

This is where she landed, fifteen months later: She was all right. There had been the wailing and the rending of garments in the early days, the nights she stared at the ceiling and thought about how loudly he'd be snoring right now, if he were still here. It was rough, to be sure. But she surprised herself. She did not start drinking heavily. She did not sit in the dark and scream. She did not spiral. She just did what she always did: she just kept stacking days together, just trying to go out there and make everything a little bit better than it was the day before. Not perfect. Not transcendent. Just better.

She began to draw. She hadn't drawn since she was a little girl, but she remembered she was good at it. When the schools shut down in the fall, she had volunteered to help with virtual education, even serving as a monitor at the YMCA for all the kids who didn't have wireless access at home and needed somewhere to log on for class. And somehow her garden had exploded. It had never looked better. She had even planted a peach tree.

A peach tree! She was proud of it, and of herself. She hadn't crumbled. She didn't know she had it in her, but she did. She still wasn't sure who she was in a world where she wasn't Judge Johnson's wife. It made her sad as the memories of Dennis faded, faster than she wanted them to, faster than they should. But she liked the direction this was going. There was something in her, she felt, that had maybe even been awakened a little bit. She was eager to find out what it was. This old lady wasn't done with the world yet. She might just be getting started.

It had all happened so fast. It was sometimes as if he had never been here at all.

1. AUNT MANDY

It was right in front of me the whole time. I just had to look. You know how that goes, right? It doesn't matter how obvious something is, how much it might be staring you in the face. If you're not looking for it, you're not going to see it. I didn't see it. I wasn't looking. But I see it now. Someday you all will.

There has always been something shady about the place, even when I was a little girl. I used to ride my bike up there after school down the road. I always loved to get milkshakes there, they made the best milkshakes. It was warm and pleasant and the sun always seemed to be shining inside there, even when it was raining. Which is why the door was so particularly scary. There was a counter that separated the diner and knickknacks part of the pharmacy and the *pharmacy* part of the pharmacy. Back there was where they mixed the drugs and gave the shots, where they wore doctor's smocks even though I'm pretty sure none of them were really doctors. To separate the two parts of Lindbergh's, there was a door. But it wasn't just any door. It was a big black metal door, locked and bolted, taller than it needed to be, taller than the average child, certainly taller than me. If you were to go in there today, as an adult, it might look just like any old door, albeit one painted a different color than the rest of the counter. But as a kid? As a kid it was massive and terrifying.

It made you wonder what was going on back there. Every kid had a theory.

I was a curious girl. I had to know. So one time, when we were having lunch there on my mom's break from work, I waited until she wasn't looking and, when they briefly opened the black door, I made a run for it. I made it past the lock but rammed straight into the man who owned the place. I didn't know it was him at the time. I just knew it was a tall man in a lab coat who wasn't letting me by. I wouldn't know it was the place's namesake until later—years later.

He bent down on one knee and said, "Whoa there." He had a kind face, because of course he did, we all have a face we wear, but he didn't let me past him either. My mom came and got me, and she apologized, and they smiled at each other, and she shuffled me out of there, and that was as far past the door I ever got. For now.

I didn't know back then, though. It was Sue, my sweet sister Sue, who had first gotten Lindbergh's stuck on my brain, years ago. It was because of Mandy.

Aunt Mandy was my mom's only sister, and neither of us ever got to meet her. Mandy was born about five years before my mom, and she had Down syndrome. Most of Mom's memories of Mandy were of her parents, my grandparents, fighting about how to take care of her. They loved her, but she required more work than either of them had necessarily signed up for. Which was why, when my mother was old enough, the job fell to her. They slept in the same bedroom, and Mom remembered staying up late watching *Gunsmoke* together and making up fairy tales as they stared up at the ceiling and fell asleep. "She was my best friend," Mom told us, in the sad way she told us everything. Mandy had the mental capacity of a child, but as she reached her teenage years, her body began to change like everybody else's. And that was a problem.

In 1937 the state of Georgia passed a law that made it the thirty-second—and last—state to allow "eugenic sterilization." The law, patterned after a California law in 1909, gave the authority for "psychiatric institutions" to perform forced sterilizations on "the mentally retarded or those afflicted with hereditary insanity or incurable chronic mania or dementia." In California, they actually had a "State Lunacy Commission" that decided who would undergo the procedure, but in Georgia it was a far more informal process. As you might expect in the South in between the years of 1937 and 1963, this became a way to target Black people. There was a North Carolina hospital that so regularly involuntarily sterilized poor Black women that the practice was given a colloquial name: a "Mississippi appendectomy."

If someone "retarded" like Aunt Mandy was deemed to be potentially sexually "of age and of desire"—and therefore a threat to reproduce—someone could report them to the Georgia Lunatic Asylum (actual name!) in nearby Milledgeville, and they would undergo the procedure.

One night, one of those nights when Mom came home from work, walked in the door, and just lay face flat on the couch without talking to us, we decided to ask about Aunt Mandy. We'd been looking at old family photos earlier and wondered why Mandy had just disappeared. Sue was always a little more curious than what was necessarily good for her. She couldn't help it. She always wanted to know.

"Hey, Mom, when did Aunt Mandy die?" Sue asked.

Mom groaned into the sofa cushion and didn't look up. She did that a lot.

"When I was about ten," Mom said, muffled. "It was complications of the surgery."

"What surgery?" I asked.

Mom wasn't sure whose decision it was to have Aunt Mandy's tubes tied at the age of fifteen, but she knew it wasn't her parents. "I get if they would have chosen that, lots of parents did, but they didn't," she said. But Mom said someone showed up at our door and said they had to do it—before she "becomes sexually active." Mom remembered that exact phrasing. Her parents loved their daughter. But they wanted to do what was right. And they did what the men at the door were telling them to do.

There were complications. She spent two weeks in the hospital. "She was never quite the same after that," Mom said. Mandy mostly stayed in bed when she came home, and one night, about a month later, she passed away in her sleep. She had many health issues, mostly heart related, as is often the case with kids with Down's. They chalked it up to that. Her heart just couldn't take it anymore.

Sue whispered it to me in our bed that night. "They killed her, you know," she said. "Someone called her in. I wonder if it was her doctor."

But I don't think it was her doctor. It was revealed years later that in many cases, states would enlist local officials to alert them to "mentally deficient individuals" that might need to be sterilized "before breeding ages." Sometimes it was doctors. Sometimes it was teachers. But often it was their pharmacists. They would receive a commission from the state for these "alerts," just a little money here or there, a thank-you for looking out for the common good. That's what these places were for, after all. They were there to serve the community.

The Lamms, like everyone else in Athens, had been going to Lindbergh's for generations. Everybody knew Buddy Lindbergh. Always friendly. Always smiling. Just like his son.

Sue always eyed the place warily after that story. So I guess you could say it was Sue who got Lindbergh's stuck on my brain.

JASON

6:48 a.m.

Jason's wife once joked that she was married to the only guy who admitted to thinking about sixteen-year-old boys when he was in the shower. Jason hadn't liked it when Helen made that joke. He'd blown his top, actually. It was a couple of years back, at a meet-the-teacher event at Oconee Middle School, where Abby, their twelve-year-old daughter, was about to enroll, and the teacher asked about what they did for a living. She was only asking about Jason, though. Everybody knew Helen. She was the top veterinarian in Watkinsville, the one who had been holding the hand of every pet owner when they put their best friends to sleep for a decade now, and she had recently performed successful gallbladder surgery on Miss Grierson's twelve-year-old cat.

Jason was the mystery. He'd come in straight from a construction project that had run late because his crew, those dipshits, hadn't shown up until noon, not that it mattered, since he spent most of the day cleaning up all the crap they'd messed up anyway. He floored it straight from the site and hadn't had time to run home to change clothes. So he'd showed up to the school in a pair of beaten-up old pants, a dirty camo Georgia hat, and, notoriously, a sleeveless T-shirt that read PRO GUN. PRO GOD. PRO LIFE. PRO TRUMP. He hadn't shown up to work wearing that shirt, just so you know. He had been wearing the company shirt, *his* company shirt, Waller Construction, but when that dumbass Tommy was filling up the gas canister to their truck, he stopped paying attention for a moment, like that dumbass always did, and sprayed Unleaded Plus all over Jason's shirt.

"Sorry, boss," Tommy said.

"You're a dumbass," Jason said.

Jason got back to the site and tried to work in the shirt, but the fumes overwhelmed him, so he just worked shirtless the rest of the day, something he used to do all the time when he was in his twenties but today just made him feel more like the old fat man he already felt like all the time. After fixing all of Harry's and everyone else's mistakes, he looked at his watch and realized Abby's meeting was in fifteen minutes, and he was twenty minutes away. "I need a shirt," he said to the crew. "Anybody got a shirt?" They had a shirt.

Jason didn't necessarily disagree with the shirt. He figured he probably was all those things the shirt said he was. But he also wasn't particularly eager to show up at his daughter's school, and meet his daughter's teacher, while wearing it. But he had no choice. So there he sat, a 235-pound middle-aged man with all his muscle and gut crammed into a desk built for a preteen, stinking of gasoline, wearing a Trump shirt, looking pissed off.

"I, uh, I run a construction company, ma'am," he told Miss Grierson. Helen had always noticed that every time her husband talked to one of the kids' teachers, he reverted back to the teenage hellraiser who'd just got caught doing something he wasn't supposed to and was about to get a whupping. "Just got back from a job, actually. Um, that's why I'm, well, uh . . . yes, ma'am, I run a crew."

Helen had a bad habit of piling on when Jason was uncomfortable like this, partly because he was so rarely this palpably uncomfortable and mostly because she was smarter and funnier than he was and occasionally felt the need to remind him.

"He also coaches baseball," she said. "Oconee Little League travel ball. Coaches Abby's older brother. That's why they're never home for dinner." Jason shot her a weary look. *Here she goes.*

"It's our family's obsession," she says. "Baseball baseball baseball. Always baseball. Who's good, who's up-and-coming, who can pitch against Athens next week, what the best lineup is. Every minute he's thinking about it." And then came the line. "I'm married to the only guy who admits to thinking about sixteen-year-old boys in the shower. Isn't that something?"

"That's enough!" Jason shouted, pretty sharp, and he both regretted it and was also glad he had said it. It had been a very long day. Helen looked startled, but also a little chastened: she probably had pushed it a little far. The commotion didn't ruffle Miss Grierson one bit. Jason supposed when you dealt with seventh graders all day, nothing much could faze you anymore. Miss Grierson stared at him for a second, gave him an "OK, then!" smile, and said, "Well, we're very excited to have Abby in class." Jason apologized on the way home. So did Helen.

But. You know. Here he was, in the shower, thinking about sixteen-year-old boys. Specifically, Jayden Richards. Jayden, a wiry kid with braces and a wicked curveball from hell, had been absolutely dominant the night before, pitching six shutout innings to beat Lavonia 8–0 in the semifinals of the Georgia Northeast Little League Regionals. That win, which also featured an absolute bomb of a three-run homer by Jason Jr., or Jace, as everybody but his mother called him, had sent Oconee into the championship game, tonight, against those snobby pricks from Athens. Jason hadn't been sure whether pitching Jayden in the semifinals was the right idea. He was Oconee's best pitcher, and their best chance to beat Athens, but in order to beat Athens, you had to beat Lavonia first. Jason was no gambler: get the win that you could, and live to fight another day. Worry about tomorrow tomorrow. But with Jayden used up, now who pitches? Jace had pitched in the quarterfinals, so he was out too. He could pitch Matt, the lefty preacher's son, but he was wild and could put them in a hole right from the beginning that they'd never dig out of. Maybe Allen Bishop? He didn't throw hard, but he'd throw strikes and give them a chance. He was also fast. Maybe he should lead off?

The key would be scoring first, putting the pressure on Athens from the start. Athens was larger than Oconee and always had the talent pool advantage, but Jason always thought they were a little soft. They were always trying to teach their kids *lessons*. The only lesson these kids needed, Jason figured, was winning. There are winners, and there are losers. Everybody—*everybody*—would rather be a winner. Jason was not about to let his kids, and his son, be losers.

But who would pitch? And should Jayden play center, or short? His speed played at either position. But could he trust Jack Duvall at second base? Jason kept rolling this all over and over in his head, and honestly he'd still be in the shower right now thinking about it had he not finally run out of hot water.

"ALLEN BISHOP'S GOTTA BE THE PICK," JACE TOLD HIM AS JASON SIPPED HIS QT coffee and turned his F-150, painted with the company logo, left onto the freeway heading into Athens. All of Waller Construction's big jobs were in Athens—that's where the big spenders were, both the elites in Five Points and the crazy rich Atlanta parents who were always overspending on homes for their children's four (or more) years at UGA, homes that the kids inevitably wrecked anyway—but this was the biggest job of all of them. It had been Jace, of all people, who had gotten him this project. Jace was playing Premier League basketball, essentially Little League Hoops, for Oconee County, and one game a couple of years ago he and a player for Athens Academy got to jawing at each other in a game, trash talking, just boys doing boys stuff, no harm in it. The other kid ended up hitting a jumper at the buzzer to beat Oconee, a three-pointer right in Jace's face, and afterward they slapped hands and hugged and shared a postgame moment the way only two people who had just been furiously trying to kill each other for two hours can. It was good for boys to have battles like that, Jason thought.

It turned out that kid wasn't just any kid: he was Timothy Tepper, the son of Georgia head football coach Osbourne Tepper, who by virtue of his job coaching the Dawgs was the most powerful and influential human in the entire state. (The Premier League had actually hired security during that game so other parents wouldn't bother Coach Tepper while he was trying to watch his son play basketball. Jason thought people could be just the biggest numb-nuts sometimes.) Jace and Timothy became buds after that, and they spent many hours playing basketball and video games at the Tepper house, in Five Points, of course. One day Jason picked Jace up before dinner, and Coach Tepper introduced himself and asked Jason what he did for a living. He said he ran a crew, and Coach told him they were wanting to add a wing to their house so the boys could have their own place to study, and maybe Waller Construction should make a bid. Next thing Jason knew, he was in the midst of a six-figure project at the most obsessed-over house in town, a job he had to get finished by the start of football season. The job had come out of nowhere, and truth be told, he didn't have the time to fit in a job this huge. He didn't have the man-power for it either. But when the most famous man in your state wants to hire you, you say yes.

And it was going well. It was going great! He'd had to kick the asses of a few guys on his crew, particularly Tommy, but that was normal. He was proud of his crew, he had good guys, but the type of person who's willing to spend all day in the Georgia heat building a shed or constructing a fence for twenty bucks an hour, no benefits, and a never-ending cycle of rich bored housewives constantly coming outside to tell you how wrong you're getting everything and how loud you're being (and not offering you lemonade) is the type of person who doesn't have a whole bunch of better options. "If they were reliable, they'd work for a bank," Jason always told Helen when she'd complain about how he'd stayed working past dinner because someone on his crew hadn't shown up. "And these ain't bank guys." But everybody understood what it meant to be working for Coach Tepper. It was something you could be proud of, something you could tell your kids, or your mom, or that foxy little number at the end of the bar who looks as restless as you do, whoever in your life you felt like you needed to impress. *Workin' on Coach's house. Nice fella too.* The job didn't feel like other jobs. It wasn't just another rich asshole.

And if word spread that Waller Construction had done that great job on Coach's house . . . this could just be the start.

"Yeah, I think you're right," Jason said. "Bishop will get the ball over the plate. He'll give us a chance."

"He throws harder than you think too," Jace said, popping a third banana in his mouth. He'd gotten obsessed recently with bananas after watching a training video of Mike Trout where the Angels superstar had said he ate fourteen bananas a day. This kid had gone from begging his mom for Popsicles to pounding banana protein power smoothies, seemingly overnight. "He's got real pop."

Jason had been coaching his son since T-ball, back when Jace knew so little about the game that he would run to third base those rare times he hit the ball. Jason really didn't care if Jace was a good ballplayer back then, or if his team won. He just wanted to make sure Jace didn't get the shit kicked out of him someday. Because if he wasn't careful, he would. Jace, in a way that had amazed both Jason and Helen from the very beginning, had an electric, vibrating intelligence that they assumed must have just been a long-recessive family gene finally coalescing and emerging in this one fortunate child. (It sure didn't pass along to Jace's younger brother J.T., who Jason loved dearly and who was also, as Jason's dad also used to say about Jason's own younger brother Rick, quite a few peas short of a casserole.) Every teacher raved about how smart Jace was, every test score had him in the top 99 percent, every indicator showed that he was, against all available odds, *gifted*. Helen was delighted by this, and Jason figured he was too, but it also worried him. He'd grown up in rural Oglethorpe County, just about twenty miles from Watkinsville, where there was nothing to do but drink, get in fights, and try not to knock up your girlfriend. (He'd once impressed Helen by taking her to see his town's lone stop sign. "This is what me and Rick did on Friday nights," he told her. "We drank beer and stared at this sign.") If a kid were smart, Jason knew all too well, there were a whole bunch of guys whose only logical response to that intelligence would be to shove that kid in the nearest locker. Jason understood how those guys were, because he was one of those guys. He knew he'd have to protect Jace. The best way he reckoned he'd do that, the only way he'd be good at, would be to make sure Jace liked sports. If you liked sports, you'd play them, and if you played them, you'd have to spend time around a bunch of smelly ape-faced jackasses who couldn't write their own name in the ground with a stick—that's to say, Jason's people. Jace would need to learn how to handle those people—it was a legitimately important life skill to have—and the best way to do it was to get him into sports. If he played sports, they'd think he was one of them. It was Jason's way to make sure his inexplicably brilliant son survived.

Eventually, it clicked. When Jace was seven, Jason took him to a Braves game on Friday, a Dawgs game on Saturday, and a Falcons game on Sunday. By the end of the weekend, Jace was rattling off every player's statistics and trying to run on the field. He was the best player on the team the next season, and he had been ever since.

"You're right," Jason repeated. "Bishop it is." Jace was always right.

"So who's on the crew today?" Jace asked. Jace had volunteered to help out his dad on the site today until lunchtime because they were putting up the east wall, and Jace would get to hammer big nails into blocks of wood for a few hours. ("Get some pregame triceps work in," he'd said.)

"Buck. Little Todd. Tommy T. Black Harold. White Harold."

"I thought White Harold was sick?"

"That was Black Harold."

"I'm pretty sure that was White Harold."

Jason turned off the Loop onto College Station. He always liked this part of Athens, where the university kids met the Five Points wealthy, where everything was bright and sunny and the grass was perfectly manicured, at least until some frat kid who got lost walking home from the bars puked on it.

"Did you see what White Harold put on his Facebook page, Dad?"

"You know, Jace, I didn't. I don't sit on the internet all day. I work for a living."

Jason had learned not to engage Jace on politics. He didn't like talking politics with anyone, an offshoot of years with his brother Rick, with whom Jason had sat through so many lectures about Hillary Clinton that one Thanksgiving he told Rick that if he brought up Benghazi one more time, "I will bomb your ass to Libya myself." But he particularly didn't like talking about it with Jace, because Jace disagreed with just about everything Jason thought about politics, and that worried Jason, because Jace was usually right about things he disagreed with his father on—not that Jason could or would ever admit it to Jace. There were certain things a son was just supposed to respect his father about, and to Jason's mind, this was one of them. Jason was a Republican, a bit of biographical information about him as immutable as his height or his eye color. His dad was a Republican, and so was his dad, and so was he. It wasn't something he had ever thought much about, and it wasn't something he felt he'd ever needed to.

At his core, Jason believed in the gospel of work. This was the Tao of Jason. You worked as hard as you could, you worked down to the bone, and if you did that, you'd end up getting along just fine. If you didn't have the life you wanted, well, the only thing that was gonna fix your situation was to shut up and get to work. You didn't complain. You didn't blame anyone else. If you want something, you work for it. Or you don't get it.

He was aware of the reality of the world. Sure: if you're Black, or a woman, your life is gonna be harder than it is for a white guy like him. Jason didn't deny that. But he also thought that if the people constantly complaining about their place in life spent all that time getting down to work instead of griping about everything, they'd be a hell of a lot better off. Jason didn't grow up dreaming of working construction, of building shelves for rich old biddies who wouldn't appreciate how good he had made himself at building those shelves, who just saw him as the help, who wouldn't even look him in the eye when they handed him the check. But he did it. He did it because he had a wife and a family and wanted a house and a dog and didn't want to be an unreliable burnout headcase who had no discipline and no control over his life. (Like White Harold. Or his brother.) Jason had earned the life that he had, every single dime he'd put in the bank, by working for it. He didn't understand people who thought money was just something you'd always had, something that existed only to be given directly to you. Money wasn't anything unless you worked for it. He'd put a lot of effort into making sure Jace and his brother and his sister understood that, understood that their cell phones and their iPads and their baseball bats didn't fall from the sky, understood that all of it was the product of his and their mother's blood and sweat and toil. It was the one lesson he knew he could pass on.

It was the one thing he knew, in his gut, to be true.

And he also was pretty sure that a whole lot of people didn't want to work, that they just wanted everything to be given to them. He had met plenty of 'em. If you gave them even the slightest excuse not to work, they wouldn't. He figured that was enough to make him a Republican right there. It had never been a thing before, though: he was pretty sure he and Helen had canceled out just about every vote either of them had ever made, and neither had never cared enough to find out for sure. You just went on with your life, dealing with the more important stuff.

But Jace, Jace didn't see it that way. He saw politics everywhere. How his school district was built and drawn. How the Black kids played football and the white kids played soccer. The guy driving the Uber. The videos that YouTube recommended for him. The ticket prices at the baseball game. The hidden fees at his mom's practice. The wages his dad paid his employees. The way everything in the world seemed broken to him, and the way no one seemed to care.

Jace was passionate about politics in a way that Jason didn't understand—in a way that Jason thought beside the point. "Politics are out *there*!" Jason had yelled, pointing out the family room window, when Jace had once ranted about immigration policy over his mother's chicken piccata. "In here we are having dinner!"

Jace had just chuckled and leaned over to his mom. "Eating processed crate poultry plucked by exploited undocumented laborers in horrific working conditions," he said into the back of his hand, and Helen did her absolute best to stifle a laugh and failed. Jason looked at her, frowned, and playfully chucked a dinner roll at Jace's head. He was a tough kid to stay mad at.

Like everything else, the pandemic had pushed this existing dynamic to its breaking point. It was fine, even pleasant, if he was being honest, at the beginning. Work was scary—it was a time when people weren't particularly eager to let construction workers into their house—but the Wallers discovered that when life slowed down to the crawl that it did during those early days, when not every day was just a constant sprint from work to school to practice to home, they ended up enjoying each other's company. They ate together, they played board games together, they spent every second together in a way they hadn't since the kids were babies. (Jason also learned that he was *incredible* at Mario Kart.) He loved his family, and his family loved him, and there's not always time to remember that when everyone's running around busy like crazy, he thought. The beginning was quieter. The early days were terrifying. But they were terrifying together.

But it frayed, like everything did, and it frayed in the Waller household the way it frayed a lot of places: it frayed over politics. Jason did not think Covid was a hoax, or some sort of conspiracy; he wore a mask, he kept his distance, he stopped going to Mama Sid's pizza buffet, all the things you were supposed to do. But he also had a business to run, and an income to earn, and he felt most of the people who wanted to stay in a state of perpetual shutdown were the ones lucky (*and lazy*) enough to sit inside on their computers all day, telling everyone else, people out in the world like him, that what they were doing was wrong without having any skin in the game themselves. Jason was grateful that Georgia had opened businesses up earlier than other states: he had work to do.

Jace, on the other hand, was appalled—by all of it. Appalled by the recklessness, appalled by the meanness, appalled by how aggressively stupid adults seemed to consistently be acting and, if you really broke him down on it, appalled more than anything else by the president himself. Jace wasn't old enough to vote yet, but he made up for it by his relentless campaigning. He knocked on doors, he phone-banked, he ran online campaigns to turn out voters. Helen was proud of him, and in a way, so was Jason. But Jace was still wrong. And Jace knew that his father believed this, which just pushed him harder, the way it has always pushed sons to rebel against their fathers, to fix whatever mistakes they think they've made. Jason always tried not to talk about it. But Jace wouldn't let him not talk about it. Eventually Jason put a Make America Great Again lawn sign in the front yard, just to irritate Jace. It worked. Jace didn't talk to his father for a week after that little stunt.

When the election came, Jace celebrated—he and Helen both cried the night they called it, something Jason found desperately silly—and Jason was all told just relieved it was over. (The exact quote from him that night was, "Congratulations. Can we shut the hell up about this now?") His brother Rick was the radical in the family; Rick was the one who had just spent the last eight months screaming about rigged elections and voting machines and My Pillows. Jason just wanted to get back to work.

He had plenty to do. It turned out that when people spent months stuck inside their houses, they started to notice all the things that were wrong with those houses, and what they'd always wanted those houses to be. That was Jason's job: to build what they wanted built. To give the rich folk what they wanted. He'd never been busier. And now that he was working on Coach's house, he'd never been in a better position to show off what he could do. He'd made it through the pandemic with his business intact; he and Helen might have enough money to get this kid through college after all. His son, so beautiful, that boy, was still on top of the world, as adept with a standardized test as he was with a late-breaking slider on the outside corner. And he sure did seem to like his dad again, as much as any teenage boy can, anyway. It had all worked out. He'd made it. This was his time.

He thought about this for a while and settled on a final decision: Bishop had to be the starter.

"Bishop's gonna start."

"Good call," Jace said. "We're gonna kick their ass." Jason pulled into Coach's driveway, secure and comfortable and grateful to know that Jace was right.

KARSON

7:46 a.m.

Karson knew he looked ridiculous in his spin class—and God forbid any of the guys from Nellie B ever saw him in here, in his tight leggings and fanny pack—but he'd never miss it. Karson spent every day running from here to there, from dropping his daughter Vanessa off at day care to shuttling the kids from the Bethel Homes to school to having lunch and chess with the middle school kids to the various afternoon fundraising bullshit that never seemed to go anywhere but still never seemed to stop to another school board meeting and all the hell that came with *that* these days. He couldn't imagine not starting the day without destroying himself on the bike for an hour. He was not the sort of spin class person who got inspired by the instructor's calls to Push It, who jammed to Taylor Swift on the loudspeakers, who really noticed anything anyone else was doing at all. He zoned out in spin class, the way he used to zone out running, before the car accident that was maybe an accident and also maybe wasn't. This was the only part of his day when someone didn't need something from him, the only time he only had to think about himself. It disturbed him a little that the only part of his day he spent thinking only about himself was also maybe his favorite part of the day.

He was in a hurry leaving class today, though, because there was an extra appointment tossed in there before Thursday's Lunch and Jam, the program he and his Athens Youth Active group—another one of his groups—ran at the Bethel Homes to keep kids active and engaged during the summer months. Karson knew better than anyone what sort of trouble could find a kid—it sneaked up on you, like a predator, like it had always been watching—when he had whole days where no one was looking out for him, and Thursdays were days to check in. To let kids know there was somebody out there, even if it was just the funny guy with the big ears and crazy long dreads who wouldn't stop bothering them, was vital. Karson's week was filled with missions like that, though, because there are more people who need looking out for than there are people to actually do so. And Karson, as much as he'd tried to be otherwise, was just one person. A person who sometimes did have to look out for himself.

The appointment was an interview with Elysian Fields Realty, a luxury realtor that bought and sold premium student housing both on and off campus. The business plan was simple and absurdly lucrative. As the cost of tuition rose dramatically at universities like the University of Georgia, parents, already spending a fortune just to get their kids through college, had begun to blanch at their kids living in broken-down old dormitories. If you're paying forty grand a year to send your kid to college, it's tough to justify them living in a state-funded shithole. So parents started making an investment out of it, buying a house or condo for the kids to live in for a few years and then, when they graduated, flipping it, usually to another parent starting the same process. This turned out to be a gold mine for young, ambitious real estate agents, who discovered a perpetual string of platonic ideal clients: wealthy out-of-towners who were constantly looking to both buy and sell. Athens was littered with these real estate companies, but Elysian Fields Realty was the biggest, run by a bunch of relatively recent UGA grads who never wanted to leave and had discovered a way to get so rich so fast that they never had to. There was more money than any of them knew what to do with.

Karson was, to say the least, not an ambitious young real estate agent. But he did play basketball with one every Monday night, games that had just recently gotten back going after being shut down during the pandemic. A couple of weeks before, after Karson had just finished draining jumpers in some fool's face all night, the selfsame fool, a chubby but friendly dude named Michael, waved Karson over.

"Hey, we're looking for someone out at Elysian, and I think you might be perfect for it," he'd said, in the affable but still sort of thoughtless way a person does when they believe they are doing you a huge favor and want to make sure you know it.

"Oh?" Karson said, not having to try too hard not to look too interested.

"Yeah, we need an in-house counsel, maybe even someone to lead the team," Michael said. "Business is getting too big, and we need a good, smart lawyer to make sure we, you know, dot all the i's and cross all the t's. Thought you might be great at it."

Karson didn't really understand the real estate business, though he figured it must not be too hard if someone as profoundly average as Michael could get rich at it. "Well, estate law is not something I really know," he said. "I studied criminal defense."

Michael frowned a little, not in an annoyed way—it was more like he was a little disappointed that Karson seemed to be missing the point. "Yeah, well, we're not too worried about that. Look, fact is, things are going real well over there, and we're looking to expand beyond our, uh, usual areas of expertise. We're looking for some new blood—some new direction. Someone as obviously smart as you, we'd find the right spot for you." He paused. "And, uh, needless to say . . . the pay is . . . well, it's very, very competitive. It's so competitive it's almost uncompetitive." He smiled, proud of himself. It was clear he loved being able to tell someone how much money he could offer them, if he wanted to.

Karson was polite. "Well, I'm flattered, dude, but honestly, I haven't even practiced in a couple of years," he said. Karson had been introduced to these guys by his friend Matt as "a lawyer," which was true, but he had suspected at the time Matt had done that because saying "political activist and community organizer" probably wouldn't have gotten Karson a second invite to the gym. And Karson had noticed how respectfully the guys had treated him after that. They knew a lot of lawyers, but not many of them had dreads or a crossover like Karson did.

Michael indicated that Karson was still missing the point. "There's a lot of value in having someone like you at Elysian," he said. "We're trying to expand our, uh, horizons. We want to be bigger, and to be bigger, we need fresh new voices. Voices like yours!" He took out a card. "Listen, just think about it. We could find a spot for you immediately, we really could. And seriously"—he looked around, as if making sure no one was listening, even though he obviously would love it if they were—"Nobody's going to pay you more than we do. Just gimme a call if you change your mind."

Karson scoffed all the way home and then spent the rest of his night, with his wife Annette and daughter Vanessa long asleep, staring at Michael's stupid card. Working for a real estate firm was the opposite of what he wanted from his life. Working with Michael felt like it'd be a headache, and he was certain the whole place was full of Michaels. His whole life had been built around being the smart kid who left the Nellie B projects and did something for all those kids he'd left behind, and all the kids that were coming next.

But in dark moments, he couldn't help but wonder what the activism and purpose he'd dedicated his entire adult life to had really accomplished. What had it come to? He'd avoided all that could have taken him down, growing up in Athens, and made it out to Clark Atlanta. He'd gotten his honors degree in political science, gone to law school, navigated the good-ole-boy Georgia Law program (so many professors in bow ties!), and, rather than joining some corporate law firm that would have made him rich but depressed and restless, immediately founded the Athens Youth Active group, which worked with Black youth year-round, mentoring and organizing, and he'd worked hand-in-hand with the Athens Anti-Discrimination Movement and the Chess & Community youth group to raise the level of political activism, to do the good work necessary to make real change, for a decade now. He'd got himself appointed to the Clarke County School Board, hoping to change the system from within, even if it took spending one night a week listening to parents complain about their school bus drivers. He'd spent the last year and a half working on voter registration drives, volunteering long hours for the New Georgia Project to try to get the vote out. Last summer, he'd even gotten his ass arrested, and his lungs full of tear gas, for his trouble. He had dedicated his entire adult life to the cause—to changing lives. To doing right by where he came from.

And yet most of these kids still saw him as just another old man they didn't have to listen to. No matter what he did, no matter how hard he worked, he couldn't change the way people were. The good kids turned out fine, the bad kids didn't, and everyone in the middle just went with the breeze the way the rest of the world did. Maybe they caught some breaks, maybe they didn't, but the random luck of their lives seemed to affect what happened to them more than Karson's hours in the trenches with them ever had. All serving on the school board had gotten him was screamed at, with half the people furious at him the whole pandemic for keeping the kids out of school and the other half furious at him for trying to get them back. And he wasn't sure if he'd changed a single mind on the politics either. Every victory felt followed by a backlash that pushed you farther behind than you were when you started. Karson had lived his whole life with purpose, a confidence that he could make the world better by pure force and relentlessness. But after fifteen years of this, he couldn't lie to himself: the world was too big and strong. It looked the same as it always did. Maybe a little bit worse.

If he was being honest with himself, too, he had to admit he was *exhausted*. It was all so much, for so little. Here he was, in this tiny apartment, making forty grand a year, with a wife working long, draining days teaching middle school kids and with a daughter sleeping in an IKEA bed that already needed replacing and in a room whose air conditioner was constantly conking out. Was this all this was for? This is all you got out of it? Would it always be like this? How could Karson take care of anyone else if he couldn't take care of his own family? Maybe that was the secret all along. He needed to take care of his own house first, and *then* worry about the rest of the world. Maybe he had all this backward. Maybe he'd always had it all wrong.

And so he'd stared at that card for an hour, and the next morning he called it, and now he was rushing out of spin class to get showered so he could meet with Michael and the fine gentlemen of Elysian Fields Realty.

Just as he was about to enter the locker room, a white woman who had been in the class approached him. Her hair was tied in a tight ponytail, and she wore a light-blue tank top over a purple sports bra. If you were the type of person who spent too much time online, Karson found himself thinking, you'd call her a Karen. But he'd met white women like this his entire life, and they were named a helluva lot more names than Karen. They were everywhere. There was a tension in their shoulders—that's where you could see it first. There was misery in those shoulders, and that, to Karson's eyes, was what these women were about: they were miserable. It wasn't that they were inherently mean. It's just that they had no place left to put their pain. So they gave some of it to you.

She was, to his confusion, pointing right at him. Did he know this woman?

Her eyes bulged and bore down on him.

"*You*," she said, hissing. The fatigue of her life startled Karson, almost knocked the wind out of him. "You're one of those school board idiots, aren't you?"

He didn't recognize her, but he didn't really need to. He had seen so many of these women last fall and spring, on their Zoom screens, spitting and howling at him and the other eight members of the Clarke County School Board. (It was always women. The men never showed up.) Some of them were screaming at them for forcing their children to stay at home for virtual schooling. Some of them were screaming at them for trying to get them back. But they were all screaming. He'd been able to numb himself to it when it only happened to him on his computer—the upside of how Zoom deadened every conversation, how he could talk to someone for an hour and twenty minutes later not remember a single word he'd said. But this was the first time it had happened in person. It was more unpleasant in person.

People cleared out of the woman's way as she barreled toward him. The spin class instructor took out her phone and began filming, which, Karson thought, was an unfortunate abdication of her role as spin instructor.

Karson inhaled and fortified himself, standing up straight and broadening his shoulders. This woman was a full foot shorter than he was, so he was careful. But he needed to stand firm.

"Ma'am, I think you need to calm down," he said, his hands out before him, his fingers spread out in a conciliatory gesture.

"Don't you *ever* tell a woman to calm down," she spat at him, but then she paused for a moment, stopped about three feet short of Karson, and took a step backward. Karson saw her take a deep breath and look up at the ceiling. *This must be what she does to stop herself from murdering her children*, he thought.

"OK," she said. "I'm sorry." She didn't look sorry, though. She looked like she was doing everything in her power not to take a polo mallet to Karson's head.

"It is going to take decades to fix what you and those assholes on your board did to my children," she bit at him, and there's really no other word for it: she bit each word at him. Each clause felt like she was being stabbed with something. "Maybe your family doesn't need to work, but my husband and I do. Didn't think about *that*, did you?" She wiped her head with the back of her hand, took another deep breath, and seemed to be mumbling to herself. She looked at him.

"You better be ready for those kids this new year. Don't you *dare* keep them home again." She turned and hightailed it to the locker room. Just before she opened the door, she turned back to him.

"Do your JOB!"

Karson watched her go into the locker room and looked back at the rest of the class, all of which were staring at him. They quickly glanced away and scattered. Karson's head throbbed. He looked at his watch, remembered he was in a hurry because he had a meeting with a real estate guy who was probably married to someone just like that lady, and rushed out to his car.

To think this was his favorite part of the day.

KARSON WAS GOOD AT INTERVIEWS, PARTICULARLY WITH WHITE PEOPLE. HE was "different" enough to be interesting but charming enough to put everyone at ease. He was really charming, he knew that. He always had been. He was at ease with code-switching, with tailoring the person he was for the audience he was with. It was one of the reasons he'd decided to go into activism and politics in the first place. It was something he knew and, frankly, enjoyed about himself. It was intoxicating to be able to make people like you, to want to listen to you, simply by force of your own will. Every person was solvable. You just had to find their on-ramp. He was outstanding at finding the on-ramps.

Not that it would have been hard in any case with the Elysian

Fields folks. Their mission was clear from the outset: do whatever it took to get Karson to come work for them. That he was the only Black person in the room during his big interview with the top executives at the agency didn't make their motivations particularly difficult to parse. He didn't know how many times they normally used the phrases "diversity initiatives" and "get outside our comfort zones" when they interviewed white agents, but it was probably less than eleven. (He'd counted.) At one point Michael, who was not actually at the meeting, something Karson found odd, popped his head inside the conference room door and said, "Seriously, you should see this guy's jumper," which wasn't an OSHA violation but sorta felt like one.

But they were nice. They were nice. He couldn't deny that. He would never mistake well-meaning for virtuous, but they were incredibly well-meaning. They did seem to want their real estate agency to have a lower percentage of pricks than every other real estate agency. The president of the company, a guy named James who was a couple of years younger than Karson and was wearing a Vineyard Vines tie, really did say: "We kinda don't want to be assholes. There are a lot of assholes out there." This was a group of young white dudes who had suddenly become obscenely rich, and that their first instinct was not "Let's now crush anyone who ever wronged us" was a positive, Karson thought, and an undeniable rarity.

They'd told him he'd technically work as their in-house counsel, but not to think of himself that way. "Think of yourself as, well, as the conscience of this group," James said. "This boat is already moving really fast, and we need someone smart, someone who can keep us honest. Someone who can see things the way we can't." Karson knew what he meant. He always knew what well-meaning white people meant when they said something like that: *Please cover our ass.* But: there were actual enemies out there, and these guys were not that. James even emphasized that not only did the agency want him to continue his work with the Athens

Anti-Discrimination Movement and Athens Youth Active, but that they'd be open to Elysian Fields Realty becoming a "financial supporter" of both those organizations, and for Karson to seek out other potential "partnerships."

Oh, and the money: the money was more money than Karson had ever earned in his life, more money than he'd ever dreamed of earning. He would make more in the first six months than he'd made in the last three years. Think of what he could do with that money. Think of what he could do for Vanessa, and Annette. Think of the good it would do. When he was young, in college and for probably too many years afterward, he believed that money was something to fight against. To have money drive your decision-making process was a sign that you were pointed in the wrong direction. He had vowed once never to do anything just for money. Money was the enemy. Money was what the bad people had, and its primary utility was to use it to try to get more of it to the good people.

He'd changed his mind on this gradually, so gradually that he hadn't noticed he'd changed it at all until James tossed out just how much this job would pay, just how much that amount of money would change his life, just how many worries, big, thorny worries, would be taken care of simply by having that much more money in his life on a daily basis. *This is why people care so much about money.* It was like he'd just discovered some element on the periodic table no one had ever seen before. *I get it now.* It was a very good deal.

Karson had shaken everyone's hand, and they'd told him to expect to hear from them after they'd had a chance to talk everything over, but seriously, you should definitely expect to hear from us. *You will be hearing from us,* James had said to him as he made sure to look directly in Karson's eyes. Karson sat in his old Volvo, one that still had a cassette player that was connected to a Discman that sat on the floor of the passenger seat, and stared out in front of him, wondering if this is who he was now, wondering if maybe that was OK, wondering if he'd had it all wrong the whole time, wondering if money truly was the only way to make real change, wondering what college Vanessa might go to, wondering if all the work he'd been doing, all the investment and time and effort and belief and hope, had all just been summed up by that white woman who didn't care a damn thing about any of it and just wanted to see him squirm and feel badly about himself. He didn't think that's what it was all about. He didn't want to think it had all been reduced to that. But the thought was in his mind. And it was not leaving.

2. WHAT HAVE I DONE TO HELP?

Ever since I was a little girl, I have wanted to help people.

I know it is not unusual for someone to say that they have always wanted to help people. Everyone always says they want to help people. But that is all most people do: they say it. They want it to look like they want to help people. They probably even think of themselves as the sort of person who wants to help people. But it is all a performance, a performance that might seem harmless but most certainly is not.

They give some money to charity, tax-exempt, nothing that will actually hurt. They show up at fundraiser events for organizations they do not know or care about, dressing up for a night out on the town that they can feel a little bit less guilty about indulging in because it's For a Good Cause. They post on Facebook, oh, how they post on Facebook, about whatever cause happens to be trendy at that specific moment, whatever will make it look like they are good people without putting any actual effort into being a good person. This is the sort of empty gesture that is worse than simply not caring at all. There is so much talking about helping people that it feels like people are being helped when they aren't. It gives the illusion that things are OK, and getting better.

And they most certainly are not.

I sometimes wish that I had this ability to lie, to trick myself into believing I was helping when I was not. It would be so much easier. But I have had this curse from the very beginning, before I even knew what helping was, of never being able to find any peace if someone else was suffering. People are suffering every single second of every single day, somewhere, everywhere. There is not a moment when something horrible is not happening. How can people be all right with this? How do people just go on with their business?

Here is what I mean. I was doing some research online one time and I came across a figure that said 1.8 people die every second. Every second! In the time it took me to type this sentence, twenty people died. You know that episode of *The Office* you love, the one where Michael burns his foot on the George Foreman grill and Dwight has the head injury that temporarily makes him a nice person? In the time it took you to watch that twenty-two-minute episode, 6,480 people died.

Well, that's not healthy, you might say, and this is what I am trying to get across to you: this is my curse. I cannot walk around the world as if everything is fine when it is quite obviously not. People find this strange, but I think all of you are strange for not being like this. You are OK with all this pain? That is not just 6,480 dead people during your funny episode of *The Office*. That number does not include their family members, or their caregivers, or their old boyfriends, or their office mates, or just people who only saw them every once in a while, enjoyed their company, and whose lives are just a little bit worse because that person is not in them anymore. How many people are affected when someone dies? I sometimes worry it is infinite. There is always a ripple effect of sadness that never, ever stops. I know that death is part of life. I know that we all must die—that it will come for us all. But that does not stop the constant thoughts of loss, of all the pain we leave in our wake. I think about this all the time.

I do not know how the rest of you do not.

This has been here since the beginning, and it has always

gotten me in trouble. Sometimes it got me in big trouble. When I was five years old, my mother, my sister, and I were sitting and watching television when a story came on the news about a little girl in Texas who had fallen down a well. She was only eighteen months old, little Jessica in Texas, when she was crawling around her aunt's backyard and stumbled down a well that was a full twenty feet deep. She had already been down there for about twelve hours when the news stations picked it up, when Dan Rather told us about Baby Jessica, on WAGA-TV Channel 5 in Atlanta, with the gravest of tones: "That little girl may not be making it out alive." We stayed up way past my bedtime waiting for updates, and after my mother and Sue fell asleep, I decided that I could no longer sit around and just hope. I put a change of clothes and my Winnie-the-Pooh bear in one of my mom's backpacks and just walked out the front door in the middle of the night. How was anybody supposed to sleep when Baby Jessica was in danger? If they were not going to help her, I would. I *had to*.

It wasn't the best idea, but I was five. I know now, for example, that it is 1,244 miles from Athens, Georgia, to Midland, Texas, and according to Google Maps, it would take 408 hours to walk straight there. I am not sure why I thought Texas was so much closer to Georgia than it is. It is asking a lot of a five-year-old to realize just how big Texas is. But I was going to do it. I was going to help Baby Jessica. At the time, I imagined running into countless other people on my quest, people who were traveling to Midland, Texas, for the same reason I was. But the only thing I came across were very loud dogs.

I did not make it far. My mother woke up about two hours after I left and found me about three miles down the road, walking alone, my stomach already growling. She pulled over and could not stop crying. But I would not get in the car with her. I shook my head at her, *NO!*, and kept on walking. My mother was slowing me down, keeping me from helping Baby Jessica. She had to physically pick me up and drag me into the car as I screamed and kicked and bit her. I thought she understood, but she did not. I had to get to Baby Jessica. I had to do something.

Baby Jessica was pulled out of the well two days later. Everyone acted like it was a happy story, now that she was saved, but I knew it was not. I looked it up online a few years ago. There's a whole Facebook group about it. There's so much you don't know. They had to amputate one of Baby Jessica's toes afterward, and she had more than a dozen surgeries the rest of her life. She still has a huge scar across her forehead today. Did you know that? And that was just her. Did you know her parents divorced three years later? Did you know the man who rescued her from the well struggled with post-traumatic stress for years after the incident and eventually killed himself? I bet you did not know that. There are always ripples. There is always more suffering.

So why am I doing this? I am doing this because I have to help. What they did to my aunt was only the beginning. People have been suffering for years from him and that family—people still are. Who knows how many more Jessicas are still in their wells?

DAVID

8:45 a.m.

If the last fifteen months had taught David anything, it was that it turned out it really was possible to get the stale beer and wet cigarette smell out of the Red Rocket. He would have always assumed you'd have to burn the place down to get that out of there. That smell was hard-earned, and nobody knew that better than David. As he flicked his cigarette to the ground, unlocked the front door, and pulled up the metal protective barricade for the millionth time in his life, he marveled again at how strangely *new* the place felt after being empty for more than a year. He wondered if everything in the world was like this. If you just left something alone for a while, if you just let it have some time away from all these *people*, it could heal itself. It could be born again.

The Red Rocket, as the website that David had taught himself to update over the pandemic said, was one of "the most famous and iconic music venues in the world." David wasn't sure about that, bit much as far as he was concerned, but it had certainly been the center of everything David had cared about for most of his adult life. He'd learned about the Red Rocket right before he dropped out of high school, back when it was in its old location on Clayton Street, back when he'd hitchhike in from Oglethorpe

County, where his shit mom and shittier stepdad made him live a shit life in that shitty Crawford camper. All he knew about it is that it was a place to go get drunk. Everyone got drunk in rock clubs back then, so that's where he got drunk. He didn't know anything about music. He was just bored and broke and useless, and there was nothing to do in Crawford, so he'd go to Athens and find enough of the right people to drink with that he'd end up with a couch to sleep on. You were sure to find those people in rock clubs.

It got in his bones without him realizing it. David didn't remember when he decided to move to Athens, or if there was even a specific move that happened at all. The choice between the nothing that was Crawford and the thrill of Athens, all the lost young people like him who stayed up all night and talked and drank and smoked and sang and danced, was no choice at all. At first he just crashed out with whoever was still bouncing around with him at 3:00 a.m. Then he was at the Red Rocket often enough that they asked him to stay after and sweep out the place. Then a couple of guys from one of the bands needed a roommate, what about Dave, Dave's a good time, a solid dude, Dave. Then he was bartending. Then he was working security. Then he was running the soundboard. Then he didn't remember he was from Crawford anymore, didn't even mention it when people asked him where he was from, he'd just say, "I'm from everywhere and nowhere," and that was always good for a laugh and maybe, just maybe, a couple of the ladies found it intriguing and that was never a bad thing. Everybody knew David, and that was new. It was nice to be known. It was nice to finally have a crew.

And there was always a party. David always found the party.

He'd met a girl there, too. She was hipper than he was, dyed her hair beet red, with a nose ring and a lip ring and occasionally a chain that connected them both. She worked for an independent punk label named Kennedy Skids, which wasn't so much a record label as a bunch of fans scraping together pennies so they could listen all day to the bands they usually had to wait until midnight to hear. He'd seen her around for weeks, but he never talked to her until one night, before a Jucifer show, she walked right up to him and asked if he'd give her a hickey.

"Hi, I'm Brit," she actually said first. "Want to give me a hickey?"

"Huh?"

"We thought it would be fun if everyone gave me hickeys up and down my arm at once," she said, pointing to a booth in the corner full of random weirdos. "We're short a person. Wanna take my wrist?"

She stuck her wrist in his face. He was happy to help. They moved in with each other a month later, she was pregnant by the time their third rent payment was due, and they got married in her third trimester. Their ceremony was at the Red Rocket, of course, before a Vic Chesnutt show with the La Di Das. David drank too much to remember much of it, but there was an incredible photo of both of them onstage on either side of Vic and his chair, David holding a bottle of Southern Comfort and screaming through his beard on Vic's left and Brit and her belly so huge it kept knocking over the microphone stand on Vic's right. It's still on the wall of the Red Rocket dressing room. David tries not to look at it.

It was around that time, when little Alice, Allie, was still a baby, that Athens music became *the Athens music scene*. David didn't notice at first what was happening. All he could tell was that parties were getting a little bit bigger and everyone was dressing a little bit nicer. He certainly didn't see any change among his friends: Michael was the same reedy, amusingly zonked space cadet he'd stayed up all night playing Uno with at the Grill downtown, no matter what *Rolling Stone* was suddenly calling him. David wasn't there for the music anyway, or at least not for the music first. He was there because he was useful. He liked being useful.

As the Red Rocket grew, eventually moving over to Washington Street, the importance of having someone who knew how the whole place worked—what to do when a breaker exploded, what times to expect what types of crowds for what kinds of bands, what motel had which discounted rate on which night, how to plug a leak in the roof, how to run lights in a pinch, how to handle a plastered shithead who won't stop bothering Justine behind the bar, when to call the cops if you had to, how to water down the drinks to run up the bar tabs, how to fix an overrun toilet, how to clean up the mess that caused it, where to get weed or coke for the band, how to talk a guy through a bad acid trip, which shows were smart to book on game-day weekends, which drummers you could let drink for free and which ones you couldn't, how closely you could push the city's curfew, what to do when someone OD'd, what the fuck to do when someone OD'd—became more evident with every larger crowd, every bigger act. R.E.M. essentially set up residency there, but all the great ones came through: Iggy Pop, the Black Crowes, the Strokes, Snoop Dogg, Hüsker Dü, Flaming Lips, Pavement, Nirvana, *fucking Nirvana played there*, a month before *Nevermind* came out, before everything was forever different (and briefly better). They tore the place apart, even grabbing the projection screen above the stage and throwing it to the ground, then inviting everybody to jump onstage and trash the shit out of everything in sight. They'd had to close the place for three nights after that one to clean it up, and nobody minded. David would tell that Nirvana story to anyone who would listen. What a time. What a fuckin' time.

Now David stood on the stage of the Red Rocket, flicking the breaker on and off, making sure everything was still connected, everything still worked, surprising himself how lost he'd just gotten in that moment. He had learned that thinking too much about the past was an express train to reliving it, and he'd come too far to let that happen. All that had happened right here, on this stage. It had never seemed longer ago than it did right now.

IT WASN'T THAT UNUSUAL FOR BRIT TO BRING ALLIE WITH HER ALL HOURS OF the night at the Red Rocket, it really wasn't. There was even a little pack-and-play in a janitor's closet right there, and if you shut the door, you could almost block out the sound from the stage. Brit and David spent so much time at the club, were so ingrained in the place, that Allie had become a sort of unofficial band mascot: you can even see baby Allie in the liner notes of the second Cracker album. (The lead singer had drawn a little mustache on her.) They were there all the time.

They just weren't there that night. He could have sworn Brit had told him they'd be there. But he was hazy about everything back then. David had always been a drinker; he'd gotten kicked out of his ninth-grade classroom for chugging Bartles & Jaymes wine coolers in the back row. But the long hours and late nights at the club had lined up the structure of his life in a way that made it nearly impossible for him *not* to drink all the time. He worked at a rock club, for crissakes. He'd wake up at noon, smoke a joint—half the time he'd have one with Brit, a fact he would always remind her of when she was screaming at him about his drinking—get to the club, have a few beers while he cleaned up from the night before and set up for the night ahead, have some shots with the bartenders, and next thing you knew, the show was starting and who didn't drink at a rock show I mean what the fuck are we doing here if we're not throwing them back at a rock show? It didn't strike David as all that unusual, and he didn't really understand how increasingly bewildered by and frustrated with the situation Brit was becoming. Hadn't this always been the life? Wasn't this how they'd met? What did she want? He sure wasn't going back to Crawford. This world had been his salvation, his escape. They were royalty here! He didn't get how Brit didn't understand that. Didn't she love this world? Didn't she like to get blasted just as much as he did?

That evening still didn't piece together well, years later. Let's see. It had been a crap night at the club, some cruddy techno disco show, mostly for college kids, which just made David drink even more: it was better than listening to that shit. He went back to their apartment on Boulevard, where Brit was waiting, irritated, she wanted to go somewhere, her sister was in town, maybe he was supposed to be home earlier, who could remember, who could keep all that straight? She left in a huff, as she always did in those days, and he sat and drank and watched some professional wrestling and smoked a bowl and drank some more. He ran out of cigarettes. He went downstairs and walked to the college market around the corner, grabbed some Marlboro Reds, and ran into Robert, a bouncer at the Georgia Theater who always was good to have some coke on him. The night was young, he remembered the night feeling young, though it couldn't have been, there was no way it was. Robert and David did a bunch of lines backstage of some pop country show at the theater and got in an extended argument about . . . Yosemite Sam? Maybe? Is there a debatable point about Yosemite Sam? Perhaps his hat. It was a mostly empty show, and David helped Robert usher everybody out and they went back to Robert's for some more lines, and drank more and played Call of Duty, and finally David left and was a little stunned by the sunlight that had already crept up on him. He stumbled toward home, but stopped on a park bench to catch his breath for a second, and when he woke up, who knew how long it had been.

He unlocked the front door to see Brit sitting on the couch with her sister. He wished she was with her mom. He'd always gotten along great with her mom—not so much with her sister.

Brit didn't look up. She held a cigarette and stared at David's feet.

"You left Allie," she said. "You *left her*."

David had been confused. Wasn't she with Allie at the Red Rocket? That had been what it was, yes?

For god's sake, if he could, 2021 David would take that David and whack him in the skull with a Louisville Slugger.

"She was in her crib, screaming," she said, finally looking at him, shaking. "She was starving, and covered in her own filth. She was looking for her daddy. *But you weren't here.*"

Brit's sister picked up a suitcase and walked to the door. "Brit is getting out of here," she said, handing David a piece of paper. "Here's my phone number. Call me, not her. My dad already has Allie. I wouldn't go bothering my father. He wants to shoot you in the balls."

Brit looked at him.

"Brit, I—" he said.

"Don't," she said. "Don't."

And they left. He didn't follow them. He just lay down on the couch and went back to sleep. That's the part that still kills David the most today. He just passed out.

This is the sort of story that is supposed to set you straight, the bottoming out everyone had before they straightened up and got their life together. But, as a sponsor later told him, if you're alert enough to think you've bottomed out, you still have a long way to go. No, this incident did not get David's head any less crooked. It made him much, much worse. Before he was drinking out of habit, or euphoria, or just boredom. Now he drank out of pity, out of self-hatred. He drank more, and partied harder, and raged louder, did everything he could to fill the maw with whatever he could fill it with. Working at the Red Rocket gave him a place to be every night, a place where he was needed and also a place where he was conveniently surrounded by everything that would blot it all out. The first two years were a blur of fistfights and 3:00 a.m. shows and snorting lines to start your shift and blacking out and waking up in strange people's apartments and stirring just in time to do it all again. It was a period his sponsor called "flooring it downhill until you hit your first brick wall." Brit would call him occasionally, but he didn't return her calls—he still can't believe he didn't return her calls. After the first year she stopped calling. After the second year she served him with divorce papers. After the fourth year she told him she was getting married, to some entertainment lawyer, and she was moving to Los Angeles with Allie, not that you would care. It all just blew past him. How had it blown past him? Did it blow past everyone like that?

Then one night, after a decade-plus of being the institutional memory of "one of the most famous and iconic music venues in the world," his heart stopped. It wasn't an overdose, though it could have been and probably should have been. He was just sweeping up between sets, after some goofball pop metal group of teenagers and before a nineties grunge band that would have sold a lot more tickets back in the early days than they'd sold that night, when he felt his right eye twitch. There was a slash of pain down his left arm, a current that made him wonder if he'd stepped in a puddle that had a live amp sitting in it. Then a wolverine came and tore him in half from the inside out. He fell, smashed his head on the edge of the stage, and collapsed into a pit of meandering kids who barely bothered to get out of his way. He was thirty-six years old.

The gang at the club made him go to rehab after that, and he failed like people always failed, but he kept coming back to meetings anyway. He always knew where one was and when he needed to get there. Maybe it was the thud of hitting the stage that still rattled around his head and even made him dizzy sometimes. Maybe it was the repulsed, pitying way all the college girls looked at him now. Maybe it was how he couldn't keep up with the staff when they went out after the shows anymore. Maybe it was that the Red Rocket, the old Red Rocket, the place that had saved him from Crawford, that had given him a community and a purpose and the closest thing to a family that a wretch like him could possibly deserve, the old bird still needed him. Whatever it was, he always kept coming back. And AA always had a space for him.

Then he realized he'd put one foot in front of another long enough that he had his five-year chip. Then his ten-year. He was at fourteen now. Fourteen years, four months, twenty-six days. He never thought he'd be one of those guys who counted the days. But he was one of those guys who counted the days.

None of the years had been harder than this last one. Routine had been his salvation. It didn't matter that he was surrounded by booze and all the spoils of rock excess if his routine was just to choose not to take part in any of it—every second of his work life had revolved around that choice. It was like how his grandpa had quit smoking when he was a kid. Gramps had for a time put cigarettes in plain sight in every room, so he had to look at them and actively *decide* not to smoke. When he no longer had to think hard about his decision, he knew he'd quit. To David, every day was like that, a decision, and as long as he always continued to make that decision, the decision of going into the Red Rocket and keeping the place afloat and functional, every day would end up in the right place. He poured all that he had into the Red Rocket, and he'd loved growing into a sort of grandfatherly figure to the forever-young staffers, the ones with hard-earned life lessons and a vaguely sad background and stories about the time Patti Smith slept on his couch and the time Nirvana wrecked the place. He'd been clean, and clearheaded, for a long time now. He knew who he was.

He'd even been, cautiously, reconnecting with Allie, who was now making music of her own after years of drumming for a group who had been opening for some jam band David had never heard of. Allie had never stopped trying to connect with him, all the way in California, even when he was totally lost. She'd visit Athens a couple of times every year, and she wrote him letters constantly—sweet drawings when she was a child, angry missives when she was a teenager, kind poems of forgiveness as she grew into her life as a musician. He'd have lost her had she not kept on him when she had every reason to tell him to fuck off. But she wouldn't let him go. When she was a teenager, she'd even come visit him over the summer, and they'd go see shows together and come home and hang out in his garage, where he'd try to teach her the only songs he knew how to play, mostly the "Smoke on the Water" riff and a few solos he could pull off from Aerosmith's "Toys in the Attic." She looked at him like he was a rock star back then. He knew how wrong she was. But god he loved how she looked at him anyway.

Today, they met every time she was in the South. It helped that Allie had been too young when David was at his worst to have been truly disappointed in him. She had her own dad now, a stepdad who had raised her in a home in the Hollywood Hills with an in-ground pool and a big-screen TV in her room and everything. Allie came to see David not as a dad but as a lost soul she'd always be connected to and could maybe help—and maybe someone who she was a little bit more alike than she might want to admit. And maybe he could even be a dad a little bit too, even accidentally. David knew he was just a small part of who she was, he'd lost the chance to be more, but he was still pleased just to be someone Allie wanted to know better but had no expectations of, or anger at, anymore. She just stopped in to see David, that's all. David was grateful. He didn't deserve that much. So he was grateful.

At this point he was grateful for all of it. Shit: the Red Rocket was about to open back up. The Drive-By Truckers, an Athens staple, were coming back to reopen the place next month, as long as the city council gave the green light, and they goddamn well better. This place, his home, his tormentor, his salvation, had been abandoned for more than a year, just him and the owner checking in, running off raccoons, waiting to return. And now they'd made it. He'd made it. He was an old fat piece of shit now, the guy all the young kids looked at and wondered what had gone so wrong in his life that he was still here, but he knew, now, that this was his place, this was his home, and it always would be. If you could get the stale beer smell out of this old dump, anyone could start anew, anywhere. You could heal yourself. You could be born again.

DAPHNE

9:16 a.m.

Grab his heart!"

"What?" The doctor couldn't possibly have said what Daphne thought she had said.

"Grab his heart!" Dr. Winingrad screamed, so loudly that Daphne wondered if the doctor was about to blow a hole in her mask. "I need you to pump his heart."

"What?"

"Pump his heart," she said to Daphne, calmer, quieter this time. "Just a couple bump-bump, bump-bumps. Until we can load up the defibrillator."

"Uh . . . ," Daphne said, but before she knew it, she was down there, with her hands up the child's chest cavity, holding . . . wow, she was really holding his heart in her hands. She'd never done that before in any of her years as a nurse. (Or in any of her years as anything, really.) She was prepared for it. She'd been at the army base in Germany for five years, and while she hadn't seen the nightmares that some of her friends from basic training had, she'd seen plenty. And anything she hadn't seen there, she'd seen in the emergency room, from severed limbs to wild animal bites to household appliances stuck in people's rectums. She wasn't really grossed out by anything anymore. She did have to admit, though, she was still a little shaken by the time she and another nurse had to flip a morbidly obese man over in his bed and found, swear to the Lord above, a dead hamster in one of his folds. It had been dead a while. The ER had a little bit of everything.

But here she was. Nothing like this.

"Bump-bump," Dr. Winingrad said, softer still. "Bump-bump. Bump-bump."

She looked at the boy's face. There was nothing. He wasn't there. She was smart enough to know otherwise, but there was still a part of her that wondered if, after one of her squeezes, he would suddenly come to, open his eyes, shake himself awake, and look directly at her. He would see her, right there, right in his face, holding his little heart in her hands. She was keeping him alive, or at least keeping his heart beating when it otherwise wouldn't be. But there was no immediate result. He didn't snap to, or stare at her, or do anything at all. His face was pale, almost translucent. It looked like there had never been any life there in the first place.

Daphne squeezed, and squeezed again. In the other room, she could hear the wails of the boy's mother, her pleas to get out of her way, to let her see her son. Daphne suddenly felt embarrassed— exposed. What would this mother think if she busted through and came to this sight, her colorless son lying on a cot with the hands of a strange woman inside his chest, caressing his heart, staring into his eyes? Daphne found herself grateful for the big security men holding the mother back. Daphne did not want her to see her like this.

"OK, everybody clear out," Dr. Winingrad barked. "Daphne, give one more squeeze, and then slowly, gently, pull your hands out and take a step backward. Are you ready for that?"

Daphne said that she was, even though she wasn't, she was not at all. Then a squeeze, *bump-bump*, and she let go and al- lowed her hands to loosen and release. She was relieved her hands didn't scrape up against anything on the way out of the chest of the ten-year-old boy she'd just been sitting on top of while hold-ing his heart in her hands, something she'd just been doing, right then, yep, that's what she'd been doing. She hopped off the gur-ney, and two other nurses and two staffers she didn't recognize gathered around the boy to prepare him. Then:

"Clear!"

Daphne sat down on the cold floor, as the gurney wheeled down the hallway past her, and began to weep. Then she did what she always did when she started to cry: she closed her eyes and prayed. She felt stronger after that. She always did.

SHE WAS NEVER PROUDER TO BE WHO SHE WAS THAN WHEN SHE SAW HER father in his uniform. It only came out for special occasions: Fourth of July parades, weddings, funerals, formal military get-togethers, Easter Sunday, Christmas Eve service. That the occasions were special was what made Daphne so proud. The other dads would be wearing faded white button-ups and ties, usually without even a jacket, their big guts hanging out over pants that looked about to split apart. Their lives were lived without purpose, so little respect for themselves, and it showed. Not her father, not her Bill Preston. SFC William B. Preston was fit and disciplined, with a perpetually fresh crew cut and the upright, shoulders-out posture of a man who took life seriously and expected the rest of the world, not least his daughter, to do the same. He wore that uniform just as tautly, lined and angular, at the age of fifty as he had when he first enlisted. Daphne always felt a few inches taller when he was in the room.

He'd lost his wife, cancer, when Daphne was eight years old, and he'd never married again. It was just the two of them. When he retired from the army, the year before she died, he took a job as head ROTC instructor at Madison County High School, running their recruitment program and also working a side gig as a driving instructor. After Daphne's mom was gone, they stayed in the same small house on the edge of Danielsville, and he and Daphne kept it immaculate; she could forever bounce a quarter off her made bed, just how his first commanding officer had taught him. They lived there the only way Bill Preston knew how: with organization, discipline, steadfast resilience, and respect for yourself and others. They never missed church on Sunday morning, they cooked each meal at home, they were up for morning exercise at 6:00 a.m., the lights were out at 9:00 p.m. every night, you could set your watch by all of it. "Care for others, and care about yourself," he'd said— he'd written it on a magnetic whiteboard on the fridge—"and you'll take care of all of us. The rest is up to God." All she wanted to do was make him proud. He was. And so was she.

Every day after school, SFC Preston would drive his daughter home for what he called, with a twinkle in his eye, "the debriefing." He was insistent that she tell him everything about her day, hold back nothing, no matter how embarrassing or unflattering the detail. He did the same, unfailingly. Daphne still laughed about the time he'd been at an officer's outreach event, and while in the bathroom, he'd slipped and pissed all over the right leg of his uniform. "Look," he'd said, pointing to the still-damp spot. "Can you imagine how hard it is to salute a man covered in his own pee?" He demanded excellence and achievement from his daughter and himself, and she was grateful for that. But it was always important that everybody still be human. God would love you, and forgive you, as long as you remembered that you and everyone else were just human beings, stupid, sinning, clumsy human beings.

That's why she knew she could tell him. She was a freshman on the Madison volleyball team, and she'd been in the locker room with the team's top setter, and she'd accidentally touched her hand and a lightning bolt had gone up Daphne's arm and sent a jolt through her whole body. It confirmed what she'd already suspected. Bill Preston had taken on the responsibility of researching what would be happening to his daughter's body and how to discuss it without shame or awkwardness; he wanted his daughter to take pride in her body, not to be afraid of it. She was grateful for that too. So at dinner that night, she just came out and said it.

"I think I like girls," she said.

"What's that?" He peered at her over his glasses with what she thought was a slight grin. Was it a grin?

"I like girls," she said. "I don't like boys, I like girls. There's a girl at school I like. As, uh, more than a friend. Is that OK?"

He cut off a piece of pork chop and slid it into his mouth. "Are you sure?"

"Yes," she said. She was. She figured he'd always known anyway. Though she didn't really know, not for sure.

He chewed slowly, then wiped the side of his mouth with his creased cloth napkin. "This is going to make your life harder," he said. "Are you ready for that?"

"I think so?"

"Well, then, you better be nice," he said. "You have to be nicer to girls than you have to be to boys."

And that was that. He would end up switching their church because one too many sermons from the fundamentalist preacher had made his daughter nearly cry, but other than that, it didn't change their life much. He pinned that prom corsage on Stephanie and beamed as much as every other father. They still went to church together every Sunday, still prayed together every night, still played golf together on Fridays when she didn't have softball practice. It might have been harder for her at Madison County High School, she knew, if she hadn't had the big scary ROTC dad roaming the hallways. But he *had* been there. And so she was fine. *You'll take care of us all.* They would always protect each other.

When she graduated, all the other girls went off to college, usually UGA, maybe North Georgia, some all the way to Clemson. But she knew exactly what she was going to do. It was partly because the spare life of a ROTC and driver's ed instructor, one who'd never gone to college himself, did not leave much money for tuition, and she was not going to put both of them in debt for the rest of their lives through loans. But she'd wanted to enlist anyway. She always had. She wanted to look good in that uniform too. She wanted him to be as proud of her as she was of him.

So she joined the army. She spent ten weeks in basic training at Fort Benning in Columbus, then signed up for the Combat Medic Specialist Training Program; in nine months she was an EMT. She wasn't scared of combat—she thought she'd be great at it, and her instructors agreed—but there was something about working as a medic that appealed to her. There was a set of clear rules to follow, procedures you followed to the letter, and if you did it all correctly, someone would be better off than they were before they'd met you. She was a star pupil, really from the beginning, and she was rewarded with a plum deployment: she was assigned to the Seventh Army Training Command in Grafenwöhr, Germany, at the USAG Grafenwöhr Army Base near the Czech Republic border. She couldn't believe it. She'd never even been north of South Carolina, and here she was, in Germany. Bill Preston drove her to her plane, took her in a massive bear hug, and told her that he'd pray for her and that he'd grow a handlebar mustache in her honor. It was 2011. She was twenty years old.

And for the next five years, Daphne lived there, in Bavaria, on the base, as a medic and—eventually, once she finished the online degree the army paid for—a nurse. There was no active combat in Europe at the time, so she never had any on-the-battlefield, tie-off-the-artery-to-stop-the-bleeding combat experience. It was, if she was being truthful, sort of relaxing. Not everyone in the army was as buttoned-up and rock-ribbed as her father, and she was able to have a little bit of fun; there are worse places in the world for a lesbian in her early twenties to be than Europe. But she approached her job with the utmost seriousness, constantly checking in on senior officers stationed there who she knew were in the danger zone, healthwise, not that they'd ever admit weakness to anyone. She was reliable and steadfast and deeply respected. She wrote her father letters every week and Skyped with him every other Sunday; she was impressed how good he'd gotten on his computer. He never looked any older on any of the videos. He always looked exactly the same.

She loved Germany, loved the base, loved being useful, had even found a church there, but she did miss home. She'd had the option to stay on past her obligation to the army, and she might have even done it—there was a girl, Catherine, who she'd even brought to the base a few times, where they all adored her. *There could have been something there,* Daphne still found herself, years later, back in Georgia, thinking, and sometimes she heard Catherine's voice just around the corner. But when she came back home for Christmas 2015, her dad's sister Jessica took her aside, when Bill Preston was in the other room, and told her her father had had a minor stroke that spring. "He'd be furious if I told you, but you deserve to know," she'd said. "He's fine. I don't notice anything different, not really. But a stroke is a stroke." She *had* noticed, when Aunt Jessica mentioned it, that the left side of her father's face seemed to be slightly sagging, and that he had been going to sleep an hour earlier than he usually did. He seemed OK. But he did seem maybe a *little* different?

So when she flew back to Germany after the new year, she told her superior officers that when her enlistment period was over, she was going to move back to America to be with her father. They were disappointed, but they understood. The army had been good for her. She had been good for the army. But she couldn't leave him alone in that house.

She moved home that spring. She even settled right back in her old room. It looked the same: Bill Preston hadn't changed it one bit. But she had been gone from home, from Georgia, from the United States, for a long time. The room hadn't changed. But, as she soon discovered, everything outside the room had. A lot.

IT HAD BEEN SO HORRIBLE THAT THE PARAMEDIC WAS WEEPING. DAPHNE couldn't tell that at first, because of all the blood. His face and beard were caked with it, caked with the blood of the boy Bryan. Daphne had always been intimidated, even actively scared, by all the paramedics who came into Athens Regional, not because they were big and burly, though they usually were, but because they always seemed so *cheerful*. She did not understand how these men, and they were mostly men, were able to be so affable all the time. By the time a patient got to Daphne in the ER, the situation was chaotic and perilous but usually, usually, there were some actionables— clear paths of forward, linear movement. *This happened, and we know that when that happens, our job is to do this, this, and this.* The patient knew something was wrong, the family knew something was wrong, the process of helping them with whatever was wrong was well in motion by that point—that's why they were there. But paramedics were the first line of defense. They came into a situation right at that pivot point between normal life and hospital world, and there they were required to restore order, to calm the stricken and to stabilize the afflicted. Daphne and her fellow ER staff were often heralded for being the "first responders," typically when some politician was trying to score a political point that had nothing to do with what anybody's jobs actually were, but these men were the true definition of the term: they confronted the overwhelming real- ness of the situation before anyone, even the sick people themselves, understood what was happening and why they were there. And yet paramedics were so buoyant. They were always smiling.

This man, however, was wailing. He had the look of someone who had been turned inside out, then back again.

He was gasping, with bubbles of an indeterminate liquid forming from his lips, as he, Daphne, and two other ER nurses loaded the boy onto a gurney and began cutting off his clothes and pants and rushing him toward the operating room. "We did what we could to stanch the bleeding, but must have hit an artery. The poor kid, he was just lying there, moaning and crying, saying he needed his mommy, until he passed out halfway here." Daphne slipped in some vomit on the floor. And then Dr. Winingrad was there, and before you knew it, Daphne was holding a little boy's heart in her hands.

Hours later Daphne would find the paramedic, and ask him to kneel with her to pray. He told her he wasn't really into all that. Then he knelt.

The boy Bryan had been spending the night with a friend in Beechwood, an older boy, twelve or thirteen, and they did what boys that age do when they spend the night with a friend: they played video games and ate candy all night until they were hyped up enough to go look for some trouble to get into. It was pretty simple, really. The older kid wanted to see if he could find his mom's gun, they found it in a closet in their shed, they were messing around with it, and the boy Bryan caught a bullet in the middle of his rib cage. That had happened around two in the morning. The paramedics had brought him in about half an hour later.

Daphne had been working the overnight shift anyway, the third shift she'd picked up over the last month. She was just about to sign out when Bryan was brought in. "That's how it always happens," her old boss and mentor, a kind woman named Sally who had run the ER for thirty years before retiring *right* before the pandemic hit, had told her. "The worst hits you right before you're about to go home." But Daphne could not leave now. Daphne could never leave when she was emotionally invested in a patient. She knew that it was not healthy, maybe not even professional, to wrap up so much of herself in the well-being of her patients. She worked in an emergency room, after all, and any experienced nurse knows that you have to separate yourself, give yourself a little bit of remove, from your patients or you'll never make it in the job. Sally had told her this constantly. You give them the best care you can, she'd say, but you cannot live and die with them and their families. You have to go home at the end of the day. That shit has to stay at work.

Daphne was terrible at this, she knew, and she'd been terrible at it for a while. She was actually a little bit famous for it. Two years back, before the pandemic, there was a high-profile case where a missing girl, a Chinese student who was studying to become a veterinarian, ended up being kidnapped by some lunatic. A man named Daniel who had a neuromuscular disorder somehow figured out who the kidnapper was, but when confronted, the kidnapper had beaten him up rather badly. They eventually caught the guy, but Daniel was seriously hurt, and Daphne was on call when he was brought in. She was so moved by this man, this disabled man who risked his life to help someone he didn't know, that when she was done with her shift she would go into his room to sit and pray with him. For a full week she didn't go home: she would do her shift, take a shower, go to his room, sleep there, wake up, shower again, go back to work. Daniel's story was so well known that eventually the *Athens Banner-Herald* wrote a front-page feature on "The Nurse Who Wouldn't Leave Daniel's Side." (Bill Preston bought thirty copies of the paper and gave them to all the neighbors and folks at church.) Daphne was a little embarrassed about it, but she also, she had to admit, sort of liked it. Sally had made fun of Daphne for the story and even scolded her a little for this sort of dedication, dedication the patient hadn't asked for (and, Sally noticed, didn't even seem to enjoy), but then again Sally had the story framed and posted at the nurses' desk and made sure to point it out to anyone who ever stopped by.

There would be a time, Daphne knew, when she'd have to leave that part of herself in service of the job. Truth be told, it had already started to wear on her a bit. She didn't pull any overnighters in patients' rooms anymore. It had started to annoy the other nurses, and those beaten-up old Athens Regional chairs next to the beds weren't the most comfortable way to rest before your shift anyway. Sally had told her she'd have to stop, and Daphne knew she was right.

But she stuck close to who she was, or at least who she thought she was. She loved every patient with the grace and glory of God—she held on to that part of herself as long as she could. This was her third year as a nurse at Athens Regional, and as awful as the pandemic had been, she was young and she was strong and she still believed. Even if she loosened that grip on each individual patient a little, she would be all right. She felt fortunate to have this opportunity to see people at their most desperate, to be the one who could try to ease their wounds and fears. She couldn't save them all. But she could help.

And that's how she'd found herself with her hands inside the chest of a ten-year-old boy about seven hours before, and that's how she now found herself holding the boy's mother, who heaved and shook and shrieked and pounded her chest and nestled her face in Daphne's shoulder before collapsing on the floor. Daphne got down with her, laid her hand on her back, and said a silent prayer for the boy, the woman, and herself. She had no doubt she would provide for this woman, and for anyone else she came across who needed His power, through Daphne's strength. This, this she could provide.

3. MOM

I went to see Mom today. I used to go every day, and then every other day, and then every week, and then they wouldn't let me see her at all. This absence would have been a lot more difficult if, during any of those times when I saw her, she ever really saw me, but she didn't. She hasn't seen me in years. This didn't make missing her during the pandemic any easier to deal with. It made it exactly as hard as it was before.

She began to fade a decade ago. There was no official diagnosis. Even though Mom was sick all the time, she refused to go to the doctor. I'd tried to drag her there for years, but she was so stubborn about it that I eventually just stopped. It wasn't that Mom was a hypochondriac, or that she had one of those conditions where she faked being sick so that people would have to feel bad for her or take care of her. She didn't complain about it, or wallow in self-pity. If you ran into her on the street, you probably wouldn't have even known there was anything wrong with her. Mom owned her pain, solely. She was sick, always, often in ways that only a daughter would notice. The suffering dripped off her like a candle. Each time I saw her, there was always a little less of her.

The reason she didn't go to the doctor, the reason she let this happen to her, the reason she let herself waste away until it was difficult to remember when she was ever there in the first place, was simple: Mom didn't want to feel better. I can't put it any more straightforward than that. It's not that Mom liked feeling bad, she didn't get off on it or anything. But she felt, at the very core of her being, as if she somehow *deserved* to be sick. I don't know when that happened. I feel like I remember a time when it wasn't like that. But I might just be telling myself that.

I never knew my father. I don't know when he left. Mom never told me. All I knew about him was a bomber jacket that hung in Sue's closet throughout my childhood, in the very back corner, where no one could see it and only we would ever know it was there. I don't know why Mom kept it. Maybe she didn't realize she had. But it hung there for decades, covered in a plastic bag, the same plastic bag the cheap dry cleaner's had packed it in the last time Mom thought about it. I wouldn't have even realized it was his had Sue not noticed his name, DEVINCENTIS, on a patch on the left breast pocket. It wasn't a military bomber jacket. It was just a jacket he probably got at a thrift store and put his name on, God knows why. There were no pictures of him. I don't know what he looks like. I used to look at Mom's face, see where it was different than mine and Sue's, and work off of that to figure out what he looked like. But I stopped doing that. That was dumb. Who cares? He was never there, and Mom never talked about him. There was just that jacket. When Mom moved into the home a few years ago, I threw the jacket away. That's not true, actually. When Mom moved into the home, I took the jacket out of the closet, dug a hole in the backyard, put the jacket in there, set it on fire, watched it burn, and buried the ashes. I wasn't mad at it, or him. I swear. I just wanted it gone. I wanted to make certain it never came back.

It was just me and Mom and Sue, from the beginning, until it all changed. Mom never had a boyfriend when I was a kid, but she had more than her fair share of options. Mom wasn't pretty, exactly, in the same way that I'm not pretty, exactly, though in a different way than the way Sue *was* pretty, but she was always shapely. She always wore these loud, bright wrap dresses, she said because they were comfortable, but even a little girl like me could tell the dresses also accentuated the parts of her that tended to be most attractive to men. (Sue, who was a couple of years older than me and a lot more comfortable talking about this sort of stuff, called them her "ba-BOOM" dresses.) Men never failed to notice. Thus there were occasional men, and some of them even visited her at our row house, but they never stayed for long, and Mom didn't want them to. "I get lonely," I remember her telling me, "but only for a little while." One time I walked home from middle school, I think I was in the seventh grade, and my science teacher pulled up in front of our house right as I got there. He looked embarrassed, but I told him not to worry. "Mom sometimes has guys over on her days off," I said. "It's no big deal." He turned around and left. Sue thought that story was hilarious. Mom was mad at me about it, but just for a second. "What in the world did you say to him?" she said. I just shrugged. She hugged me and made some mac and cheese, and then we watched *Survivor*.

That duplex was, still is, old and beaten down, but it was, and still is, ours. We didn't have cable or internet or anything like that, so I spent all my time with Sue in the basement, playing Connect Four and Clue, staying awake late at night reading or making shadow puppets on the concrete wall, waiting for Mom to come home. We had a cat who lived down there, Sylvester was her name, and she was in a constant state of pregnancy. I must have seen hundreds of kittens born in that basement. Sylvester would feed them for a couple of weeks, and then she would usher them into a little hole mice had bored into the wall. I don't know what happened to them after that, but she'd come back and do the whole thing a few months later. Sylvester ended up getting eaten by some sort of wild animal. I found what remained of her bones on the front porch one night, along with part of her skull. The next night I went out looking for that animal, whatever it was. I did not find it. But I know what I would have done if I had.

Anyway, Mom was never too happy, but I'm not sure she was ever *un*happy, at least not until what happened with Sue. She was just always a little tired, a little ill, a little confused. But it was fine. Mom did her shift at the restaurant, then she came home, and then she'd watch some TV with us, and then she'd make us go to bed, and when we'd wake up she'd still be on that couch, sometimes asleep, sometimes awake, but always on the couch. It was who she was. Mom was sick. She wasn't well. I don't know how she was sick. She was just sick. Sue always told me not to worry about it. "Mom's got problems just like everybody else," she said. "It's not our fault, and it's not hers."

She was like this before Sue left us. And she was like this before him. I have to remember this. It is sometimes hard to remember this.

Mom looked worse today. It has been a few weeks since I last saw her, and a little bit more of her goes away each time. There was something particularly faded about her today, like each breath she took vanished into ash. I don't know how much longer she will hang on. I am not entirely sure how much of her is left in there, how much of my mother, such as she was, remains. But I suspect whatever part of Mom is left has stopped fighting. I suspect she's ready for this to be over. I wonder, I worry, if maybe she always was.

THEO

10:47 a.m.

The old woman was staring at him, shaking her head gently, like she was just looking at the damnedest thing. The damnedest thing.

"You look just like him," she said. "I mean, I thought I was looking right at him when I walked in here. If I didn't know any better, I'd say he was standing in front of me right now." She patted Theo on the cheek. Theo wasn't sure how many times other people got their cheeks patted in their lives, but he figured the contours of his life had lined up in such a way that he soared far above the national average. We all are blessed with that one special thing.

Theo smiled a toothy grin. He'd had braces for nearly three years, throughout high school, way too old to have braces on that long, and he was so embarrassed of them that for two decades he only smiled with his lips closed, as if hiding the inside of his mouth. But he'd noticed that ever since he moved back to Athens, he was showing his teeth when he smiled. *Like the kid in the Lindbergh's logo.* He palpably refused to keep that fact in his mind longer than a couple of seconds.

"Yes, Ms. Keniley, been getting a lot of that lately," he said. "We Lindberghs, we've got strong genes."

"It's the cheekbones," Ms. Keniley said. "Your family has the most handsome features. Your dad had them, your grandpa had them. Your mother . . . she looks so . . ." Ms. Keniley paused, and Theo suddenly had a vague flicker of recognition, a memory of his youth, of his parents screaming at each other, of Theo putting on headphones and a Nirvana CD, as loud as he could play it. It was almost certainly because of someone like Ms. Keniley. It usually was. He tried to push the thought out of his mind.

"Well, your mother, she's her own woman," she said, as if she'd been about to say something else but changed her mind. "I do hope she's doing well. Tell her I said hello, would you?" Ms. Keniley, well into her seventies, appeared to be batting her eyes at him, if you can believe that. Was that what she was doing? He was faintly certain that she had done the same thing to his father, and maybe his grandfather. There was a small, somewhat gross little child behind her, fat, stupid, sneering, with snot hanging out of his nose, whacking her in the back of the knee with some sort of plastic tube. "G-Ma, you said I could have the iPad when we got out of the car," he wailed, and Theo thought that maybe it was a good thing he'd never had kids, because he would constantly be smacking them. "You *promised!* G-MA!!!!"

Ms. Keniley looked behind her, returned to Theo, and frowned slightly. "Sorry about that," she said. "You know children and their electronics!" She batted her eyes again, and there was no question about it, she definitely did it that time. "Well, I'll see you back in here tomorrow, I'm sure," she said, and she rubbed the bicep of his right arm. Theo knew he had puny little-girl arms, and he instinctively pulled back for a second before returning his arm to her hand. Customer satisfaction was Lindbergh's number-one goal, it was right there in the ads.

"It sure is great to have you back where you belong," she said. The shitty little kid grabbed the iPad out of his grandmother's purse and dropped it and screamed. "Noooooooooo!" he wailed, again, probably forever.

Theo took his arm from Ms. Keniley's grasp, for good this time, and smiled at her. "Well, it sure is great to see you," he said. "Please let me know if you need anything else, Ms. Keniley." She gave him one final eye-bat and went back to her lousy grandson, who would sit at the soda counter and continue pitching a fit for the next hour.

The last time Theo saw his father, Theo had been very much not at his best, but Jack wasn't either, a fact that, if Theo was being truthful, had brought him a modicum of comfort. The Dinner Party disaster was a few weeks in his rearview mirror at that point, and while Theo hadn't really come to terms with it yet—unless you counted sleeping until noon, eating Frosted Flakes, playing video games in his underwear, and feeling sorry for himself as coming to terms with it—he had to pull it together for his dad, who he still hadn't talked to since the restaurant had gone down.

Jack had been openly contemptuous of the Dinner Party idea from the beginning, but then again, he'd been openly contemptuous of just about everything Theo had done since leaving Athens. The two weeks after graduation Theo spent hiking the Appalachian Trail, the two months he lived in Spain with a college girlfriend, the summer he waited tables in New York City, the forever-aborted attempts to make some sort of name for himself, or at least a name for himself that wasn't the name he already had and everyone had forever associated him with, in the cutthroat Atlanta restaurant scene—it all seemed pointless to Jack, a waste of time, energy, and money. If Theo wanted to run a restaurant, well, there was one right there in Athens, waiting for him, just like it had been waiting for Jack. Theo hoped Dinner Party would strike his father as an impressive bit of ambition and go-get-'em-ness, but the very second Theo mentioned it to him, Jack had told him that it was an idiotic idea, and he was killing his mother, and what the hell did Theo know about South Asian food anyway?

The last time Theo saw his father, then, had been when he was still actively trying to avoid his father, a feat that wasn't particularly difficult: Jack rarely left Athens, within a three-block radius of Five

Points, all told. So it was a surprise when Jack rang the buzzer of Theo's Atlanta apartment at three on a random Tuesday afternoon.

"Hey, it's your dad," Jack's muffled but unmistakable baritone blared over the intercom. His deep voice was a Lindbergh's signature, how everyone knew their milkshake was made, their medicine was ready, *ORDER THIRRRRRRRRTY-FOOOOUURRRRRR.* "In town, thought I'd come by. Buzz me up."

At that moment Theo was wearing boxer shorts, his bathrobe, a T-shirt with a picture of ALF on it, and about twelve days of ragged, twisty beard. This was not going to be pleasant.

Jack was clean and pressed as always: light-blue button-up, pleated khakis, penny loafers, not a hair out of place even though he'd just tromped up four flights of stairs. Theo noticed that his black hair was unusually shiny, which he knew meant he'd just gotten it dyed.

"Well, it looks like you're keeping busy," Jack said, scanning the room, barren except for the television, a couple of pizza boxes, a half-empty wine bottle, and a bong in the shape of a Georgia football helmet. He picked up the bong. "Hey, go Dawgs."

"Sorry," Theo said, and it surprised him how much energy he suddenly had. He was horrified that his father was here, seeing him like this, and knew there would be hell to pay in the short and long term for it. But he also couldn't help but notice that he was moving around the apartment, cleaning up trash, wiping down counters, putting on non-Melmacian clothing, with a vigor and purpose he hadn't shown in weeks. Parental humiliation, he thought, was a potential source of sustained power that perhaps our nation's energy conglomerates had spent years tragically overlooking.

"I've had, uh, a lot going on around here lately," he said.

"I'm not sure there's a lot of evidence of that," Jack said, and a jolt of shame went through Theo so fast and so powerful that he almost jumped. Jack walked over to the bathroom closet, pulled out a folded towel, sniffed it, decided it was acceptable, draped it over one of the two folding chairs on the opposite side of the coffee table from Theo's old Barcalounger, pressed it straight with the back of his hands, and sat down. Theo took this as his cue to stop the mindless fidgeting he was doing with an SOS pad to look busy and sit down across from his father.

"So, hey, good to see you," Theo said, and in spite of it all, he meant it.

"You too, Theo," Jack said. "I was in the city today, and I didn't realize I was so near your apartment. So I thought I'd check in and see how you are doing. I think I have a pretty clear idea now of how you're doing."

The rest of Athens had of course adored Jack for decades, but not *this* Jack. This was the Jack only Theo and his mother knew: exacting, judgmental, and supernaturally smug. It was as if several decades of being the public face of Athens's oldest and most lasting institution, of acting as if everything was crisp and perfect and pressed and smiling, had convinced Jack that he was really like that, and that when either his son or his wife failed to live up to this entirely invented, extremely incorrect ideal, it was their fault, not his.

"I'm doing fine, Dad," Theo said, fifteen again.

"Well, I'm not so sure, but there's nothing I can do about that." Jack unbuttoned the buttons on his sleeve and buttoned them again. "But how I feel about this doesn't matter much. It clearly doesn't matter to you. But what you're doing to your mother . . . it's tearing her apart."

Theo knew this wasn't true, knew all too well that this was an old strategy of his father's: deflect his feelings about something onto his wife, act as if *he* didn't care but *she* did, as if emotion was foreign to him, but his wife, well, she was downright overcome by it, *Look what she's going through.* This served two purposes. It made Jack look like the calm, rational one, the person trying to be *logical* about everything, the one keeping his hands clean. And it made his wife look emotional and fraught. The second thing, not coincidentally, reinforced the first. Which fit Jack just fine.

Betty had always been seen as the *other* Lindbergh, the one who wasn't from Athens, the outsider, the one who had married into the Lindbergh's tradition but wasn't *of* it. This meant that if any sort of disagreement or conflict ever spilled into public view, Jack could count on the town having his back and not hers, and not her son's, who was thought, growing up, to be more his mother's son than of the hearty Lindbergh stock. It also meant that Jack could get away with anything. Athens would cover for him.

Everybody knew about Jack. The kids at school. The other employees at Lindbergh's. Betty's friends, who were at first supportive but then got exasperated with the whole situation and no longer mentioned it. All those rich men in their bow ties at the country club, sitting around the table talking about their golf games—they all nudged and winked at Jack anytime Betty went to the bathroom in a way that suggested they thought Theo wouldn't understand. It had only made it into their home twice. The first time involved one of Theo's teachers; he only vaguely remembered that one and felt no particular need to explore it any more deeply. The other he knew no details about other than the fact that Betty, when Theo was in the fourth grade, on a school night no less, woke him up at two in the morning and told him to get in the car, they were leaving, they had to go right now. They made it to a Holiday Inn in Winder, where Betty wept in the front seat for about half an hour, then started the car and drove back home, not saying a word the entire time. Theo just looked out the car window and tried to figure out what he'd done to make this happen. Then he fell asleep. He never brought it up again, and neither did Betty.

"Mom's fine," Theo said, with more spine than he meant to have.

"Oh, you would know that, yes?" Jack said, picking up a dirty rubber band off the carpet and flicking it into the garbage with disgust. A nice shot, actually. "I'm not sure how you'd know much of how anyone is doing. She never sees you. You're never home.

Though I do understand you are"—he paused, standing up to wash his hands in the kitchen sink—"obviously preoccupied."

It was not in Theo's nature to stand up to his father, which he figured was definitive proof that he was indeed his mother's son. He had rehearsed so many comebacks to his father, had even woken up in the middle of the night from dreams where he was screaming them at him, but he never used any of them. He was angry with his father, how could he not be? He was angrier at him, he thought, than he'd ever been angry with anyone else. He also loved him and wanted him to love him more than anything he had ever wanted in his entire life. Even Jack coming by and making him feel like shit felt like a gift. It had been a long time since Theo's father had just popped by.

"Well, I'm glad you came by," Theo said, meaning it. "You look sharp. Plans in the city?"

"Yes, I have, uh, a friend who lives near here," Jack said, and instantly Theo understood everything, the woman in her late forties who lived in the apartment two floors down and three doors over, the one who recognized him when her dog ran up and licked him while he was reading, the one who said, "Oh, yeah, I used to know your dad, I, um, still see him around from time to time, tell him Amy Shepherd said hi," the one who took great care of herself, the one who always seemed to be looking at him when he walked by, the one, if he was being honest, he was a little attracted to himself.

"Ah," Theo said, and the whole Amy Shepherd process he'd just gone through must have flickered across his face, because his father cocked his head slightly at him and said, "Oh, what is it now? What grand offense have I caused you this time?"

Theo looked at him and wanted to say something—wanted to pour it all out, really let him have it. But he didn't. He never did. Instead he stood up, said he needed to go to the bathroom, and left the room. He opened the lid to the toilet and saw unflushed urine from the night before. He wanted to vomit, but he didn't. He just put the lid down, flushed the handle, splashed water on his face, and stared at himself in the mirror. He saw Jack; he always saw Jack. *I look like shit*, he thought. *But I still look like him.*

Jack knocked on the door. "Do you need anything?" he said, not unkindly.

Theo opened the door, shook his head, and sat back down on the couch. "No, sorry, Dad, I'm just not feeling that well. I'm perfectly fine."

Jack took a handkerchief out of his pocket, soaked it with water from the sink, and put it on the back of Theo's neck. It felt good. Jack's phone vibrated and buzzed. He took it out, he chuckled lightly to himself, he put it away.

"Theo, I need to go," he said, and he bent down on one knee and lifted Theo's chin so their eyes met. He stared at him, gently, with a look that Theo knew Jack didn't want to look like pity but absolutely, 100 percent, no fucking question, was nothing but pity.

"Your life doesn't have to be like this," Jack said. "Let me help you. Will you let me help you?"

"I'm fine." Theo looked away. He stood up and began aimlessly wiping down the kitchen counter, trying to look busy, trying to look like he no longer noticed that Jack was in the room at all. Jack nodded at him and silently walked out of the room, and out of the apartment, and almost certainly two floors down and three doors over, and three weeks later he was dead and now Theo had his old job and it was just the damnedest thing.

THEO HAD NEVER TRIED HEROIN, WOULD NEVER TRY HEROIN. HE CONSIDERED himself a better class of drug addict than that. Sure, if you were going to be all pedantic about it, the Opana he popped a little bit more of each day was in the same family as heroin, all descendants of the same poppy field in, oh, probably China, or Afghanistan maybe—OK, all told, he didn't really know where you grew opium. (A field, though, definitely. Or a cave? Probably a field.) But a pill made it different. Pills were normal! Everybody took pills. He doled them out all day, after all. Old ladies took pills, high school kids took pills, babies took pills. Pills were as large a part of Lindbergh's history as the little York Peppermint Patties they sold at the checkout register. (Still just a dime!) There was nothing wrong with pills. Heck, what kind of fake pharmacist would he be if he wasn't comfortable with pills? Can't trust a pharmacist who doesn't trust pills. Pills were life. Pills made the world go around. Pills pills pills, yeah yeah yeah, pills pills pills, whaddya say?

"I think it's probably clean now."

Theo was snapped out of his scintillating internal dissertation on oral dosage via compressed tablets and their musical accompaniments by the young woman whose arm he had been mindlessly dabbing with rubbing alcohol for about eleven seconds longer than he needed to.

"Oh, sorry," he said. "Spaced out for a second there." He followed this with a giggle that was louder and more demonstrative than he meant it to be.

"All good," the woman said. "My arms are too hairy anyway. I appreciate your makeshift wax."

This was the point when he was supposed to ask her if she had any questions about the vaccine, but Theo was pretty sure he wasn't qualified to answer them. First off: he wasn't a medical professional, no matter how far you tried to stretch that definition. The most complicated medical procedure he'd ever performed was giving one of his hostesses at Dinner Party the Heimlich when she'd started choking, and he was terrible at it; he nearly cracked her rib. You technically needed a pharmacist's license, or some sort of, you know, medical degree, to administer vaccine shots. That was the law.

But at a place like Lindbergh's, customers didn't want some stranger in a mask and plastic gloves and a face shield giving them shots. They wanted a face they could trust. And there was no face you could trust like a Lindbergh face. They might not have known Theo at all—they certainly didn't know he was so stoned all day at work that occasionally he'd catch himself staring at the blood pressure pump long enough that he thought it was starting to look a little like Eleanor Roosevelt. They knew his face, though. They knew he was that little kid on the sign, and if you couldn't trust that little kid on the sign, here in this place that had served their parents and their grandparents and their children, there was no one in this godforsaken world you could trust anymore. So he had the pharmacist and the nurse train him on the correct way to jab a person, and it really wasn't hard, why did you need a medical degree to do this anyway, and now when someone came in and asked if maybe Theo could be the one to give them the shot, he could do it just fine. He liked it. It made him feel like he was helping.

That was what this woman in front of him had done. Alexis was her name, and she'd walked into Lindbergh's, the rare face no one had seen before. She had told Sandy at the register that she was here for a vaccine and was told to ask if "a Theo" could do it. That got Theo away from his brief Hyde Park vacation, and he greeted her. He was rubbing the hair off her arm before he knew it.

"Aren't you supposed to ask me if I have any questions about the vaccine?" she said. Theo, his fog starting to clear, noticed that he could not stop looking at her. She had straight burnt-brown hair that always seemed to be strategically hanging over one eye, and she had a wry grin that made Theo think she understood something about him that he didn't, even though she had never met him before this very moment.

"Uh, yeah, I think," he said. "Do you?"

"Covid is bad. If I get a shot, I don't get Covid. Therefore getting the shot is good. It's not terribly complicated, no?"

Theo smiled. "I suppose I can't put it any better than that," he said, and dropped his syringe. He stared at it as it fell, in slow motion, carried along by the wind and the fates, as it skittered and spun across the floor. It was beautiful, he thought.

He looked up at Alexis staring at him, wearing that grin. "Uh, you OK, dude?" she said, and Theo was so relieved that she was laughing that he wanted to hug her.

"Yes, yes, sorry," he said. "Morning jitters, I apologize. Shall we try again?"

"I mean, I guess so," she said, flipping that hair out of her eye. Theo watched it fall right back there again; it was somehow magic. "Eventually one of those is going to have to end up sticking me."

Theo prepared another shot and, when he realized he'd been wiping her arm for too long again, started up some normal human regular person nothing the least bit strange here nope conversation. "So, are you a student here?"

"I'm not, though I'm flattered," she said. "I'm thirty-three. You really don't look at that paperwork closely, do you?" The wry smile again. "I just moved here from New York. My mom's a professor here, and I'm up for a bit trying to get my shit together."

"I know the feeling," Theo said. "This isn't the worst place to get your shit together."

"It kinda is when you're stuck inside with your mom for thirteen months," Alexis said. "But that's what we're trying to do here today, right? This is my ticket to rejoin the world." He noticed that she was fidgeting a bit. "Hey, do you all sell cigarettes here?"

"Here? At a drugstore?" He chuckled. "Uh, no, no we don't."

"Oh, don't act so surprised," she said, laughing, actually poking him in the shoulder. "This place was probably selling cocaine in soda pop forty years ago. Didn't places like this used to be involved with *owwwwww*!"

Theo found it better to just give people the shot rather than warn them it was coming.

"Sorry," he said. "I didn't drop that one."

"That hurt like a fucker," she said, and put her hand over her mouth. "Can I say that in a family establishment?" Theo noticed she'd started to move a little closer to him on her chair.

"I think it's OK," he said. "We stopped caning people for

vulgarity a couple of years ago. Did a number on our insurance premiums."

He put a bandage over her arm, taped it up, and gave her some paperwork to sign. "Would you like to make your appointment for your second shot right now?"

"Yes, actually, but I have a question for you first," she said. "My mom actually told me to come in and get this shot with you today. That's why I asked for you. She apparently knew your dad from when she first moved here years ago, and she said we should meet."

Theo felt his stomach drop to his feet, as if someone had instantly replaced all his bones with uncooked Polish sausage.

Alexis noticed. "Oh, don't worry, he's not my dad or anything, though she told me you might think that if I said that, which is actually really sad, now that I said it out loud." Theo must have looked so ghastly. "I think she knew your mom a little better anyway. She just, you know, suggested I get my shot here, and here I am."

The hair fell back over her eye, but he could still see it staring at him, up and down. "And here you are," he said. "Getting your shit together."

"Trying to," she said, popping a York Peppermint Pattie in her mouth. "But hey, isn't everybody?"

"Don't I know it," Theo said. He felt like someone had just put a warm rag on the back of his neck.

"So," she said, looking around the pharmacy, "no offense, but you don't look too busy." She shifted her jaw subtly in a way Theo sensed she wanted him to notice. "You wanna have lunch?"

Theo had known this woman for exactly twenty-one minutes and was riding a pretty serious Opana high, so he wasn't exactly sure about this, but he also had a vague sense that he might want to have lunch with this woman more than he'd ever wanted anything in his life.

DOROTHY

11:21 a.m.

The pleasant Australian voice told of horrible things, of the death of poor Edna Gibson, a seventy-three-year-old woman, just a little younger than Dorothy, a library worker who disappeared back in January 1992 while waiting for a bus not far from her home in Owensboro, Kentucky. She was living a quiet life, and then one day she vanished. They found her body two months later, next to two college girls, both presumably murdered by the same person who murdered her. They never found the person who killed them and three other girls and women, and police are still trying to solve the case more than thirty years later. The podcast floated the names of a couple of suspects, but all the evidence was circumstantial. As Dorothy watered her hydrangeas and swatted away a sweat bee trying to nestle under her right ear, she wondered if eventually the police would just stop trying. Sometimes, people are just gone. Nothing much else you, or anyone else, can do about it.

Dorothy had gotten into podcasts during the pandemic. It was Wynn's suggestion, on a Zoom call, when he thought his mother had sounded lonelier than usual, a little more out of touch, a little bit too lost. Wynn always had a feel for what his mother needed,

96

and he was right: listening to podcasts was good for her. In the first months after Dennis went, she did everything she could to stop herself from spinning out. She drank for a while, but that stopped working; she swam laps in their pool, but it got too gross. (Dennis had always been in charge of cleaning it; eventually she just hired somebody.) She tried reading novels but ended up stopping anytime something sad happened (and something sad always happened). She'd had some luck with going on long walks, but it was too quiet, too easy to get trapped in the catacombs of her own grief, and listening to music didn't work because all the songs were about love or sex or loss. She started out listening to political podcasts, because it was 2020 and everything was about politics in 2020, and she got herself hooked. She loved how a well-orchestrated podcast discussion made her life fade away, how listening to smart people have smart discussions about the world in which she lived made her feel like a silent, invisible observer—like they were talking to each other just for her, even if they didn't know it. She didn't think about Dennis or her grief or how alone she was. She just tuned out and listened to the smart people tell her what she should be thinking about the news. It was a relief. It was nice to have someone else be in control.

After the election, Dorothy, like everybody else, needed a break from politics. So she discovered true crime. She'd always had a thing for grisly crime stories—she and Dennis used to order dinner in on Friday nights and watch *Dateline NBC*, where they tried to find the missing girl, where the wife vanished and the husband was the prime suspect, where you tried to imagine how you would handle all of that if it were happening to you, in your life. (Dennis loved making fun of the preening prosecutors, who always got to look like virtuous geniuses on those shows. "This guy spent more money on his hair than paralegals," Dennis whispered into Dorothy's ear as she nestled her head in his chest.) And the great thing about true crime podcasts was that there was a never-ending supply of them. As soon as you were finished with one series, there was another just waiting for you. She loved getting lost in the stories, in solving the mysteries, of trying to comprehend the motivations of everyone involved, even the bad guys—especially the bad guys.

Dennis had never felt this way. His judicial philosophy was simple: there were laws, and if you broke them, you had to face the consequences. He was aware of, and empathetic to, the circumstances of crime. But he had little interest in the psychology behind it. Life was a series of choices, he thought, and if you made the wrong ones, well, that was on you. He didn't find crime intriguing, or mysterious, or compelling. He saw crime as a way of sorting people. If you committed a crime and ended up in his court, it was his job to decide how long you needed to be separated from society until it allowed you back in again.

But Dorothy didn't think that. She loved her husband. She thought he was a great judge. But she thought he was wrong about that. Sometimes people just did things because they were scared—too scared to make much of a choice at all. She was pretty sure she had proof.

IT WAS WYNN'S JUNIOR YEAR OF HIGH SCHOOL, WITH WILLIAM ALREADY off in New Haven, when Dorothy answered the front door and was welcomed by a handgun in her face.

When the doorbell rang, she thought Wynn had ordered a pizza or something. It had been one of those busy fall evenings when Dennis was still at the courthouse and Wynn had gotten back late from Clarke Central baseball practice and Dorothy had been putting together her speech at the Starry Starry Night event for Brightpaths, an anti-child-abuse charity that had its annual gala that upcoming weekend. She was proud to have this busy, active, *striving* family: you were expected to achieve in the Johnson household, to make your mark in the world, and that meant working or studying or practicing well into the dinnertime hours.

Wynn was upstairs preparing for a science test tomorrow and must have ordered a pizza. Poor thing probably hadn't eaten all day.

And then there was a gun in her face.

"You're the wife, right?" the man said. He was short, so short that he was pointing the gun up at her. He was wearing a logoless black baseball cap, a black leather jacket, tight black trousers, black gloves, and black sunglasses, even though the sun had gone down hours before.

She looked down at him. This was the first time she'd ever had a gun pointed at her, and it surprised her how little it bothered her. She was calm—focused. She would tell Dennis later that it felt like the whole incident was happening to someone else, as if she were in a movie theater watching a character go through the experience onscreen. That character didn't have to worry, because Dorothy was in her seat, watching from a distance, assessing, whispering in the character's ear what she was supposed to do.

"My name is Dorothy," she said. "Can I help you with something?"

The man looked at her and cocked his head to the left slightly, like a dog watching a hummingbird. She saw a bead of sweat roll down his left cheek.

"The judge," he said. "Judge Johnson. He lives here, right?"

"I—"

"Shut the fuck up, I know he does," the man said, and shoved the door open, pushing Dorothy backward into the front hallway. He pointed the gun at her, and then at the couch in the front room, the really nice room of the house, the one without a television, the one Dorothy never let anyone walk through with their shoes on. It was also the room she and Dennis sometimes had sex in when the boys were gone for the night. You need to mix it up sometimes. "Sit down there."

Dorothy walked over to the couch, but before she sat down, she motioned to the antique chair across from her on the other side of the coffee table.

"Would you like to have a seat?" she said, and he gave her the dog hummingbird look again. Dorothy wasn't sure what her plan was, but she knew both that it would likely be many hours before Dennis got home, and that Wynn was going to get hungry and take those headphones playing that rap music off his head and venture out of his room long before that happened. She needed this man calm.

He sort of grinned for a split second—amused by her, Dorothy thought. That was good. Amused was closer to calm. He sat down in the antique chair. He took a short breath, pointed the gun at her, and looked her in the eye.

"Where's your husband?" he said, waving the gun at a photo of her and Dennis with Michelle Obama that sat above the fireplace. "He working late?"

Dorothy put her hands in her lap and thought for a second. Telling this man and his gun that Dennis would be home later tonight would keep him here until Dennis arrived, whenever that was. Lying and telling him he was out of town would either get him out of here more quickly . . . or make it so that he felt like he could do whatever he wanted while he was here. There was also Wynn to deal with. Wynn was not calm or collected like Dorothy or her husband: he would freak out if he came across this scene, and that would freak out the man and, perhaps, his gun. Wynn might stay in his room for hours. Or he might come out at any minute. Dorothy felt like the arrivals of Dennis or Wynn were alarm clocks hovering over the whole proceeding. Eventually one of them was going to go off. She needed it resolved before either did.

She would have to do this herself.

Dorothy sighed and looked at the man. She was surprised by how not threatened she was by him. This was the first time someone had pointed a gun at her. It was no big deal, she thought. How did she know this guy wasn't going to use it? There was no way she could know that. But somehow she did.

She smiled at the man. "He's out of town for the week," she

said. She could handle this guy. "At a conference in Richmond. Is there anything I can help you with?"

The man raised an eyebrow. "I'm not sure I believe you," he said.

"Well, you don't have to," she said. "He's not coming home until Sunday, and what you believe has nothing to do with that. So I ask you again: What can I help you with?"

"Fuck!" the man yelled to the ceiling. Dorothy very much hoped Wynn had his headphones on. "He told me the judge was going to be here. Goddamned idiot, don't know shit! Should have my head examined, listening to that asshole." He stood up from his chair and began to pace. Dorothy stood up with him, slowly, with her right hand out in front of her, palm facing out.

"I work very closely with my husband. Again, I can help you, if you just sit down," she said. "Can I fix you a drink?" *Can I fix you a drink?* The version of Dorothy sitting in the movie theater watching all this was astounded by how calm the version of Dorothy in the really nice room was being through all this. *Maybe I should have been a spy.*

The man took off his ball cap and revealed a few sad strands of thinning hair and all sorts of splotchy red spots on his scalp. Dorothy understood why he wore a hat.

He shook his head back and forth like a dog trying to dry himself. He spat a "Fuck! Fuuuuuuuuck!" at the ceiling again, coughed, whispered, "All right, all right, focus," to himself, and sat back down. He did not point the gun at Dorothy again, instead cradling it in his lap carefully. "So you know so much about your husband's work. You know about Teddy Crosby, then, do you?"

Who didn't know about Teddy Crosby? Teddy Crosby had been all over the news. He was a student at Athens Technical College who, one night about a year ago, was out drinking and smoking crack, or something, Dorothy never could tell any of those drugs apart, with one of his buddies when they decided, in their infinite wisdom, to rob a Waffle House. These were not skilled criminals—they didn't seem to Dorothy to be particularly skilled at anything—so when one of them (and it was a matter of considerably contentious testimony at the trial which one it was) pulled a gun on the cashier, he didn't notice the family eating quietly at the booth behind him. That family was the family of Trent Curbelo, the associate athletic director at the University of Georgia, who had just come back from a softball game at Jack Turner Stadium and was enjoying some smothered and covered hash browns with his wife and their three children. Teddy, or the other guy, Dorothy didn't remember his name, one of them, addled by whatever weird drugs he was on, quickly spun around startled when he heard one of the children drop a metal fork on the checkered linoleum floor. He pulled the trigger—all sides agreed it was an accidental pull, not that it mattered—and fired a bullet directly into the brain of Curbelo's lovely wife Doreen, killing her instantly as her husband and their three children watched, their food still warm in front of them. It was a horrific tragedy that had become the only thing that could knock the president off the front page. Curbelo and his children had come out at halftime of a Georgia game that last fall and received a thunderous ovation. That poor, poor family. Teddy's buddy, whatever his name was, testified that Teddy had fired the weapon, that in fact it was Teddy's idea to hold up the Waffle House, that Teddy had dragged him into all sorts of other crimes, that he was "a damn wildman." The jury, presided over by the honorable Judge Dennis Johnson, believed the friend. At sentencing, Dennis was thunderous and rageful; Dorothy had told him, after watching him on television, that he had "gotten his Old Testament on." He sentenced Teddy to the maximum possible punishment, three consecutive forty-year sentences, without the possibility of parole for thirty-five years.

"Is he your brother?" Dorothy said. "You look like him."

The man looked down, then looked back up and snarled at her. "He didn't deserve what your husband did to him," he said, eyes cold, nostrils flaring. "He didn't fire the gun. He didn't even want to be there. It was that asshole set him up. I'm sorry what happened to that family, I really am, and I know Teddy was too. But he's just a kid. It was Wallace, he fired the gun, he got Teddy hooked on drugs, he was the one always causing all the trouble. He sold my brother out. And your husband believed him."

Wallace, that had been his name, *Wallace*, he had made a deal with the DA and only had to do a year in county. Wallace knew what was good for him, and when his time was up, he moved the hell out of North Georgia.

"So what were you going to do to my husband, had he been here?" Dorothy said. She noticed that the man had begun to sweat, and that he was compulsively tapping his left foot. "Were you going to shoot him with that gun?"

He looked at her, then at the gun in his lap. "I don't know," he said, and sighed deeply. His nostrils were no longer flaring. Whatever mad force that had driven him to do something as self-destructive as invading the house of a judge to get leniency on his brother had left him now. Now he was in even deeper shit. He clicked his tongue. "I don't think so." He cracked his neck and looked incredibly tired. Dorothy almost felt bad for him.

"I was hoping I could get him to listen to me," he said, and Dorothy thought she saw a tear welling in his left eye. "My brother doesn't deserve to die in prison. He really doesn't. I just . . . I guess I just don't know what my plan was." His eyes met hers. He looked like he wanted to crawl underneath the floorboards.

"I wasn't going to shoot him, though," he said. "I just wanted him to list—"

"Hey, Mom, why is the front door open?" Wynn said, ambling into the room with headphones around his neck and a slice of cold pizza halfway in his mouth. "Wait, wha—"

The Dorothy sitting in the movie theater watched everything go down in slow motion. The Dorothy in the really nice front room, as the man turned his head to her sixteen-year-old son who had a big science project due tomorrow, grabbed the poker next to the fireplace and swung it at the head of the man. She took a big enough swing that she didn't slice his face with it; instead the metal rod met his skull with a thick, wet *thwack*, knocking him out of the chair. She grabbed a massive book off the coffee table called *The Golden Age of Couture: Paris and London, 1947–57* and landed it on the back of his head, bashing it against the floor so hard that she thought she heard the flooring wood crack. The man groaned and lay there. Dorothy picked the gun up off her wool and silk rug, ran to her bedroom marble-top side table, pulled out a pair of handcuffs that she and Dennis always kept in a drawer there for *no reason whatsoever*, and slapped one cuff on the man's left hand and the other on the leg of her grandmother's antique Victorian chest that had taken four movers three hours to get through the front door.

She pointed the gun at the man's head. "Stay the fuck right there."

"Holy shit, Mom," Wynn said, pizza still in his mouth.

Three hours later, after the police had taken the man away, after Dennis had come home and wept for hours as Dorothy and Wynn tried to calm him down, after everyone had gone to bed, Dorothy poured herself a glass of brandy and sat on a rocking chair on her front porch. She'd found an old cigar in her husband's desk, unwrapped it, and lit it. It filled her lungs and her nostrils and made her cough and cough and tasted terrible, but also a little sweet and burning, in a not-unpleasant way. She was flushed from the evening, but not with fear. She was, she had to admit it, excited. Her heart was pumping, in fact. She had been in charge the whole time. She, or the Dorothy in the movie theater, had known this man was more lost and scared and sad than he was particularly dangerous. He did what he did because he didn't know what to do—he did what he did because he felt like he didn't have a choice. He hadn't thought it through, because when you are sad and you are scared and you are backed in a corner, how can you think anything through?

But Dorothy, she thought it through. She saw it all unfolding in front of her. She knew what to do from the very first second, something her son or husband hadn't known about her, something she hadn't known herself, until she suddenly did. She smoked her stogie and drank her brandy and felt in charge. She felt strong. She felt indestructible.

Later she would lobby her husband, successfully, to convince the judge who presided over the man's case to take it easy on him. He had suffered enough, that was true, but that's not why Dorothy did it. Dorothy did it because he had given her so much. She did it because she was grateful.

DOROTHY WALKED BACK TOWARD HER HOUSE, LISTENING TO THE AUSTRALIAN man wrap up the story of the Owensboro murders, pausing to pick up some trash off the ground and pet a cat that lazily strolled across her path. It was quiet out here, still, just her and the voices in her head, the people telling stories that seemed to exist just for her. The podcasts, and the lives of the people in them, made her feel less alone, made her feel like no matter what happened to her, or Dennis, or the people she loved, somewhere out there, people would still be telling their stories, and those stories would find a way to make someone else feel less alone. You didn't really have a choice on how it all turned out, she thought. You had no control over what happened to you. What mattered was finding out who you were in the wake of it.

Dorothy was proud to keep learning new lessons about herself. It made her feel good. It made her feel like she was doing all she could do.

4. SUE

Sue was one of those older sisters who let her younger sister hang out with her friends. Most older sisters aren't like that. Sue's friends certainly weren't. They were always annoyed that I was there. They wanted to talk about boys, and Leonardo DiCaprio, and how creepy Mr. Barreto was in art class, and I never understood what they were talking about and they never made any effort to let me in. But Sue let me be there anyway, and always defended me. She wanted me there. It's important for a little sister to feel wanted.

Sue was always the one with the good head on her shoulders. Mom used to say, "Sue, sometimes I feel like you're the mom," and Sue always gave me a little "Don't we know it!" nudge. Sue took care of everything. She made dinner every night, she checked on my homework, she fixed Mom her drinks, she made sure all the lights were off at night, she always was the one who answered the door when someone knocked. Sue never got good grades—I was the one who had the book smarts—but she always seemed to know how to do everything. Any device that needed hooked up, any piece of technology we couldn't figure out, any blinking light no one knew how to turn off, she always took care of it. It was Sue who talked me through my first period, not Mom; it was Sue who told me never to have sex without a condom; it was Sue who, after the guy sitting behind me in algebra class snapped my bra strap and made me cry, grabbed him by the back of the neck, smashed his head into a locker, and slammed the door on his face. She made sure everyone in the school saw too.

Whenever there was bad news, she handled it for us—she guided us through it. I remember when the Oklahoma City bombing happened, I was a freshman, she was a junior, and after they announced it in class, and the teacher was crying, and all the kids were scattered and rattled, when I opened the door once the school bell rang, she was out there waiting for me.

"Are you OK?" she said. It was as if she had been there all day.

"I am," I said. "It's really scary."

"It's all right," she said. "I'm here." And she was.

She kept us on track. Mom was wrong to feel like Sue was the mom. Sue was more like our dad—had our dad been a real dad. She was stable and solid and strong. She had earned that bomber jacket, not him. We depended on her. The house would never have worked without her.

She was going to college in Atlanta, Kennesaw State. She wanted to be an engineer—"I want to wear the little railroad hat," she used to joke, though I was never quite sure if she understood that wasn't what engineering was—but didn't have near the grades to pull off Georgia Tech, and we wouldn't have been able to afford a full four years there anyway, so she had applied to Kennesaw State as a general studies major. Her plan was to get straight As her first year, "by hook or by crook," she'd said, and then transfer to Tech. I never knew why she wanted to go to Tech so badly. Maybe she just wanted to get out of here.

She was a senior. She went to homecoming with some dork none of us knew who was six inches taller than Sue but felt a foot shorter. She had some other weird guy who would always call her on Thursday nights, but she wouldn't tell us anything about him. She always wore big hoop earrings. She really liked going to Pearl Jam shows. She had a tiny tattoo of the mask of comedy and tragedy on her left ankle. She sometimes sneaked sips of Mom's wine coolers in the fridge but otherwise thought drinking was gross and stupid. She had black hair that went down just below her shoulders. She thought her breasts were too big. She had a vein that always popped out of the left side of her neck. She had a tendency to call people "bud"—"Hey, bud, what's up, bud?"—when she met them. She had played basketball in middle school before injuring her knee but still had a flawless jump shot. She subscribed to *Entertainment Weekly* and *Rolling Stone* but never seemed to read either one of them. She laughed too loudly at dirty jokes, like she wanted to sound like she was cooler with them than she really was. She always caught me when I picked my nose, and she'd say, "Pick me out a Cadillac!" She snored. She loved Popeye's chicken. She never wore a wristwatch. She had hazel eyes. She was allergic to penicillin. She once broke the DVD player and blamed it on the cat. She was really good at Tetris. She made me laugh. She made us all laugh. She was better than we were.

Was she? Or am I just remembering her that way? It doesn't really matter.

Mom was working a shift at the Texas Roadhouse that night. She had little odd jobs like that back then, after she'd stopped working full-time at the walk-in clinic, after she'd exhausted all her sick days and they'd issued her one last ultimatum that she couldn't meet, back when she could still work a full shift on her feet, before she went on disability, before she gave up. She waitressed at a lot of places, and Sue and I found the fancier the place and the higher her nightly take-home (a night or two a week at Five & Ten, Saturdays at the Last Resort), the less we liked the food; I wished she could just waitress at Steak & Shake. We were fine with the Texas Roadhouse, though. She always brought us back a steak sandwich and a baked potato wrapped in tinfoil.

I was home, as usual, watching a movie with Billy Crystal in it, I don't remember which one, it wasn't very funny. I didn't know where Sue was, only that she was out with her friends. I didn't know which friends, though of course I can recite their names by heart now: Nicole O'Neill, Veronica Westin, and Alice Verdan. Sue didn't tell us who she was with, or where she was going, because she didn't need to—Mom and I were too disorganized to do much with the information anyway. I guarantee you Sue knew where we were, though. She always knew where we were.

We discovered later what Sue and her friends were doing. There was nothing untoward—no one was even drinking. Nicole was driving, and everyone was bored on a Friday night before all the parties started, so they drove out to Watkinsville to see the Iron Horse. It wasn't even dark out yet. The Iron Horse—official name *Pegasus without Wings*, for some reason—is an old metal sculpture made back in the 1950s by a Georgia artist, and it used to sit on campus until, inevitably, college students started defacing it. So a farmer in Watkinsville bought it and placed it on his property, just off Route 15. There's nothing that special about it. It's not a particularly impressive sculpture. But it's weird, and it's definitely weird to find it in some random farm twenty miles outside of Athens, so bored teenagers and UGA students like to drive out to it and take pictures with it. I've seen it. It's no big deal. But it's something to do.

No one is quite clear what happened, or why it happened. The woman in the other car—she'd just left her job answering phones for a dermatology clinic—told the 911 operator that she'd been driving home on the two-lane Route 15 when a car, a 1993 white Toyota Camry, Nicole's 1993 white Toyota Camry, all of a sudden swerved into her lane, right in front of her. "I slammed on the brakes," she said on the call, a call I could listen to right now on any number of websites if I wanted to, "but there was no way either one of us could have stopped." Nobody had any booze or drugs in their systems, which wasn't a surprise. Sue wouldn't have been so foolish and wouldn't hang out with anyone who was. She was always looking ahead to something, whatever it was. Maybe Nicole's hand slipped on the steering wheel. Maybe she wasn't paying attention. Maybe she was trying to avoid an animal crossing the road. That doesn't really matter either.

The other car hit Nicole's car on the passenger side, which is surely where Sue was sitting: Even when she wasn't driving, she was up front, telling everybody where to go and what to do. The investigators calculated that the woman was driving the speed limit, actually a little bit under it, they guessed. But a Ford Escort hurtling directly at you at fifty-three miles per hour will kill you just as dead as a Ford Escort hurtling directly at you at eighty miles per hour will. Nicole's car spun around and flipped down Route 15 an estimated seventeen times, coming to a stop in a ditch five and a half miles away from the Iron Horse. They'd barely even left.

They told us they all died instantly. I never knew if they were just telling us that to be nice or not.

The police had found Sue's driver's license with her address on it and called the house, about two hours after the accident happened. Mom was still at work. I was at home by myself, still bored by Billy Crystal. The phone went to voice mail two full times before I answered it. I hated answering the phone back then, and I hate it even more now. The third time, I finally got annoyed enough to answer. I was 15 years old. Mom was at work. I was by myself.

I didn't scream. I didn't cry. It didn't feel like it was really happening. It felt like a joke Sue was playing on me. I told the sheriff that my mom was working at the Texas Roadhouse, they should call her there, he said they'd send a squad car over there, I told them thank you and hung up the phone. I went back to the movie. I don't know why I did that. It wasn't real. I didn't want to accept it. I was fifteen years old. Mom was at work. I was by myself.

There was a police car, lights flashing, twenty minutes later. Mom got out of the back seat. She didn't say a word. She walked to the front door and opened it. I turned toward her and saw her walk into the screen door. I'd closed it, I don't remember why, but Mom walked into it so forcefully that it fell straight to the floor. She tripped on it and fell down hard on her left knee. She was still wearing her Texas Roadhouse uniform.

She glanced toward me on the couch. I glanced back at her.

"Are you OK?" I said. Her knee was starting to bleed.

"Did they tell you?" she said. There was no emotion in her voice. It was like it was all already gone.

"Yes," I said, but I wasn't crying yet either. I felt like all my bones had turned to metal—like my body had gone cold and rigid and fused into steel, the Iron Horse, Pegasus without Wings. "They called me first."

My mother looked into my eyes. She closed her eyes and passed out, right there on the mud room floor. I let her lie there. Waking her felt cruel.

They buried Sue a week later. Neither Mom nor I went. Neither one of us even left the house. She had hazel eyes and she was allergic to penicillin and she was better than we were and she always will be.

JASON

11:58 a.m.

"You gonna hold the rope up there, or are you too busy hold- ing your pecker?" Jason yelled up to Tommy T, who was on Coach Tepper's roof, fidgeting with some stray branches and barely keeping a fiberglass mop fifteen feet in the air.

"Yeah, yeah," Tommy T growled down at him, his long hair dripping with sweat and matted to the back of his neck. "I ain't dropped it on your head yet, have I?"

This afternoon, Tommy T was in charge of tarring the roof of the new wing of Coach Tepper's house, where little Timothy Tepper would spend the next couple years of his life telling his father he was studying while really playing video games. It was hot already, but Tommy T would be applying the roofing tar in the afternoon cauldron, when even the most basic task, done in the scorching Georgia sun, makes you feel like a convict on a chain gang. So as he tugged the mop up the side of the new room, trying not to scrape any of the paint primer Buck had put on yesterday, he was in a grouchy mood. It was going to be a long day.

"Heat's good for ya," Jason said. "Maybe it'll finally get ya to cut your stupid-ass hair."

Tommy T held the rope with his left hand and flipped Jason off with his right, which was hilarious because Tommy T had chopped off his middle finger on a job about three years ago—they were cleaving some branches and he got his hand stuck in there—and thus could only half-flip anybody off. He always joked he had to flip people off twice as often as everybody else just to catch up.

"Oh, shit, he's got out the stump," Jason yelled to Buck, who was smoothing out cement for a sidewalk leading out to the pool just down the way. "Now I've really pissed him off." The crew all laughed. Tommy T gave him another half-bird and laughed too.

Jason was always more relaxed and jokey with his crew than he was with anyone else. He probably felt more comfortable out on a job than he did anywhere else in the world. The crew loved him, he knew it, and the reason he knew it is because they'd stopped trying to screw him. The hardest part of Jason's job was finding a good crew, but it wasn't because the work was particularly complicated or complex. Nobody grows up wishing to have a job where you stand on your feet in the Georgia heat all day, wrenching your back and smashing your fingers for twenty bucks an hour, and therefore the only people who have that job are either people who truly love it—and those people usually end up running a crew, rather than working on one—or people without any other viable options. People generally worked for Jason because they'd fucked up their life in one way or another, and people who have spent their life fucking up tend to continue to do so. Waller Construction rolled through crew like toilet paper—all construction companies did. Jason had seen people who couldn't make it through the first day. A young kid once showed up clearly high on pills and nodded off two hours into their first gig; Black Harold had stuck French fries up the kid's nose at lunch, the rest of the crew got a big kick out of that. One time a Mexican guy—Jason thought he might have been Mexican, anyway—had responded to a homeowner asking him to wipe his feet before coming in the house by telling her, a fifty-five-year-old economics professor, to "suck his dick." One guy had clearly just shown up to try to steal tools; he'd gotten away with two hammers, a crescent wrench, and a reciprocating saw before Little Todd caught him. Jason had to stop Buck from killing him right then and there. He probably would have.

But it was usually about money, and work. People would ask for advances and not show up again. They'd claim they worked eight hours when they were barely on a site for two. They'd say they were going on a "tool run" and not return. They'd make their lunch hours stretch all day. They'd do anything they could to avoid putting in a full day's work; it was exactly how jobs that were supposed to take six weeks ended up lasting four months. Nothing angered Jason more. He'd rather you try to steal his tools. He'd spent years whittling these guys out of his crew, gently at first and then very much not gently. He'd once decked a guy, dude named Dax, for not showing up for a job for four days straight and then trying to shake Jason down for cash. Dax, bigger than Jason but a weak coward from the day he was born, had gone flailing into Mrs. Porter's cloudberry bushes. He slunk away, muttering about lawsuits and not standing for this bullshit, but Jason knew Dax wouldn't dare come within a half mile of him again after that, and he was right.

Depending on the size of the job, though, Jason didn't have to worry about this problem anymore. He had his loyal crew: Buck, Little Todd, Tommy T, Black Harold, and White Harold. They weren't perfect—White Harold, in particular, was always grousing and carrying on quite a bit for a guy whose work Jason always had to end up fixing—and, with the exception of Buck, they weren't the craftsmen Jason was. But they showed up on time, they stuck to the schedule, they worked when they were supposed to, they took the jobs seriously and dedicated themselves to doing them well. This was not the same thing as *actually* doing them well, but for twenty bucks an hour, you couldn't expect perfection. They respected Jason, and he paid them on time and even gave them bonuses come Christmastime, and that was about as well as you could reasonably expect any of this to work. And Jason didn't have to worry about them embarrassing him at Coach Tepper's house. This was one job you had to get right. He was, he realized, proud of having this crew working for him on this job. They were knuckleheads, but they were his knuckleheads.

Jason knew he had the only crew in town that was still working at noon without having bolted for a three-hour lunch break, and he was proud of that.

But this little twerp standing in front of him wouldn't know any of that.

He had pulled up in his compact Tesla, a shitty little car, Jason had always thought. Piss-poor craftsmanship—the cheap, flimsy frames of those things would make his great uncle Fred, who had worked on the GM assembly lines in Michigan for forty years, roll over in his grave—along with faulty tech that broke down all the time, tech that couldn't be fixed with a wrench and a jack like a normal car, all wrapped up in fake-rich yuppie bullshit, a status symbol for people who pretend not to care about status symbols but care about them more than they care about anything else in the world. The Tesla was an idiot's version of the kind of car fancy people drove. Of course this dipshit drove one.

"Wow, I'm surprised to see your crew still working." He was dressed in a light-blue golf shirt, khakis, and sunglasses connected to a strap he wore around his neck. This was the way all these peckerheads dressed, Jason thought, like they wanted to look important but didn't want to put even the slightest bit of thought or effort into doing so, like he couldn't even be bothered to change shirts after he left the country club. "Are you, uh . . ."—he riffled through some papers he had on a plastic clipboard, a cheap purple one—"Jason? Are you Jason Waller?"

"I am," Jason said. "Can I help you with something? You're on an active worksite."

"Yes, yes, I suppose I am," the man said, and he looked up and squinted, like he expected a two-by-four to drop on his head. Jason figured that could be arranged, if need be. "I'm Derek Peters, I'm from the UGA athletic department. I work in our public relations division." He extended his hand to Jason, and Jason shook it. It was as smooth and as unfettered a hand as Jason expected it to be. You'd think at some point he might have at least scratched it with a pencil, maybe caught some stray fire from a staple remover, but nope.

"I wondered if I might have a moment of your time?" Derek Peters said. "Something has come up that I think we might need to discuss."

Jason didn't have the slightest idea what Derek Peters would need to talk to him about, but an uneasy sensation began to rumble up from his lower left side and into his stomach. Guys like this never showed up out of nowhere with anything helpful to offer. He'd met all sorts of Derek Peterses in his life. Anytime he did any sort of corporate job, they always came out of the woodwork. It took Jason a while to figure out what job these guys did, exactly. They didn't make anything; they didn't sell anything; they weren't the boss. They seemed to just sit at their desk all day and only pop up when the people who actually made something were just about to finally start working. They showed up at the worst possible time, always, just to muck everything up. At first Jason was confused by these people. If your company's business was to make and sell widgets, and these people weren't involved in either the making or the selling of widgets, why were they there? What did they do all day? But the more he got to know them, the more he understood: their job was to keep their job. Their job was to *slow things down*. They popped up with "suggestions," or "concerns" or "potential issues," and everyone always had to stop what they were doing and listen to them, and right there they've already won: they've slowed the process, ground down the gears, and made themselves look critical to the whole organization. Their interruptions became self-sustaining. By creating the problem, they persuaded all the bigwigs that they were the only people who could solve the problem. And they were *everywhere*.

It had not escaped Jason's notice that these people always had bigger and nicer houses than he did.

Yes, he knew Derek Peters, he'd known Derek Peters forever. Derek Peters right now was doing what all the Derek Peterses around the world were uniquely skilled at: stopping Jason from working.

"Sure," Jason said, with a grimace. He made sure to spit off to the side when he said it. He didn't need to spit right then, but he thought it made sense. "Let's go over by the pissers."

Jason waved to Buck, an *I'll be over here with this moron go ahead and keep doing what you're doing we'll get lunch when I'm done here* scowl. Buck nodded back, pointed at Derek Peters behind his back, and made a jacking-off motion with his hand.

Jason led Derek Peters to the end of a row of Port-a-Potties. He was about to growl "OK, what?" at him when Jace came out of the last row.

"Hey, Dad!" Jace always looked so happy when he was on a job with his dad. He'd once told his mother that even though he probably wouldn't end up working a crew, and his dad would strangle him if he tried, he loved the physical labor so much more than boring schoolwork. "None of the other kids in AP History could build a freaking Ikea cabinet," he joked. "They're so smart, but they're also so stupid. I like getting to make things." Sometimes when Jason was low, he would remember that story and feel better.

"You finish that second coat around the top window of the guest cottage?" Jason asked. He hadn't wanted Jace to overexert himself on game day, so he'd given him the simple job of painting, a job that Jace hated, because who wouldn't, but it needed to be done nonetheless.

"Just about," Jace said, and wiped some sweat off his forehead. Jason loved how Jace lowered his voice a little bit when he was on a site, all *manly* like, how desperately he wanted to be one of the crew. This did not stop them from calling him "College Boy," a name they'd used for him since he was in the third grade.

"All right, finish up, then we'll break for lunch," Jason said, and Jace bounded off, more pep in his step to go paint than the rest of the crew had ever had to go do anything. He turned back to Derek Peters.

"OK, what?"

Derek Peters watched Jace go off. "Is that your boy?" he said. "I didn't know your son worked on your crew."

"He doesn't," Jason growled. "He's just helping out for the day."

"Does he have a work permit? He doesn't look like a legal adult."

"He's my son, that's all the work permit he needs."

"Well, I don't—"

"Buddy, how can I help you?" Jason could almost *hear* the minutes of his workday ticking away.

Derek Peters wiped his hands on his light-blue shirt and straightened up his khakis. For him and his stupid life, this was showtime. "So, I work with Coach Tepper in the athletic department."

"You said that already," Jason said.

"Well, yes, you see, it's my job to make sure that the athletic department, and of course the university, is, uh . . . protected."

"Protected?" Jason said, nervousness rising in his chest but still enjoying his height advantage on Derek Peters. "You work in protection?"

"Well, we have to make sure that the university, and the athletic department, and specifically Coach Tepper and the football team, are not involved with anyone that might damage the reputation of the school or the team."

"I see," Jason said. "So what does whatever they're involved in have to do with me and my job?"

Derek Peters looked down at his feet, at the ground, at a disturbing liquid leaking out of the Port-a-Potty, anywhere but up, at Jason.

"Perhaps *involved* is the wrong word," he said. "Maybe *associated* is better. And there's an, uh, association, then, that I wanted to talk to you about."

As if slapped in the face with it, Jason suddenly knew exactly why Derek Peters was here and what he was going on about.

"Don't tell me this is about my brother," Jason said.

"I'm afraid it is," Derek Peters said, and it must be noted that he did in fact look a little afraid.

RICK HAD ALWAYS BEEN A LITTLE OFF, THERE WAS NO QUESTION ABOUT that. He was always too intense, even as a child, always doing crazy-ass things that Jason would end up bailing him out of. Rick was the type of kid who would pick a fight with a senior as a freshman just to see how hard a punch he could take. (He could take one pretty square, all told.) This caused Jason nothing but headaches; he was constantly apologizing to his friends for his younger brother. Rick was shorter than Jason, but he was compact, a rampaging boulder of a person; he'd had some brief potential as a competitive Greco-Roman wrestler until he started skipping all his practices because "them fuckers don't know shit." In Rick's world, no fuckers knew shit, and they were all fuckers.

Jason had always tolerated his little brother, and he made sure to watch out for him. But they were so different, in temperament, in intellect, in body size and shape, in basic human social function, that no one could believe they were brothers, including, sometimes, Jason. Rick never could get anything in his life straight. He'd dropped out of high school, worked at a chicken factory out in Gainesville, quit, moved back home, got arrested a couple of times, nothing serious, but nothing much good either. He got caught up in drugs for a while, inevitably, but even the effort of being an addict seemed too much for Rick. Drugs were just another dumbass thing that didn't mean shit because fuckers don't know shit. He worked in the deli department at Aldi's for a couple of years but got fired because a customer kept changing his order and Rick got so annoyed by the customer that he threw a whole half pound of ham at him. On his way out of the grocery store, Rick took out his dick and pissed on the self-checkout counter. Rick had a tendency to struggle with polite society.

Jason still had Rick's back, though, if just for his parents' sake. Jason was the kid who had his act together, who did the right things, who never got in trouble, who got a job and found a nice smart girl, a doctor no less, which is all to say that he was the kid who his parents thought about so much less than they thought about his troublemaking brother. It was remarkable how much more concern and care parents gave to their screwup kids than to their relatively stable ones. Jason could win the Nobel Prize, and his parents would skip the ceremony if Rick had a stomachache. Jason had always vowed not to make the same mistake with his kids, though Helen had pointed out to him, many times, how much more time he spent with Jace than he did with J.T. He supposed his parents had probably at some point vowed the exact same thing.

Jason had even briefly brought Rick onto his crew, a few years back. It was right when Waller Construction was just getting started, before either of the Harolds were hired, when it was just Buck and Little Todd and half the jobs involved replacing windows and fixing door hinges. Rick lasted exactly four days. The first day he was two hours late. The second day he didn't show up. (He claimed he was confused about where the job site was, even though he'd been there just the day before.) The third day he was on time but never returned from lunch. The fourth day he left early, went to the Applebee's bar, and got a DUI on his way home—his third, costing him his license, for good this time. Jason bailed him out of jail and fired him in the car on the way back to their parents' house.

Jason loved Rick, the way a brother loves a brother, in ways he'd never understand and never really try to. But he didn't like him. And he doubted Rick liked him much either. He wondered if this was true of all brothers.

Then came 2015. Rick had always been politically active, though saying it that way, Jason thought, gave him too much credit. It's not like Rick had political *views*; he wasn't exactly out there writing detailed policy papers on the virtues of trickle-down economics. Politics just gave him a vessel to find more fuckers who didn't know shit. There were many fuckers, but, perhaps not surprisingly, Hillary Clinton was the lead fucker. (When he was pulled over, he had a HILLARY SUCKS COCK bumper sticker on his truck. Jason wondered where you even bought a bumper sticker like that.) And Rick embraced the Trump candidacy as if he'd been waiting for it his whole life—as if, for the first time, his life had direction and focus. At first, Jason thought this might be a good thing. Anything that kept Rick occupied was a positive in Jason's book. It even briefly provided a connection between him and his brother. Jason admired Trump, how he'd built a business into something so huge that his name was on the side of buildings, and Hillary struck him as a bit of a ballbuster, though he'd never say that aloud around Helen. There was a brief moment there when the brothers could almost enjoy getting together and complaining like old men.

But Rick got too carried away with it, like he always got too carried away with everything. First it was the hat: he never took that ugly-ass thing off. Then Rick wouldn't wear anything that didn't have TRUMP on it. He started volunteering for Trump, showing up at political rallies with a megaphone and screaming. He began ranting and raving about the pedophiles, and the deep state, and all sorts of other weird stuff that Jason didn't understand. At Thanksgiving 2016, Rick screamed at the poor boyfriend of some random cousin Jason didn't even remember the name of because he was part of the ELITE MEDIA CONSPIRACY, though Jason was pretty sure the guy had just said he sold advertising for a website. Rick ended up challenging him to a fight, right there on the front steps. The guy refused, so Rick grabbed him and threw him off the porch. At that point their father, who was too old for any of this and look what you're doing to your mother, had had enough: he made Rick move out a week later. Jason drove a truck with all of Rick's stuff, what little there was, down to Jacksonville and helped him move into a ratty apartment under a highway overpass. He'd given him a thousand dollars and his first and last month's rent.

"Get it together," Jason told him.

"Go fuck yourself," Rick said, and they hugged.

No one saw Rick much after that. Rick came home only twice, both during the pandemic. The first time was in April, when he just showed up one day and walked right into his elderly parents' home, like nothing was going on, like he'd never left, and they kicked him out again. The second time was during a protest to take down a Confederate monument that summer, where he'd shown up dressed in a Hawaiian shirt and carrying an AK-103. Tommy T had been drinking at the World Famous nearby, saw him, and texted Jason: Your asshole brother's in town. Jason drove into downtown Athens, found Rick, and told him to put that gun away, what kind of idiot are you, you don't even know how to use that thing. Rick looked at him blankly, coldly, like he was a stranger he'd just met. "A storm is coming," he said. "Get your family ready."

That was the last time Jason had seen Rick in person. So he

was not the least bit surprised when Jace knocked on his bedroom door one morning a couple of months later.

"Dad," Jace said. "I think Uncle Rick is in trouble."

Jace showed Jason a message from the official Twitter account of the FBI. It read, "The #FBI is still seeking information on people who took part in the violence at the U.S. Capitol on January 6. If you know this individual, visit http://tips.fbi.gov. Refer to photo 4022 in your tip." And it featured a picture of Rick, right there, screaming, on the floor of Congress, like an idiot—like, as ever, a fucker who didn't know shit.

"That's not him, doesn't even look like him," Jason said. Jace knew he was lying, but he was OK with it.

Rick was arrested three weeks later. Someone posted his bail, but it wasn't Jason and it wasn't his parents. No one had heard from him since, which was a relief to everyone involved.

And now here Derek Peters stood, with the FBI tweet printed out, and a news story from the website of a Columbus, Georgia, television station, and that sissy little clipboard, asking Jason about his brother. "Obviously, this is not something that we can have Coach Tepper connected with in any way, shape, or form," he said. "Now I am not saying that you were associated with this at all, but he is your brother, and it has made the news, and . . . well, you understand, yes?"

Jason was looking past him, barely listening. *Goddamn Rick*, he thought. *You stupid son-of-a-bitch. If you cost me this . . . goddammit.*

Derek Peters looked at him, expectantly but haltingly, like a student teacher who had caught a student stealing his erasers red-handed and knew he was supposed to demand an explanation but didn't really have the stomach for it. Jason wasn't sure what he was supposed to say, but whatever it was, he wasn't going to say it to this putz, that was for damned sure.

"Well?" Derek Peters said, fidgeting with his glasses.

Jason took a deep breath and touched the bridge of his nose

the way he did when he wanted to make sure he was calm so he didn't say anything he shouldn't—so he didn't throw this guy in the Port-a-Potty and flip it over right then and there.

"Well . . . ," Jason began.

And then there was a crack.

Jason heard it behind him and instantly knew what had happened. Derek Peters's eyes, looking at a spot over Jason's right shoulder, widened and flared, and his mouth made a cartoonish O. He raised his left hand and said, "Whoa, look out there now." Jason knew he wasn't talking to him.

The sound was like a tree branch falling: a snap, a groan, and then a *whoosh*. It was strange, Jason thought, how the act of someone falling made its own distinct sound. You could hear it more clearly than the person falling could.

But the clearest sound, the thing you couldn't miss, was the one that the men around a worksite accident made when an accident occurred. They would all inhale at once and then make a short, nasally *uuuuuuuhhhh*, like they'd been popped right in the solar plexus—it was the sound of people simultaneously seeing something happen, feeling guilty that they didn't or couldn't do anything to stop it, and being grateful that it hadn't happened to them. Accidents weren't usually a result of someone doing something wrong, a mistake they'd made that the universe was punishing them for. They just happened, randomly, resulting from circumstances no one could have reasonably foreseen. That randomness was the scariest part. That randomness meant it could just as easily have been you.

Jason's eyes locked with Buck's. Buck looked terrified. He mouthed:

Jace.

Jason sprinted away from Derek Peters, faster than he'd thought his fat old body could go, and took out two Harolds as he made his way to his son, his beautiful son, the son that he knew was the best thing he'd ever been a part of.

Jace was lying on the ground, fifteen feet from the top step of the ladder he'd just been standing on. He looked up at his father. His eyes were clear, and to Jason's relief, there didn't appear to be any blood. Jace was holding his right arm, groaning. But he was looking right at his father.

"Sorry, Dad," he said. "I think you might need a new short-stop tonight." And he put his head down in a mud puddle.

KARSON

12:47 p.m.

The purple car would not move. There was no reason it could not move. It was a car: it was supposed to move. It was built to move! But there it sat. One car back, Karson glared at the college girl in the driver's seat, lost in her phone, nowhere to go, nowhere to be, not a care in the world. How wonderful that must be, he thought. To have no one waiting on you.

As always, Karson was in a hurry. Had he always been in a hurry like this? He supposed he always had. He figured early on that he wasn't getting out of Nellie B if he didn't get on his horse right from the get-go. He'd been sprinting since that first teacher told him, when he was seven years old, that he was gifted, that he was special, that he needed to "keep his nose in those books or he's gonna end up stuck here like the rest of us." When he was seven, Karson wasn't so sure what was so terrible about where he lived, but he'd figure it out soon enough, and once he did, he'd been nothing but forward momentum ever since then. And yet here he was: right where he'd started. He had sure moved a lot. But had he really gone anywhere?

He'd had an early lunch with those kids at Clarke Middle,

where half of them didn't show up and the other half, when he tried to ask them about their lives, just yawned and asked for money for the vending machine, but he'd gotten out of there late. He floored it down 316 to go meet with a bored, stoned manager at the University 16 Cinemas out in Watkinsville to confirm a charity screening this coming weekend of a self-made documentary about the Chess & Community group that Karson had invited all those kids to, not that any of them would show up, not that any of them would give a rat's ass about it. After *that* meeting was over, he had to drive right back into Athens, through Five Points, out to East Athens, to pick up a meat and cheese plate for a church mixer he'd forgotten he'd committed to that evening, and there were still four or five items on his agenda after that, and if he had time maybe he'd briefly wave to his wife and daughter, though probably not. He had seven items to check off his to-do list between the Elysian Fields meeting and the church mixer, and they sure were starting to seem more like busy work than anything particularly useful.

And he was going to give himself a heart attack wading through these idiotic drivers to get to each of them. Karson was now behind a tiny green car witlessly drifting from lane to lane; he felt his blood pressure go up and a vein pop out the middle of his forehead. He was always in a hurry. And he was never going anywhere. For a meat and cheese plate.

He crawled his way up Milledge Avenue, behind a college student playing Uno on her phone with her hazards on and, somehow, her left foot hanging out the window, before turning right onto Southview Drive. He noticed he was leaning toward the windshield, like he was trying to see through a rainstorm, and he was gripping the steering wheel so tightly his hands were starting to sweat. Annette had bought him a bike for Christmas a few years ago, saying he'd be less likely to have a coronary embolism on "one of those." But there were always too many papers to carry, too many kids to drive around, too many errands and stops along the day, for a bike to be of much practical use. Not that it mattered. It was stolen the third week he had it anyway.

As he sat at the four-way stop at Southview and Pinecrest, waiting for three men, all wearing ties and driving pickup trucks that had never been used to haul anything, to decide which of them could possibly be roused to determine the right of way, he looked out the window to his left. He paused.

Wait, he thought. *Is this where it was?*

He drove through Five Points regularly, but he rarely stopped and looked around. This was not a place where he was needed. As he well knew, all too well, this was not a neighborhood with a lot of Black people in it.

But was he really here? Was that actually the street where it happened?

After a honk from the pickup behind him, he made a quick left turn onto O'Farrell and then pulled the car over. This was where it was, he thought, finally certain. As if in a sudden trance, he put the car in park, turned off the engine, and opened the car door. This was all incredibly familiar. He felt like an animal who had picked up a scent and would not relent until he had tracked it down.

University Drive was the widest street in Five Points, with the most expensive houses and thus the wealthiest, most powerful families. The Clarke County attorney general lived here, as did the university athletic director, three trustees, four assistant football coaches, all the economics professors, and the longtime morning radio personality Big Buck, as they called him, even though his name was Joe and he'd grown up in the ritziest Atlanta suburb as a progeny of a prominent family of financial advisers. This was the street where everyone came from all around Athens to trick-or-treat on Halloween. The rich folk gave out the best candy.

This was definitely the street. Karson walked up a block to Scott, and sure enough, there was that same telephone pole. Oh, this pole. The last time he had seen this pole up close, he'd been lying on the concrete sidewalk, with a broken leg and two fractured ribs and missing four teeth, teeth that flecked the grass beneath this very pole. He remembered staring at two fire ants crawling up this pole and worrying that he'd landed on an anthill and would soon be crawling with the buggers, biting and attacking him at the very moment he had no way to escape. But they'd left him alone. It was the one break he'd caught that day.

This was the street. He had just been thinking, while waiting at the stop sign, that Five Points was probably the Athens neighborhood he spent the least time in, knew the least about. He now remembered why.

The pole. That fire hydrant. This grass. Those teeth. That truck.

That truck.

IT WAS . . . 2013? IT HAD TO HAVE BEEN 2013—HE'D JUST STARTED GETTING serious with Annette, and he had told her he was a runner, one of those little white lies you tell when you first meet someone and are so desperate to impress them that you just start making up stuff. She had told him about the AthHalf, a half marathon that Athens ran every October, always on a weekend when there wasn't a UGA football game because the last thing anyone wants to do on a football tailgate weekend is *run*. She said she ran it every year, maybe she'd see him out there, and he liked her so much that he was willing to try to make the lie true by training for the AthHalf. Running was a lot harder than he'd realized. He was still smoking at the time, and going up Athens hills, those satanic hills, instantly sapped him of any remaining lung capacity. Training for a half marathon was miserable at first. When someone runs a half marathon, when it's over, all their friends clap them on the back and congratulate them and buy them beers—they're a little hero for a day. But when you're training for a half marathon, there are days where you run eleven, twelve miles, and when it's over, no one cares: you just have to go back to work like always. He knew he had to train. But he did not want to train. He loved Annette's lips and her neck, though. He loved her quiet confidence and obvious intelligence and how he thought that the fact that she existed was a sign that whatever mistakes The Man Above might have to answer for, that she was here walking around the planet at all was proof that the Guy had *some* sort of plan for the universe . . . he loved all that, yes, it was becoming very clear. But when he ran, he just thought about her lips and her neck.

After a while, though, it hit him: *I might be a runner.* He was starting to come around on it. He was most struck by how, when you got on a good heater of a run, you could forget everything about your life, both the good and the bad, and just concentrate on some elevated plane of pure physicality. You hit a certain *click*, around the fourth mile, and the fog just lifts. Your breathing calms, your stride locks in, and you are moving without having to try to move at all. Karson found peace in running. He blissed out. He couldn't believe it had taken him this long.

He was two weeks away from the race that October Tuesday. He had worked himself up to nine miles, mostly by avoiding the awful inclines of downtown Athens and sticking to flat stretches like Milledge Avenue, where your only real obstacle was all the sorority girls singing their songs and the groggy frat bros staring at their phones while waiting for the bus. Toward the end of his run, at the four-way stop at Pinecrest and University, he spotted a Ford F-150 with oversize tires, so high that you needed an extra metal plank just to get in the driver's-side door, start to roll through the stop sign. Annoyed, Karson stopped running, took a step backward, and, in an exaggerated motion, put his hands in the air, mouthed "Whoa," and rolled his eyes. The truck—Karson is sure of all of this, still—paused for a moment, and a man with a thick beard and a brown hat turned to him and flipped him the middle finger.

Karson knew not to escalate situations like this, particularly with white men with big trucks. So he put his arms out, gave the guy a little sneer, said, "Good for you, man!" and kept running.

When he reached Milledge, he turned around again, back down University, just three-quarters of a mile to go. He'd lost a little time with the truck guy, so he sped up: he had a chance to make it through this whole nine miles at an eight-minute pace, and this was just the straightaway to do it. He pushed. He felt the click, and his legs stretched out in front of him, and it felt a little bit like he was floating above the ground, and there were also Annette's lips, and her neck.

There was a gunning of an engine, and a sudden immense pressure behind him, and he was flying, he really was floating above the ground.

He landed about six inches in front of the curb—he knew still today he'd be dead if he'd gone headfirst into it—and rolled, faster than he'd thought a body could spin, before smashing into that telephone pole. The doctor later would explain that he hit the pole ribs-first and then rotated around the pole, where, to his great misfortune, there was a fire hydrant. That's what broke his leg. "I'm not sure where you lost the teeth," the doctor had told him. "That's a bit of a mystery."

On the ground, he opened his eyes and saw the pole. And those teeth. That made him close his eyes. The next thing he remembered, he was in the emergency room at Piedmont, not in any pain, not understanding much of anything, just lying there as people he didn't know did all sorts of strange things to his body as he drifted in and out of consciousness. He dreamed of Annette's lips and neck then too.

The next day, with his leg wrapped in a cast and Annette and his mother keeping constant watch around his hospital bed, a police officer took detailed notes. Karson was not as much help as he wanted to be. The officer told him he'd been hit by a "large vehicle," which was the first Karson had heard of it. Karson didn't have any idea what had happened and couldn't provide any context to the officer. Karson would remember a couple of days later that he had briefly been flipped the bird by a large white man in a large black truck just a few minutes earlier, and he called the officer and told him. The officer asked Karson why he had been in the neighborhood, accepted his answer, and said thank you. And that was it. Nothing ever came of it. Whoever hit Karson, whether it was the guy in the truck or someone else, took off, and was never found. No one saw anything; even the lady who called 911 said she just did so because she saw Karson lying on the ground, had no idea how he got there. He was just a Black man jogging in a white neighborhood who suddenly got hit by a truck, and no one knew who or how or why or even when. It just happened, and then it was over.

Nine months later, Karson's leg was healed, and he asked Annette to marry him, and she said yes. His life had mostly been the same since then. But he'd never run again. And now that he was here, he realized he'd never returned to University Drive, and this telephone pole, either. Now he was here.

He'd been lucky. He knew that now. He also knew it would never, ever feel that way to him.

How did he feel being back here? He had no idea. He had only just now realized he was here. He bent down on one knee and rolled over to lie on the ground, so that he could see the pole the way he had then, to try to remember what that was like, how it had felt. He realized, lying there, that the memories that rushed back were not the ones from when it happened, but instead the ones from afterward, when it was clear that nothing was going to be done, when he had to wrestle with the fact that someone had *hit him with a fucking truck* and just sped off like he was nothing, like he was just some burden they didn't want to deal with, like maybe that's what he had coming all along. That was why Karson never thought about the accident anymore. It was because it meant nothing. Some asshole almost killed him, they never found the asshole, Karson's bones healed, move on with your life, all of you. It didn't matter at all. Karson had never thought of it this way before. He never liked talking about it, but when he had to, he told the story in a way that made it sound like an unlucky accident, and never mentioned the guy in the truck. Annette didn't either. It was bad enough without that. But now, suddenly, it was all he could think about it. He lived, he died, nobody gave a shit. *Shouldn't have been in that neighborhood anyway. Probably shouldn't have been running so fast like that anyway. Maybe it was your fault.* Doesn't matter. Doesn't matter one goddamn bit. You can work your whole life to make a difference, and not only are you not going to change anything, no one is going to care that you ever even tried. No one is going to care that you were ever here at all.

Karson lay in the grass, now looking up at the sky. *What the fuck am I doing?* he thought. He'd never thought of himself as depressed. But he figured this was probably what depression was. He hoped this was depression. Because if it got worse than this, he didn't want to know what it was.

But still he lay. The sun bore down on him, and he began to sweat, but it felt right, it felt almost soothing, just to lie down there in the grass and dirt and anthills, on a wealthy street in Athens, Georgia, sweat staining his shirt, knowing he had so much to do but not only not wanting to do any of it but also not sure any of it needed to be done at all anymore, staring up at the sky and feeling like everything he thought was right had turned out to be wrong and that his entire life up to that point was a series of well-intentioned decisions that had added up to nothing. He had never felt so small and inconsequential. He had never felt so pointless.

Take the job. Get the money. At least that's real. At least that's something you can touch.

He should work for them. He should work for Elysian Fields and do whatever the hell they asked him to do. He'd buy Annette a dress and they'd have dinner at the nicest restaurant in town and they'd take Vanessa to Disney World and let her ride all the rides she wanted, maybe they'll even buy her the fancy bracelet that lets you skip all the lines. He'd get a nice big house with a yard—maybe a dog, he'd always wanted a dog. If he couldn't help anyone else, and he clearly couldn't help himself . . . he could at the very least help them. Take the job, idiot. Why the fuck not at this point?

He closed his eyes to stop himself from crying.

When he opened them, he was briefly blinded by the sun before realizing that a figure had emerged, just to his left, and was standing over him. He put a hand over his left eye for shade and tried to focus on the figure.

It was not a concerned neighbor, or an angry policeman. It was not, he shocked himself by briefly thinking, the man in the truck.

It was a little girl. She had light-brown hair pulled back in a ponytail, and she was wearing athletic shorts and a soccer jersey, an Atlanta United Josef Martínez jersey. Karson pegged her at about five, maybe six. She looked at him matter-of-factly, not the least bit surprised to randomly see a large Black man lying in the grass on her street, a man trying not to cry. She just looked at him the way a five-year-old looks at everything: like it was put there just for her.

She was holding, Karson noticed, a green plush stuffed turtle doll. He looked closer and realized that it wasn't a doll: it was a puppet. And it was on her hand. And it was talking to him.

"Hi!" the turtle said. "I'm Asa! I'm trying to help Kyla find her school! She didn't want to be at home anymore so she decided to go to the school but now she can't find it. Can you help her? I'm Asa. I'm a turtle. Do you know where the school is?"

Karson wiped his brow and coughed. He pulled himself up,

went down on one knee, took the girl's hand, and looked the turtle right in the eye.

"I can help you," he said.

"Good," said the turtle. "Because Kyla is getting hungry. And so am I! I like to eat tadpoles. Tadpoles are yummy." And then Asa the turtle licked Karson's face, and he smiled so wide he couldn't believe how close he had just been to crying.

5. COLLAR SPITTLE

The thing about this little town is that everybody knows everybody, and if you've been one of those everybodies longer than people like us have been nobodies, you can get away with whatever you want. When you've got your fingers in every pie, and the whole town knows it, you have power wherever you go. And you will always win.

I was a wonderful teacher. The key to teaching kids—little kids, my grade was fourth grade—is not having kids of your own. That might sound strange, but it shouldn't. The comedian Sarah Silverman once had the best advice on how to deal with your family at Thanksgiving. "Pretend they're someone else's family," she said. Everything about your family that drives you crazy, everything that has made you want to claw your eyes out since you were a little kid, it suddenly stops bothering you when you pretend you're a stranger just visiting them for a little while before you get to go back home. If Uncle Dave farts at the table or says something horribly racist, that sucks, because you're related to that guy—you have to deal with him for the rest of your life. But if you pretend he's just some random guy named Dave, you can treat him merely as an odd duck who, when you drive home at the end of the day, you don't have to think about anymore. He's someone else's problem now!

That was my secret for being a terrific teacher of nine-year-olds: always remembering that, at the end of the day, they're someone else's problem. You do the best you can, you care for them, you try to educate them, you try to help them, but when that bell rings, you hand them off to someone else and hope they make it through the night without someone setting them on fire. You're there to make a difference, but there's a limit to what you can do. Treat them like temporary amusements, a jacket you get to try on for a while before taking it off and giving it to someone else. It makes them so much less frustrating. It makes them so much easier to deal with. You do what you can. But you also know they're ultimately on their own like the rest of us.

After Mom left for the Winterville home, I began working on my teaching degree from UGA. It was cheap and easy. I won a scholarship put aside for "orphaned children," which required a little fibbing on the application, but only a little, and by the time they came by the house to check, Mom was gone and it was an easy sell. College is super easy if you live in a big house, for free, by yourself, and you don't have any friends or sorority sisters always trying to talk you into doing Jell-O shots with them. I had my degree in three years and my certificate in four, and at the age of twenty-three I was an assistant fourth-grade teacher at Fox Mountain Elementary School in Watkinsville, and after two more years, I had my own class. The job was an excuse to get out of the house, and it gave structure to my life. I'd show up in the morning, teach class all day, visit Mom on the way home, and grade papers in the basement before falling asleep down there. (I still sleep there today. It always feels more like home than upstairs. Plus, the wireless is faster.) I loved having a routine. I miss those days. I'm not sure what the other teachers thought of me at Fox Mountain. I never really talked to them, I just sort of got in and got out. But the students liked me. They treated me kindly there. Nine-year-olds are great because they're old enough not to wander off into traffic if you leave them alone for a second but not old enough to be monsters yet. They still believe they can be happy. Being around them makes you believe you can still be happy too.

I used to play this game with the Fox Mountain kids. On Monday morning I would tell them five facts—Richard Nixon was the thirty-seventh president, the capital of Illinois is Springfield, Groundhog Day is on February 2, little factoids like that. They were not allowed to write down the facts. They just had to remember them. The student, or students, who remembered the most facts on Friday afternoon got to play a game of Mario Kart with me, with the whole class watching and cheering us on. I am terrible at video games, and that might have been what they liked the best: children are elated when they get to be better than an adult at something. No one called me Ms. Lamm there. I was just Mommy Mario. Just last year I had a former student who is now a junior at UGA see me at the supermarket and get all excited to see Mommy Mario. There are worse marks to leave on the world.

I loved that job.

And I was good at it. So good that I wanted more. I was so prideful. I could have been happy there forever, if I would have just allowed myself to be. But I wanted to get back to Athens. Fox Mountain is a lovely little school, and Watkinsville is a lovely little town, but it was a twenty-minute drive from our house in Five Points. Just down the street from the house, though, just like it had been for fifty years, was Murray Elementary School, where I went to grade school. I knew its classrooms, I knew its hallways, I knew its hidden corners, I knew its smells, I knew its secrets. I knew how wonderful it was too, and I also knew how difficult it was to get a job there. The Athens–Clarke County School District has its issues, particularly once you get into middle school, but Murray is the finest school in the whole county, maybe the whole North Georgia area. The place is clean and safe and diverse and hopeful: *Be a Murray Buddy!* It is even right across the street from the University of Georgia athletic department, and on Fridays during football season players come by the school and greet the kids on their way in. Not a lot of elementary schools in the country have had random drop-bys from Nick Chubb, running back for the Cleveland Browns, who went to school in Athens. It's the best. It's where every teacher in this area wants to go. I didn't know then what I know now, so I wanted to go there too.

When an opening for a fourth-grade teacher opened up, I was ready, and I pounced. I put on one of Mom's old wrap dresses—a little bit of a tight fit, I'll admit, but that's why you can loosen the strap around the waist—and I went to Supercuts for a nice haircut, and I even put on some of her old makeup, just the way she used to. I looked perfect. I looked like a teacher. I looked like a Murray Buddy. I aced the interview with the lady principal. I know how to be charming when I need to be, and I was extremely charming that day. I told her I'd been a Murray student and it had always been my dream to teach at the school I'd grown up loving so much. That wasn't entirely true, but it was close enough for me to believe it, which meant it was close enough for her too. They hired me two weeks later. I'd made it. It was all going to work out. How little I knew.

Some people just have it in for you. That ever happen to you at your job? The very first week, Ms. Holliday, who had been at the school for years, walked up to me in the hallway while the kids were filing in.

"You have spittle on your collar, Miss Lamm," she said, wiping it down with a handkerchief.

"Oh, I'm sorry," I said, stepping backward.

She looked me up and down. "Hmmmph," she said, and walked away. *Hmmmph!* That's what she said to me. She hated me ever since, just never gave me a chance after that. And she was very powerful there, I could tell, because after that, I couldn't get any teacher to so much as speak to me. I think she was after me from then on. Every time I turned around, there was Ms. Holliday, waiting for me to screw up so she could pounce.

She found her excuse in Freddy. Did I overreact with Freddy? Or was she going to get me no matter what? You tell me.

Freddy was a real snot of a fourth grader. You always saw him out at recess, running around, pushing people, bullying the girls, forcing everybody to play tackle football. There are always Freddys, and you can always tell who the Freddys are by their parents, usually their dads: these dads all strut around like they are in charge of everything, like every single person in the world is working specifically for them. They all think that if you just get forceful, if you raise your voice loud enough, if you're willing to shove harder than anyone else, you can get away with anything. And they're usually right. These dads are everywhere—these dads were always a problem for my mom, especially of course him, always him. Freddy was one of those kids.

One day I was monitoring the playground during the after-school program when I saw Freddy go up to a girl who was standing by herself, playing with a little truck set in the sand, and pinch her bottom. He took the truck from her and yelled "Trucks are for boys!" Then he pinched her nipple and yelled "Kiss my penis!" before running away. The girl, I didn't know her, she didn't cry. She just stood there, stunned.

I am not an angry person. But I could not let her think that was what her world would be. I ran over to Freddy, grabbed him by the ear, and dragged him to a nearby bathroom, the only bathroom connected to the playground, with a door that lets out right next to the teeter-totter. I bent down on one knee and made him look at me.

I didn't think I was yelling, though he later claimed I was. I was pretty mad, though. "You know what? You're a little jerk. You need to think about how you're a little jerk." Then I threw him in the bathroom and told him not to come out, or he'd be expelled from school.

I didn't think he'd stay in there for two hours. In retrospect I'm kind of impressed he did.

Ms. Holliday called me at home later that night. I didn't even know she had my number.

"Did you lock Freddy in the bathroom at ASP?" she said, almost before I had a chance to say hello.

"I didn't lock him in there," I said. "That door doesn't even lock."

"He stayed in there for two hours," she said. "His parents are furious. In what universe do you think it's OK to lock a nine-year-old boy in a bathroom for two hours?"

I explained to her what had happened with the little girl, and that he'd said the word *penis*, and also that I thought he would leave the bathroom the second I walked away. Wouldn't you have thought that?

"I'm sorry, but I'm going to have to report this," she said. She did not sound sorry. "This shows a serious lack of judgment."

She filed a formal complaint with the principal against me, and I had to go through all sorts of boring, pointless meetings, just the school system covering their ass as always. They asked me if I was sorry, and I told them I was, I even signed something saying I was sorry so we could all move on because I liked that job and I loved those kids and someone had to protect them from the Freddys of the world. And I even think I was a little bit sorry at the time. But I'd do it again. That was unacceptable behavior. Should I have come back and checked on him in the bathroom? Maybe. But if those were the worst two hours of his life, he's lived a pretty good life. And I made sure that little girl saw what I did. I made sure she knew someone would do something about it. I'm not sorry. Even with what happened.

After the Freddy incident, it was over for me—I realize that now. Ms. Holliday had been there a long time, and she started to turn the other teachers against me. Teachers have cliques at school, just like students do. They might be worse.

Still: I believed I could make it work. I got to walk to school, walk home, and the old hallways were the same and the kids loved me. I'd put in five years, I wasn't Mario Mommy at Murray yet. But I was getting there.

The district was on spring break when it happened, so most of the kids and teachers were all away on vacation. I was home, of course, and I was stunned when they told everyone to stay in their houses after spring break, not to come back on Monday. The school year was sacred, and here we were, messing up the whole thing. They gave us laptops, as if anyone could teach or learn on those things, and after three weeks of doing five minutes of class and five hours of yelling "Move your screen down" and parents calling me to help them figure out how their own wireless network was constructed, they gave up and canceled school for the year. I spent the summer on Facebook. I think a lot of people spent that summer on Facebook.

But they weren't ready to go back to school that fall either, said it wasn't safe. By that point, I didn't want to go back either. I had a new focus. I didn't need to fight them anymore.

Because by then I knew what I had to do.

DAVID

2:05 p.m.

"Can I let 'er rip?" Brock said. "Can I just tear it up right now?" He was smiling as widely as David had ever seen him. He was smiling a lot wider than a rock god is supposed to smile.

David nodded. "Ten-four!" he shouted. This was the first time the Red Rocket stage had seen a real live guitar player, plugged into a real live amp, for more than a year. There was no one better to be the first guy up there than Brock Cockburn. He was an Athens music legend. He'd been part of the Vic Chesnutt crew back in the day, a guitar virtuoso who made a couple of rough but lovable solo albums in the early nineties but ultimately discovered he had more of a talent as a producer. "I know what it's supposed to sound like," Brock told *Pitchfork* a few years later. "I just can't make it sound like that. I know how to tell other people to, though." He'd made the career of many an Athens band, from the B-52s to Cracker to the Drive-By Truckers to Of Montreal, and was so renowned as a producer that he'd actually worked on a couple of songs on a Kanye West record, though Brock admitted that he'd mostly just turned a few random dials, watched a bunch of guys he didn't know take naps, and collected his biggest paycheck in about fifteen years. Brock had been in New York when the pandemic hit, working on the Truckers' new record, and had absconded upstate with his wife when it started getting real in New York City. He'd only returned to Athens the week before, and the first person he wanted to see was David. It had been Brock's idea to have the Truckers be the reopening show for the Red Rocket, the place that had made them like it had made so many others, and with the show just a couple of weeks away, and tickets so sold out David wondered if they'd just block off the street and charge people to listen out in the parking lot, Brock wanted to return to "hear that old Red Rocket sound again."

So David got a private show, on a Thursday afternoon, from a rock god who couldn't stop grinning like an idiot. "How about a little hair metal?" Brock said, taking a swig of Corona and launching into Ozzy Osbourne's "Crazy Train," which morphed into Mötley Crüe's "Kickstart My Heart" and the closing Slash solo from "Paradise City." At the end of the medley, Brock stuck out his tongue and banged his head wildly, but just for a second; the last thrash made him pull something in his back, and he set down the guitar and grimaced. "I always forget I can't thrash like that anymore," he said.

"Sounded great," David said, and he meant it.

Brock looked around the empty music hall. "So, there really hasn't been anything here since March?"

"Nope," David said. "Some other places, college bars mostly, opened up last fall, but the city didn't give the green light to music venues. Sucks." He took a swig of vitamin water, some cucumber concoction that someone, maybe Allie, told him would clean out the toxins, though David was pretty sure it'd take a lot more than some cucumber water to do that. "It's been a tough year, no question about that."

"Well, we're gonna do what we can to put an end to that," Brock said. "We're gonna blow the fuckin' roof off the place." And he launched into the Pixies' "Debaser" and started smiling like a goon again.

David sat and listened to him play. It was sorta weird, he thought, two grown men standing right across from each other in an empty room, one playing guitar, the other silently nodding along with him, but that's what great music did: it was so transcendent and transporting that it rendered weird things normal—it made all that had been wearing you down just drift away. David listened and floated off. It was all going to be OK.

And then there was a pounding at the front door. It was a frantic, urgent pounding, the sound of someone being chased by a lion. Brock stopped playing and raised an eyebrow. David shrugged for a second, then heard more desperate pounding and a "David! David! Are you in there? Are you in there? David Gallagher! David Gallagher! Hello?"

David sprinted to the door, toward the unfamiliar but terrified voice. He unbolted the lock, unspooled the chain, and pulled up the security gate.

David didn't really recognize him at first. Nobody looks the same in real life as they do on Zoom. But then his eyes focused, and the man looked at him with pleading, stricken eyes.

"David! David! It's Joe!" he said. "I drove straight here from Tennessee, man. I need . . . man, I need some help. Can you let me in?"

It sure looked like Joe. He had a long white beard with salsa and cheese stuck in it, a shirt that had no buttons exposing a massive, hairy chest, and a St. Louis Cardinals tattoo on the left side of his neck. He was also holding his keys in one hand and what appeared to be . . . an iguana? . . . in his right. David also noticed that his hair was matted with blood.

It was definitely Joe.

THE FUCKUP BRADY BUNCH GREW OUT OF A FACEBOOK GROUP OF FANS OF the rock band Dinosaur Jr., which is to say, it was a bunch of fat old Gen Xers who had fucked up their lives and had no one else to ride out the worst global health emergency of the last hundred years with other than fellow bald, bearded Gen Xers who think *Beyond* is a totally underrated record. David started out sharing live mp3s of some old Dinosaur Jr. shows with Brad from Berea, Ohio, and Kevin from Mattoon, Illinois, and Greg from Austin, Texas, and they just kept talking to each other because they were lonely and scared and, as Kevin put it, "it was you boys or QAnon."

There was a stretch in March and April when David didn't see a single human being in person—he only talked to Allie, who was stuck in some weird part of Romania on a tour, on FaceTime twice, and he had a short conversation with Theresa, the Red Rocket's owner, down on the street from his window one night, but they both had worked in a music club for thirty years, so neither one of them could hear what the other was saying. So the Bunch was salvation. Brad and Kevin were both in the program—cocaine for Brad, Oxy for Kevin—so they ended up splitting off from Greg (who didn't have any substance abuse problems, he just wanted to trade some vinyl) and talking deep into the night. Eventually they found others, all guys in their forties and fifties, all people who didn't have anyone else, who were alone and who needed someone to keep them accountable because they'd run off anyone else who might have cared to. It had been Kevin's idea to keep Zoom on everybody all the time after Anthony from Aberdeen, Washington, missed three straight check-ins and then showed up piss-drunk with unexplained cuts all over his chest and neck. "We need eyes on all of us, always, until this is over," he said. "But no jerking off on camera."

No matter what they were doing, their camera stayed on. David saw a lot of old guys naked, but they got themselves through it. Just him and eight strangers, staying online, staying straight, keeping each other sane.

Even among this crew, Joe stood out. Everybody in the group, at a certain level, was a narcissist. They were addicts, after all, and when you're an addict, the only person you care about is yourself—or, more accurately, all you care about is your addiction. All must feed that. Everyone in your life—loved ones, coworkers, bosses, that fucker down the hall—they're all supporting characters at best, unwitting accomplices at worst, in the never-ending quest to get high or drunk. They are either helping you get high, or they are standing in the way of you getting high. Part of recovery is understanding that, that you're just another helpless addict like everybody else. One of the first things you have to do, David knew in his bones by this point, was recognize that there's nothing special about you. You ain't shit.

Joe did not know this, or he had purposely chosen to ignore it. Everything was always about Joe.

Whatever story anybody else told, Joe had something worse. If you had to sell your car for drugs, Joe had to sell his house. If you once got so drunk you shat your pants at a party, Joe would tell you how he once wiped his ass on his girlfriend's mom's couch. That sort of shit—please-look-at-me shit. Even in a room of dirt-bags, Joe was a pain in the ass. (David didn't even know what Joe was addicted to. He wondered if he was ever addicted to anything, if he was just lonely and making up shit to have someone to talk to.) Still: David knew this was about giving everybody every benefit of the doubt, even if you probably knew you shouldn't. Brad didn't feel this way. He'd been trying to get David to kick Joe out of the Bunch for months. But this was David's group. And he wasn't giving up on anybody. He knew how it felt to realize that there was nobody, *nobody*, who gave two Irish shits about you, how much that feeling froze in your veins and spread to the rest of your body, how it turned you nihilist and destructive. David knew all too well what a man was capable of when he was truly lost. Even Joe, dumbass, passive-aggressive, aggro-narcissist Joe, even Joe deserved to be protected from being that lost. David couldn't stand Joe. Nobody could. But David wasn't leaving him behind either.

They'd lost two Bunch guys in the pandemic. One was a happy story. Paul from Idaho logged on to Zoom one day in March with, of all things, a woman. It was his ex-wife: the pandemic made her realize she missed the old bastard after all, and she was moving back in with him. She offered to let him check back in with us, but he smiled for the first time in twelve months and shut off his laptop camera for good. The other story was not so happy. Geoff from Pittsburgh, who used to be a drummer for some punk bands before cocaine ate the last twenty years of his life, vanished from his Zoom screen one night; the Bunch only saw a live shot of his empty bed, for about three days, running continuously. Around 2:00 p.m., Brad noticed, after a banging on Geoff's door, two cops barging into the shot. They walked past the camera and into his bathroom. Two hours later paramedics came and wheeled Geoff's dead body out of his ratty apartment with the Rancid poster on the wall. No one really knew how to react to that. They'd tried to have a moment of silence to honor him, but moments of silence on Zoom weren't that much different than every other moment on Zoom.

The Bunch had mostly disbanded by May: everybody had their shots by then, ready to rejoin the world and close the laptop. They checked in with each other every few weeks, usually one-on-one, but they'd all pulled each other through. They'd made it. David was relieved, too, not to be responsible for the whole group of guys anymore—the Bunch was sometimes more responsibility than he'd meant to take on. And if you really pinned him down on it, he'd admit that he was relieved to have Joe off his plate. He'd done all he could do. They were all on their own now, back to the world, even Joe.

Joe, who was here, now, at the Red Rocket.

"Christ, man, get in here," David said, opening the door for Joe, less out of eagerness to deal with Joe than out of fear that the passersby of downtown Athens would start to notice a shirtless, screaming three-hundred-pound man with blood in his hair, carrying an iguana.

"Shit, David, thank you, thank you." Joe pushed through the door brusquely, like he wasn't entirely certain David had unlocked the door entirely and couldn't chance it. "I've been driving a long fuckin' time, long fuckin' time, LONG fuckin' time." He slapped his face with both of his hands and swept his hair around dramatically like a dog getting out of the bath. He smelled so ghastly, David wasn't sure which of them would vomit first.

"Yeah, Joe, god, are you all ri—"

"Can I use your shitter?" Joe blurted. "I don't need to shit or anything, I just, you know, long drive, long fuckin' drive."

David stared at him for a second. "Do you want me to hold the lizard?"

"What?"

"The lizard," David said. "That big fucking lizard in your hand."

Joe looked at his left arm like he'd just noticed he had one.

"Right!" he said. "Kirby! I named him Kirby." He held the iguana out to David with no further explanation.

David didn't remember Joe ever having an iguana on Zoom, but he took hold of the lizard, which was a shit-ton heavier than he thought it would be, and directed Joe to the men's room downstairs. Joe said, "Thanks, David, you're the fucking man," and groaned as he navigated the stairwell. David could hear his joints pop and crackle as they echoed through the hallway. The iguana began to gag on something. David set him on the ground, and he proceeded to follow Joe down the stairs.

"Was that a Gila monster?" Brock had noticed the commotion and walked over. He was carrying his guitar case and clearly angling to leave, as one might when one is suddenly confronted with a massive man with no shirt, covered in blood, carrying a wild animal.

"Iguana, I think." David was pretty sure it was an iguana.

"Those things kick ass," Brock said. "I always wanted one. My mom would never let me have one. Anyway, sound check was golden. Place still has it. Good luck with your iguana and your, uh, your friend."

David watched Brock leave the Red Rocket and strut amiably down the street. All rock stars know when it's time to own the stage, and when it's time to walk away.

Joe came back up the stairs, sans iguana, looking just as much of a disaster as he had when he went down them.

"So, Joe, uh . . . what brings you to Athens?" David said, trying to sound like he wasn't worried, nope.

"Man, I needed to see you," Joe said, and David felt a thick bead of sweat start to run down his back. "I remembered that this was your club and figured you'd probably be here, so I just got in the truck and drove." David looked outside and saw an old Ford pickup with holes rusted through the passenger-side door, parked across three handicapped spaces and in front of a fire hydrant.

"Why did you drive all the way from Tennessee to see me?" David wasn't doing as great a job of hiding his worry this time.

"Well, you're the only guy I could turn to."

"Joe, are you drinking?"

"I'm not! I'm not! I never drank, man, that wasn't my thing." David sort of hoped Joe would follow this up by explaining what his thing *was*, but he didn't, because Joe never did anything you hoped he would.

David poured Joe a cup of Folgers he'd just brewed from a can that had been sitting open, without even a lid, behind the Red Rocket bar for fifteen months. Joe drank it like a tequila shot and didn't so much as blink.

"So what can I help you with?" David said.

Joe paused and looked into his empty cup. "I'm sorry to say this, but I need some money."

David tried to imagine being so alone, and so desperate for money, that he would drive four hours to the workplace of a man he'd never met to ask for it.

"What happened?" David said. "Why are you bleeding?"

"Am I bleeding?" Joe said, and David pointed to his hair. "Oh, yeah, this. Yeah, that's the thing, turned out, well, there's this guy, and I owed him some money, and I'd sorta thought he forgot about it because of, you know, but he hadn't, he hadn't at all. So he came back and told me he'd kill me if I didn't pay him, and we got in a fight, and then I got in the truck and took off."

"And you came here?"

"I was trying to think of where I could go, who I could ask, because this guy, this guy was really gonna kill me, I think, and I was remembering, well, I remembered that you ran a music club, and I figured, man, music clubs have tons of money, it's a club, you're a big shot, you're a big music club owner, and this guy's gonna kill me, so, uh, well, I didn't know where to go. So I went here."

"Uh-huh," David said, knowing, as a longtime purveyor of the form, a bullshit addict story when he heard one. "So where did the iguana come in?"

Joe looked at him blankly. He turned around and glanced at the floor, then looked back up. "Uh, I don't know where the iguana came from." David actually believed him.

David took Joe's coffee cup and began to walk back around to the bar. Joe stood up from his stool and began to follow him.

"Look, Joe," David said, "I don't think you know much about music clubs, but if you think I'm somehow rich, you really weren't paying very much attention on the Bunch calls."

Joe inched closer to David as he walked behind the bar, in a way that David found odd and uncomfortable. "Come on," he said, eyes scanning the Red Rocket. "This is a big music club, you guys have to have lots of money around here. There's a cash register right there."

David felt the hair stand up on the back of his neck.

"Joe," he said, taking a step backward, "This place hasn't been open in a year and a half. There ain't no cash here. I barely remember what a customer looks like."

"You're telling me there's no cash in that register right there?" he said. "I've never seen a register without any cash in it."

David found himself securing his balance, left foot locked in front of him, right foot a couple of feet back, like he'd been taught, ready for what sure seemed like it was coming. "There's no cash, Joe," he said. "I'm not sure I like what you're getting at here."

Joe scratched his nose and snorted. "Never heard of no business with no cash," he said, and suddenly grabbed a knife off the bar that Brock had just been using to cut limes for his Corona. "I don't want to push you here, David, but you're not really giving me a lot of—OOOOFF!"

David had taken boxing classes at his third rehab spot, someplace in South Carolina, and he knew how to shift his weight, how to ball his fist, how not to hesitate. Joe hit the floor of the bar and rolled over, moaning. David leaned over him, kicked the knife away with his foot, and stepped on Joe's back. This was not the first guy David had flattened in this bar, and he realized, with a surprising excitement, that it wouldn't be the last. The Red Rocket would rise again.

Joe tried to get up, but David kicked him, and he relented.

"Christ, Joe," David said. "Stay the fuck down, would ya? I don't want to have to do that again."

David pulled out his phone and called Lt. Anderson, his buddy who worked for the Athens police force, the guy he'd always called when a drunk got out of control and he'd had to put him on the ground.

"Hey, got a live one for you," he told the cop. "Wanna send somebody by?"

"Well, holy shit," Anderson said. "Just like old times. I'll send a car by, they'll be there in five. And nice work. Feels like nature is healing, my friend."

After, David pulled Joe up and sat him on a barstool. David had broken his nose, no question. It was a clean shot.

Joe began to cry. "I'm sorry, man, I'm so sorry, I'm all fucked up, man, I'm all fucked up."

David grabbed some napkins from the bar, handed them to Joe, and sat on the stool across from him. "I know you are, man. We all are. But we ain't done yet. They ain't killed us yet." He hugged Joe, and Joe hugged him back.

When the cop came fifteen minutes later, David locked up the Red Rocket, got in the back of the squad car with Joe, held his hand, and whispered in his ear for the entire ride to the station. *We ain't done yet. They ain't killed us yet. We ain't done yet. They ain't killed us yet.* The police tossed Joe in the drunk tank and said David could come get him in the morning if he wanted. He wanted.

David drove back to the Red Rocket to make sure he'd shut all the lights off. That iguana was sitting on the stage, next to an old Tomson Splendor Series guitar with broken strings, like nothing had changed, like nothing had happened at all.

DAPHNE

2:58 p.m.

'm Becky," the woman had said that morning, her face caked
black with mascara, back when this was going a lot better than it
would go that afternoon. The woman wiped her ashen eyes with
a paper cocktail napkin she'd taken out of a massive tote bag she
had with her. She was bigger than Daphne had realized. She was
also much louder. "I figure if I've been blowing my nose into your
tits for the last two hours, I should probably tell you my name."

Daphne giggled slightly and extended her hand. "Daphne."

The two women sat alone in the room that had been assigned
to the boy Bryan once he made it out of surgery. *If he makes it
out of surgery*, Daphne couldn't help but think, darkly. Daphne
had helped the woman off the floor and guided her into a chair
at the foot of the bed. She poured her water from a pitcher another of the nurses on the floor had brought in and wiped off
her mascara and makeup. The rag she used was yellow and black
and damp. The nurse, an older Black woman named Cheryl, was
assigned to this room through the afternoon, but Daphne told
her that even though her shift was over, she'd sit with the boy's
mother and take care of anything pressing that came up until
he returned from surgery. Cheryl nodded and said thank you,

and even though it was hard to tell sometimes with the mask, Daphne thought that maybe she rolled her eyes at her a little.

"How old are you, Daphne?" Becky asked. "You're a little bitty thing."

Daphne tried not to blush and failed. "I'm twenty-nine," she said. "This is my fourth year here."

"I don't know how you do it," Becky said, blowing her nose into her sleeve. She lifted her head, a large bubble of snot hanging from her left nostril. Daphne instinctively wiped it away. "You must see, my god, you must see awful shit like this all the time." She broke back down into tears and dropped to the floor again. Daphne kneeled down with her, but Becky waved her off.

"I'm fine, get back up, Christ." Becky pulled a rubber band out of that huge bag, tied her hair back with it, and stood up. She let out a big "BLAAAAAAGGGHHHH" of a breathy scream to the ceiling and shook her head back and forth and up and down violently, like she was in the crowd at a death metal show. Daphne noticed, for the first time, that she was wearing a black Iron Maiden T-shirt and had multiple tattoos on her neck. "Pull it together, Jefferson, pull it together," she said to herself.

She took another sip of water.

"All right, all right, I'm cool." Becky looked down at her blouse, discovered that her left breast had popped out, and folded it back in. "I'm all right. I'm all right." She burped slightly, excused herself, and continued. "So . . . what happens now, Daphne? What are we in for?"

Daphne quickly shifted into professional mode. She explained that Bryan was in surgery, that they were trying to get him stabilized, that they needed to make sure the bullet hadn't pierced any major organs, that he might need a blood transfusion, that we won't know anything until the surgeon is completed, that it's just too early to jump to any conclusions, that the boy was in the capable hands of the best medical professionals in the entire state of Georgia. She didn't know if any of this was true, or explicitly true, or applicable to Becky's son, but it was what you were supposed to say if you didn't have any updates and didn't know anything: you were supposed to be vaguely reassuring but also to be careful to promise nothing. Daphne did know nothing. All she knew was what it felt like to have the heart of this mother's son in her hands. It was as if she could feel it, all slippery and wet and . . . thin. That was what Daphne kept thinking about. His heart was so *thin*. It was so fragile that tiny Daphne could have crushed it. There was a part of her that still worried she had.

Daphne's professional mode must have been particularly droning and mechanical, because Becky immediately stopped her. "Don't give me any of that," she said. "Just tell me," she said, beginning to heave again, "if he's going to be OK. And don't lie to me, Daphne. I'll know if you're lying. I can always tell when a bitch is lying."

Daphne looked at her. What do you say to a mother whose son is barely alive, and quite probably not for long? What do you say when you touched his heart? What do you say when it was so, so thin?

Daphne started to answer but began to choke on her words. "I . . . I don't know. I'm sorry. I don't."

Becky stared at her for about two beats too long and exhaled, right in Daphne's masked face. "Well, I appreciate the lack of bullshit," she said, and chuckled into her arm. She took both of her earrings out of her ears, big hoop earrings with silver moons hanging from them, and put them in that bag.

"Daphne," she said.

"Yes," Daphne said.

"Will you pray with me?"

And Daphne did. Daphne knelt with Becky, and she prayed.

THE FIRST HINTS THAT THIS WORLD WAS DIFFERENT FROM THE ONE DAPHNE had left five years earlier came from church. The minister, an earnest clean-cut young man named Adam who used to go fishing with Bill Preston every weekend until his wife had his infant daughter and he started looking so exhausted on Sundays that you worried he'd fall out of the pulpit, was in the receiving line, seeing everybody out to their cars. He'd given a normal, boring sermon about loving your neighbor, about how Jesus taught that we must be welcoming and compassionate to the entirety of His flock, one of those sermons that Daphne, she had to confess, had trouble keeping her eyes open during. She was standing with her father, waiting to shake the preacher's hand before leaving, when the man in front of them, a man Bill Preston had once described as "wound a little tight," stuck his finger in Reverend Adam's chest.

"You got a lot of nerve," the man said. "I go to church for God, not for politics."

Reverend Adam stared at him, confused. "I'm sorry?"

"I see what you're trying to do," the man said, his voice rising. "That 'love thy neighbor' crap plays a lot different when you got a new neighbor every day. You can be compassionate, sure, but you also have to be tough. You come in here acting like you know what we face every day, trying to sneak that lib stuff past us." Remembering he was talking to a preacher, he took a tiny step back and tried to collect himself.

"I'm sorry, Reverend," he said as his wife tugged on his jacket. "Just try to keep the politics out of here, would you?"

Flustered, Reverend Adam, said, "OK, Tom, have a great rest of your Sunday," and shook Daphne's father's hand.

"What was that about?" Bill Preston asked.

"I haven't an earthly idea," Reverend Adam said.

But he'd know well enough soon, because within the next six months, a quarter of his congregation was gone. They'd migrated to a new church, just on the outskirts of the county, run by a former biker who'd cleaned up his act and now preached the gospel of the prosperous, how Jesus wanted you to thrive so you could spread his word, and how there were enemies everywhere—enemies even within. Reverend Adam seemed to look a little older every week, seeing his flock slowly dwindle, seeing people who had been in his church for years, people Reverend Adam had grown up with in that very same church, people he'd fished with just like he had with Bill Preston, call him "soft" or "not willing to fight for Jesus." At one point Bill Preston came home from a late Sunday afternoon at the lake with Reverend Adam with a scowl Daphne had rarely seen on him. "People are losing their damn minds," he said, cursing, another Bill Preston rarity. "Yelling at the preacher! Sorta thing people used to figure would send you to hell." He asked Daphne to pray with him, and she did, she always did.

By that point, Daphne had certainly noticed how much had changed, how, in the five years she'd been gone, suddenly *upset* everyone was all the time. It was partly politics, which was so much larger a part of her daily life than it had been before she left. When she'd shipped off to basic training, not only did she not know whether anyone in her life was a Democrat or a Republican, she never even thought about it; it would have never occurred to her to ask. (She knew her father had voted for George Bush twice and Barack Obama twice, but only because she'd interviewed him for a social studies class her freshman year of high school.) She'd never even registered to vote, herself. But when she got back, out of nowhere, people were screaming whatever their political views were in your face at every opportunity. And they were screaming at you for not screaming yours.

But it was more than that. Everyone was, to use a Bill Preston term, "dialed up." Family members at the hospital were always shouting at her and the rest of the staff. Sally told her they were calling the police twice as often as they used to. She noticed a disturbingly high number of people with their concealed-carry weapons on them at the hospital, to the point that exhausted security guards, not paid near enough to deal with all this, had mostly stopped asking them to leave them in their car anymore. Every time Daphne turned on the news, something was inevitably on fire, or about to be. It felt like everyone was just on the edge of losing it, all the time. She had never worried about the world before she left for Fort Benning, and then for Germany—she had never thought to. The world would always be there, you could always put one foot in front of the other and know the ground would be there for each step. But now it felt like the earth was always unsteady under her feet, almost vibrating—like it could crack and send you plummeting to its core at any moment. It made her knees wobble. It was a new and most unwelcome sensation.

Maybe, she thought, the world had always been like this, and she was just too young and naive and protected to notice. Maybe she was seeing it for the first time, later than she should have, cocooned in the ordered and logical world of the military. Maybe it was that.

But deep down: she didn't think so. Something had changed. Something had definitely changed.

She didn't know how to handle it. So she threw herself into her work. She could not fix what was wrong with the world, but she could fix what was in front of her. The world might have gone nuts when she was away. But if she could keep everything in front of her safe, if the person in her care could be better than they had been when they'd come into that room with her, she would have done all that she could do. Maybe it wasn't enough to make the world better, or back to what it was before. But it was a start. It was a small piece.

IT ALL STARTED TO FALL APART AFTER LUNCH. DAPHNE HAD BEEN SITTING IN the child Bryan's room, on her constant vigil, when Becky began to scream at one of the doctors at the nurses' station. She had blown past the door with such velocity that Daphne briefly thought some sort of wild animal had been unleashed. There was just a *whoosh* of air, and a stomping of bear feet, and then an unceasing torrent of profanities that taught Daphne a few words she didn't know. She wasn't even sure all of them were profanities. Any word can be a profanity if you say it with enough rage.

Daphne leaped out of her chair and sprinted toward the nurses' station. Dr. Brooks had stopped by to look at pictures of Amy's new granddaughter, who had just been born in South Korea, where her daughter and her husband, both Marines, had been stationed for a couple of years. Dr. Brooks had been cooing a bit at the baby—a baby Daphne secretly thought was kind of ugly, though she felt guilty thinking a baby was ugly, even a truly ugly baby like Amy's granddaughter—and eating a Snickers bar when Becky came barreling toward him.

"Get that candy bar out of your mouth, you cuntbag!" Becky blared at him as she blew through the two doors to the ICU that were supposed to be locked but were never, ever locked. Becky was trailed by two security guards who, with the word Becky had just yelled, had just lost their patience. She stopped in front of Dr. Brooks and poked her finger in his chest. The security guards were about to grab her, but Daphne put a hand on the bigger one's shoulder. "Wait," she whispered. "She's OK."

The guard narrowed his eyes at Daphne. "She doesn't look OK," he said, and pulled Becky by her left arm. She spun around and smacked him right in the face. He stepped back and looked for all the world like he was about to put her through the wall.

"Get your goddamned hands off me," she spat at him, and the other guard grabbed her and pulled her arms behind her. He was older, and calmer. He was not about to suplex a grieving mother in a hospital. He guided her into a chair and sat down next to her.

He began rubbing her shoulder. "Ma'am, we can't help you like this," he said with the tone of a man attempting to coax a child into handing over that rocket launcher. "This is only hurting. You and everyone else." Becky looked at him, flared her nostrils, and snorted. She did take a deep breath, though, which was clearly more than anyone else had been able to get her to do.

"I want to know why that guy"—pointing at Dr. Brooks—"is

eating a candy bar while my son is in there in surgery right now. How can he sit there, with his stupid goon face, doing nothing. Why isn't he in *there*?" She turned back to Dr. Brooks, who Daphne had always thought had a bit of a goony face, now that Becky mentioned it. The doctor had crouched down behind Amy's desk and appeared to be desperately searching for a hole in the earth he could hide in.

The guard, who Daphne had seen plenty around the hospital but never talked to before, wore a metal name tag that read UNDERWOOD. He kept his right arm on Becky's left shoulder but put his left hand, gently, on her elbow. Her body eased up, almost instantly, as if Underwood had pressed a button.

"Ma'am," Underwood said to Becky, "that's Dr. Brooks. He's a resident, and he just got here. He doesn't know anything about your son. From what I understand, your son is still in surgery. I know that you are scared and upset, and I understand that. I would be scared and upset too. But you are not helping your son, or the people who are trying to help him."

Dr. Brooks slowly poked his head around the corner of Amy's desk and carefully approached Becky. "Ms. . . . I'm sorry, uh, I would be happy to go check in on your son's progress, if you would like."

At this point Daphne sat on the other side of Becky, who looked at her and burst into tears again. "I am right here, Becky," she said. "We will get through this together."

Everyone sat there for a second, silent except for Becky's sobs. Then Becky stood up, wiped her hair out of her eyes, and pointed at Dr. Brooks. "Yeah, why don't you fucking do that, you prick."

Becky took Daphne's arm and dragged her into the child Bryan's still-empty room. Daphne looked behind her and saw that the whole staff had, in an instant, already gone its separate ways, moving on to another patient, another emergency. There was always somebody screaming somewhere.

"So what the fuck is going on?" Becky said an hour later,

quieter but not calmer. It had been six hours since her son was brought in and five hours since she last saw him. Daphne did not know the specific surgical procedure for saving the life of ten-year-old boys who had been shot in the abdomen with high-caliber handguns, but six hours of surgery did not strike her as an unreasonably long period. But she didn't really have any idea.

"I don't know," Daphne said. "All we can do is wait and pray."

Daphne was not usually comfortable talking so openly about her faith with her patients, not because she felt awkward—talking about her faith was the easiest thing for her, in many ways, the only time she felt confident and assured—but because she was always worried someone at the hospital would report her. There were other Christians who worked on her floor, including an older woman who sat two pews down from her every Sunday, but Daphne, partly because of the Daniel incident and partly because she would occasionally post church flyers on the communal bulletin board on the wall of the nurses' station, had a particularly strong reputation for it. Sally had always been tolerant of it, even a little amused by it, but the supervisor who took over for Sally, a tall, angular woman named Deborah who always looked at Daphne like she was a ten-year-old girl, had admonished her when she walked into a patient's room and found Daphne kneeling and praying with her. Deborah was waiting for Daphne in the hallway, her eyes cold.

"You are here to take care of them, not to save their souls," she said. "This is not a Catholic hospital. We are a publicly financed institution. It is literally illegal for us to preach to our patients. You could get us sued. Did you realize that? You could get us sued."

Daphne had not realized that. How could such a law exist?

"There is a chapel in the lobby for anyone who needs it," Deborah said. "They do not need spiritual guidance from their nurses. They need their nurses to take their temperature, to switch out their IVs, and to change their bedpans. They need their nurses to be nurses. Can you do that?"

Daphne wasn't sure that she could, but she said yes anyway. She'd tried to be stealthy ever since then, and she thought she'd been rather successful at it. But then she held a boy's heart in her hands.

"Yeah, I'm not feeling too kind to the big guy upstairs at this moment," Becky said now. "It's probably best He and I not talk too much right now. He wouldn't much like what I have to say to him." She chuckled a little, and Daphne took that as a good sign, or at least a sign that Becky wasn't about to attack another doctor.

"We don't always know His plan," Daphne said. "But I also know He forgives. I'm sure He would forgive anything you said to Him on a day like today." She didn't know if she'd said that as well as Bill Preston, or Reverend Adam, might have. But she thought she did OK.

Becky turned her head back over to Daphne. "You ain't heard what I've got to say to Him yet, honey."

Daphne's shift had been over hours before, but of course she was still here. Ordinarily when she did this, other nurses would silently cluck at her when they came into the room to check on a patient or a patient's family—"Saintly Miss Daphne," she'd heard them call her—but after the incident with Dr. Brooks, no one dared to come near little Bryan's room, not with him not in it yet. Daphne wasn't on the clock. But she was on the clock.

Becky sighed, blew her nose, and walked over to the bed. She fluffed the two pillows, smoothed over the sheets, and sat down on the edge of the bed, knocking the patient clipboard to the floor before picking it up and putting it back on its hook. She wiped her eyes and began picking up another pillow, switching its position, setting it back down. "Bry always has been very particular about where he sleeps," she said. "Even when he was a baby, if one pillow was out of place, or one bit of the bedspread was hanging off the side of the bed, he wouldn't be able to sleep. He'd just roll over and toss and turn and kick all night. I used to let him sleep with me, back when he still wanted to do that, but it was so hard to get any rest. It had to be just perfect for him. The bed had to be just right."

She laid the pillow back down once more. "Have you slept on these beds before?" she asked Daphne. "Are they comfortable?"

Daphne told her she had, often, and they were. One of these answers was a lie—a big one, the beds made your spine feel like gravel—but Daphne thought Jesus would understand.

"That's good," Becky said. "He's going to be so tired. He's going to need a lot of sleep. I hope he can sleep." And she began to lightly sob again. Daphne handed her another tissue. Then they both sat and tried not to stare at the door to the room, the door where someone, sometime, would show up and tell Becky whether her ten-year-old son, the boy who had gone to spend the night with a friend and left with a huge hole in his belly, was going to live or die. They looked at each other, but only for a second. All they could see was that door.

6. HIM

Mom fell apart after Sue. So did I. Anyone would have. But she didn't truly break until he showed up.

We had a lot of visitors in the first few weeks after the accident, which we hadn't been expecting. I didn't seem to know any of the people who were suddenly in our house. We were never much of a hotspot before Sue's death, but the bigwigs of Athens were all making a beeline for our door once we were a part of the Tragedy of the Georgia Girls. The other three girls, Nicole O'Neill, Veronica Westin, and Alice Verdan, they were all from prominent Athens families. Their parents were big real estate types, lawyers, socialites, rich country club people. There were stories on the front page of the *Athens Banner-Herald* every day for a week. We were celebrities at the exact time we wanted attention the least.

People kept coming by. They brought food, they brought prayers, they brought whatever they thought might make themselves feel better. A preacher from one of the suburban Atlanta megachurches came by and got his picture taken holding my mom, making it look like he was comforting her, but he had just grabbed her and put his arms around her, without asking, and made sure his perfectly coiffed hair was in the exact right angle for the photo. We never heard from him again. Last I saw, the picture was still on his church's website.

Eventually, inevitably, he came by.

The first time he came by, it was with his wife. They brought us by sandwiches that first time, along with some necessities from the pharmacy—toiletries, soap, paper towels, milk, that sort of thing. It was nice. We needed all that. Neither of us were in any position to shop.

But a couple of days later he came back with another armful of stuff, this time without his wife. He was back again over the weekend. The next Tuesday, when I came home after returning to school for the first time, he was sitting on the couch next to Mom. He stood up when he saw me and offered to take my backpack. My mom was sitting up straight—straighter than she had since the accident. She didn't look better. But for the first time in a while, she didn't look worse.

She always perked up when he came around. We knew him already, because everybody knew Jack Lindbergh. His smiling face was on that sign, on T-shirts worn by coeds and little kids and old men five towns over, with his daddy and his little boy and a little dog. I'd seen him, behind that counter, and he'd always ignored me. But now we'd go to Lindbergh's, we were actually getting out of the house, and Mom would buy me a milkshake and tell me to sit down and stay there, and the woman behind the counter would give me another milkshake, and then another. She poured each milkshake with a little chuckle, like she did this for awkward teen girls with shapely moms all the time. We went by there the next day, and a couple of days later, and then we suddenly stopped going there altogether because he started coming by our duplex twice, maybe three times a week. Mom would make me a grilled cheese and some popcorn, she'd put me in the basement with a book or a board game, and when he left, she'd come down and get me. We'd watch a little television, and she'd send me to bed. She'd still be on the couch in the morning too.

For a long time, I couldn't fathom what he was thinking. Of all the women in Athens, why the grieving mother? Was he initially trying to help her, and it just got carried away? Was he simply unable to help himself? As I've gotten older, I realize it wasn't that complicated. My mother was at the weakest point of a rather weak life, and he couldn't resist taking advantage of someone who was that weak. He didn't do it to help, and I don't think he did it as some sort of sexual conquest. I just think he saw something broken and liked how it looked. He liked broken things. He didn't want to fix them. He just liked them broken. There's no complex emotional motivation. There wasn't for his dad either. You just take what you want. Whatever gets you what you want, that's what you do. That's how they are. They don't know any different.

I only remember him talking to me once. I had to use the restroom, so I went upstairs, and he'd just come out of her bedroom and hadn't expected to see me standing right outside it. He gave me a dark look, but caught himself and gave the same grin he had on the sign. He told me I was a cute little girl, and if I ever wanted anything, all I had to do was ask him. Then he went right back in the bedroom, and I ran to the basement as fast as I could.

One day, about four months after the accident, I came home from school and he was just pulling out of our driveway. He looked at me, blinked, and drove away. I walked inside and found my mother sitting in the middle of our kitchen floor, wearing an oversize Georgia Bulldogs T-shirt and no pants. She was holding a manila envelope in her left hand. She was just staring at the refrigerator, or past it—somewhere off in the distance where she couldn't see or hear me or anybody else. I got her a cold rag and wiped her face down, but her slack expression didn't change.

"Mom, are you OK?" I asked.

She turned her head to me slowly. "I need you to stay in the basement tomorrow," she said. "All day and all night." She touched my face. "Can you do that for me, honey?" I told her I could. I skipped school, just stayed down there, playing Clue and napping. I occasionally heard the front screen door open and close, and some muffled voices I didn't recognize, and every half hour or so the phone would ring and no one would answer. I remained down there until the next morning.

I went upstairs and saw Mom on the couch, staring straight ahead. She looked back at me.

"I don't think people are good," she told me. "I do not think we are going to be OK."

Those were her exact words. I even wrote them down. Her eyes were as clear as I had ever seen them.

Jack Lindbergh never made an appearance at our house again. I only remember Mom staying in bed all day and all night. She got disability shortly thereafter, and then the insurance company—the one Nicole's parents had; they had a really nice one—paid us a bunch of money, so much that there really wasn't much reason for Mom to leave the house after that. Shortly after Christmas she developed some sort of pituitary disorder and gained about fifty pounds in a month. That just accelerated her other health problems. It crumbled, fast.

Then her mind started to go. I don't know what it was. They never found any evidence of Alzheimer's, or dementia, at least not anything the doctors could determine. But they could not deny that she was going. Her uncle came from Nashville and told me that he was the executor of her estate, that she couldn't be trusted to stay in the house anymore, that I'd be an adult soon, in college, that they needed to find a place for her to stay until that happened, and that he could be my legal guardian until then. Then he took her to the Winterville Retirement Center, an old folks' home where she was thirty years younger than anyone there but more gone than any of them. I got her car, her duplex, and her life. I stayed in town for college, got my teaching license, taught, and it was fine, before it all got ruined, before they messed it all up. I would go see her. But she never spoke. She just sat there, looking out the window, not responding to me or anyone. I still went. I had to.

We were never going to be right after what happened to Sue. But Mom might have had a chance, had it not been for him. She was in pieces, and he broke her into smaller pieces. Like she was nothing. Like the world existed solely for him.

I had done my best to put him out of my mind, even as I knew I could feel his tentacles everywhere, his attempts to discredit people like me—people who knew who he really was—to make us disappear, to make us seem foolish. His father had surely done the same thing. All the stories about what doctors and officials did to those poor girls, those people who were complicit, so many punished for what they did and what they allowed to happen. But not them. Not the Lindberghs. They danced between the raindrops.

And then he died. The *Athens Banner-Herald* had a story about it, I saw it on Facebook. I'm just sitting on my computer, minding my own business, and up shows his face on my scroll. Lindbergh's Scion Dies Of Heart Attack, right there, with a big picture of his smiling face, like he was a former president or the founder of a bank.

The story treated him like the revered civic treasure he painted himself to be: he had been quite successful in that. I remember thinking, as I read it, *He's going to get away with it now.* No one would ever know, not what he did to my mom, not what his dad did to all those girls, whatever else he and his family had been involved in over the decades. He got to die a hero to this town, while everyone he knew picked up the pieces.

And then I read it.

Jack Lindbergh was such a meticulous chronicler of Lindbergh's place in the community that he kept every piece of paper from every business transaction the pharmacy ever made, in the belief that it should be preserved as part of Athens history.

"He's got boxes of stuff in the back," said Sandy Lucero, a longtime cashier at Lindbergh's. "He never threw anything away. Everything this place has ever been a part of, it's back there. He truly cared about every detail."

And then I knew what I had to do.

THEO

5:21 p.m.

"Your mother has to be the happiest mom I've ever seen in my life," Alexis said on the drive back to Lindbergh's, after Theo set a land speed record for the earliest he had ever introduced someone to his mother. "Everyone's mother I know is completely miserable."

Theo knew that his mother, for the first time in his entire life, was happy. He saw it in her every day. He saw it in her walk, the way she used to hunch back on her heels as if about to run away from something but now leaned forward, almost on her tiptoes, like she was always trying to get wherever she was going as quickly as she could. He saw it in the way she had begun reading over the last year and a half, ravenously, three or four books a week, like she was trying to take in all the parts of the world she'd missed over the last forty years in huge gulps. He saw it in the way she came by Lindbergh's, a building where she'd been a faint, oft-whispered-about ghost for decades but now strutted around like she owned the place, which, by the way, she totally fucking did. He saw it because his mother was lighter. She had a monster off her back.

She'd said it exactly like that: "I have a monster off my

back." She was behind a closed door, quarantining with Covid, when she said it, but he knew how she looked then, and exactly what she meant. She'd said that to Theo behind that door nine months before, and she'd apologized, but Theo said she shouldn't, and they cried, and then she was so much better, she was better than she'd ever been.

Betty had long been a figure of curiosity in Athens. As Jack's mostly absent wife, the one who was always at home with Theo or somehow away from whatever Jack was up to, she'd been the subject of gossip her entire life, gossip that she ignored by focusing on keeping Lindbergh's solvent, raising her son not to be like his dad, and not asking any questions. She knew what people thought. She figured they were sort of right to think it. Jack was out there making a fool of her, had been doing so their entire marriage. But he was who he was, and Betty knew there was nothing to be done about it. Years before, after he was caught the second time and Betty didn't do anything—didn't leave him, didn't ream him out, didn't go out and bonk the carpenter to get back at him—he stopped trying to hide it, and Betty stopped caring enough to notice.

Jack never said a cruel word to Betty, but he didn't have to. All he had to do was look like the pressed, clean, composed public face of generations of Lindberghs, the one with everything under *control*. If you cracked at all, if you lost your shit for a second, if you called him out, if you expressed anything other than cool, collected remove like he did, *you* were the one having an emotional outburst, you were the one who was causing a scene. Jack had a way of weaponizing your response to him and everything he did: to say that you were upset was, to him, confessing weakness. The only way to be, for Jack, was a placid, affable, forward-facing public figure, keeping your emotions under wraps, and if you were unable to do this, well, you'd already lost. You couldn't argue with Jack because arguing with Jack was playing tennis against a wall.

You could hit the ball as hard as you could, but it wouldn't matter; the wall would always dispassionately return the ball to you.

Jack had decided at some point—and Theo suspected it was long before he met Betty—that he was forever going to do whatever he damn well pleased, and the way he would get away with it was to paint it like it was all your fault if you had a problem with it. People who didn't know Jack well would find him charming on the surface, and that was exactly how he wanted it. If you didn't like what you found when you dug deeper, well, that was your fault for digging deeper.

Betty had married him because of that charm, but she had no idea what she'd gotten herself into. That charm curdled into toxic, relentless smugness quickly—but not quickly enough for Betty. By the time she saw behind the mask, Theo had arrived, and he was so beautiful, so guileless and earnest right from the get-go, that she knew if she didn't protect him—from Jack, from all of it—he'd be forever lost. Or worse—he'd be like *him*.

She would not let that happen. She stopped fighting Jack, stopped caring, stopped hitting the tennis ball against the wall. What could you do? To fight with Jack was to lose—to give him a part of yourself that he didn't deserve. So she battened down the hatches. She gave him nothing and expected nothing. She made sure he would have no weapon against her. She had to. She had to protect Theo.

So she made sure Theo was shielded the best she could, smiled in public when she was expected to, and got the hell out of there as fast as she could. Her marriage became less like two old roommates than like two separate renters sharing the same duplex. She didn't share a bed with Jack for the final decade of their marriage, which had to take some stress off both of them: she didn't have to ask, he didn't have to hide. The less they spoke to each other, the easier this could be. This was why Theo was honestly sort of surprised that his father was so upset when

Theo left for Atlanta rather than running Lindbergh's alongside Jack, as Jack had alongside his father. Sure, it was a break with tradition, but it wasn't like Jack and Theo were ever as close as Jack and Buddy . . . though Theo supposed he didn't really know how close his father and grandfather actually were, all told. Did Jack legitimately want to spend that much time with Theo? Could have fooled him. And Theo's departure allowed both Jack and Betty to end their charade, the brave front they kept up for Theo's sake. Once he was gone, they no longer had to pretend. They could ignore each other in peace. Theo did sometimes notice, when he came home to visit, that his parents always seemed to be in different rooms of the house, even when they were sitting right next to each other. He had to admit they were more pleasant this way.

Theo didn't think *that* much about any of this until that night, or at least not how deep it went. He knew his parents didn't really like each other, and he knew who his father was. He always had. He knew his mother was the one to go to for everything, that reaching out to Jack Lindbergh for love or help or advice or even a second of his time was only inviting Jack to hurt him. He knew Jack saw him as weak, his mother's son in every way, a useful prop when needed and hopefully occupied with something else when not. (It sent a shudder through Theo, after Jack died, to realize how long he had known this about his father. He'd felt this way about his dad in *kindergarten*.) But he didn't know the details. Who would want to?

But that night, he learned. He had been taking care of his mother all week after her positive test, all day and all night: with the reduced capacity, Sandy, the front cashier at Lindbergh's, who had been covering for Lindbergh family squabbles for forty years, could easily run a smaller shop without him. (He did suspect she was sneaking a smoke when there were no customers without Theo there to bust her, though.) He stayed downstairs while his mother was upstairs, communicating with her through two old walkie-talkies he'd found in the basement. It was really fun, actually. She'd buzz down, "Roger one-nine, Roger one-nine, calling for pasta reinforcements," and he'd make some spaghetti, pop open a bottle of wine, pour her a glass, put it all on a tray, and leave it outside her door. Then he'd head back downstairs, pour a glass for himself, and they'd have dinner together through their walkie-talkies. It felt good, *worthy*, to take care of his mother, to provide for all her needs, to keep her safe; he began referring to himself as "The Nervous Butler." He mapped out little exercises that she could do alone in her bedroom; he programmed playlists for her upstairs Amazon Echo; he texted back and forth with her while watching terrible television.

And most of all, they talked. They talked about the pandemic and the election and the pharmacy and this old house and the failed restaurant and that Susan girl he used to date and everything they'd never had the time to get into before, because who has the time to get into anything? It was one of the last nights, just two days before she was clear of quarantine, when they stayed up too late, drinking too much wine. They'd been careful, during all of their talks, not to bring up Jack too often—they'd been enjoying themselves too much. But that night, on their third bottle of wine, Betty said it: *A monster off my back*. And Theo knew exactly what she meant.

Two days later, Betty left the room. She was smiling. She was positively beaming.

"And she hasn't stopped smiling," Theo told Alexis as he drove her back to her mother's house off Mel Street in Five Points. They'd had lunch, and then they just hadn't quit talking, and next thing you knew five hours had passed—such was Theo's status as a Lindbergh that two customers let him give them vaccines with some random lady chattering next to him—and his mom needed him to drop off some medicine so Alexis just came with him and the three of them chatted and next thing you knew it was time to take Alexis home, though Theo sort of wondered why she had to leave at all. He'd just told her about the most personal story he'd ever told anyone, after all.

"That's really sad," Alexis said. "And also not."

"Yeah," Theo said. "Makes you look at that sign at the store a little differently, doesn't it?"

Alexis, who had pulled her hair back around 3:00 p.m. and no longer had that little strand hanging over her eye, grinned at him as he pulled into her mom's driveway.

"Probably time for a new sign anyway, isn't it?" She leaned over, kissed him on the cheek, and looked him in the eye. She took a deep breath. "I have to confess something to you."

"*Oh shit*," Theo said, and it was out of his mouth before he realized that he said it rather than just thinking it.

Alexis grinned. "Christ, it's not *that* bad."

"Sorry. I have a bad habit of always thinking there's a piano about to fall on my head."

"Well, there might be. I'm a huge mess. You really need to know that."

"I don't think I have much room to talk on that one," he said.

"That's clear," she said. "But that's not what I wanted to confess." She pivoted in her car seat and, swear to God, Theo saw that bit of hair pop out of her ponytail and pop right back out over her eye.

"So you know how I told you that my mom told me to come in to you and get my shot today?"

"Yes?"

"Well, that was kind of a fib," she said. "I told my mom I was just going to the CVS on Alps Road."

"OK?" he said. "That seems a dumb thing to lie about. Though I'm glad you're shopping local."

"Well, the thing is, it was actually *your* mom who set this whole thing up," she said. "I'm . . . uh . . . I actually play tennis with your mom at Jennings Mill, every Tuesday night."

A grin slowly crept onto Theo's face. "Oh my god," he said. "You're the unemployed writer!"

Alexis's nose wrinkled. "That's not exactly how I'd put it!" she said. "It's a tough market. You know how expensive a Brooklyn apartment is? Sheesh, Betty."

Betty had been talking for weeks about her tennis instructor, a cute "sorta gloomy, the kind of gloomy you like" unemployed writer who'd moved back from New York City when the pandemic hit. She had tried not to make it look like she was trying to set Theo up with her, even though she talked about her constantly and kept trying to get Theo to meet her for lunch at the club to introduce them. Theo had thwarted every attempt, partly because he didn't want to be dating anyone, partly because he was embarrassed that he was an unmarried failure of a man in his mid-thirties whose mom was trying to set him up with strangers, and partly because by lunchtime he was usually too stoned on Opana to do anything but stare at the milkshake machine. Betty had curiously stopped bringing the unemployed writer up over the last couple of weeks. He now knew why.

"So you two, just now, were pretending like you didn't know each other?"

"Well, we didn't know you were going to bring me over to meet her, like, an hour after I came in," Alexis said. "We had to improvise!" She smiled, a little sheepishly, but only a little. "I guess you must like me."

Theo had been wondering why his mother was talking about New York City and blogs so much.

"Are you mad?" Alexis asked.

He wasn't. He trusted his mom. He always had. And anyway: it sure looked like she was onto something.

"As long as she doesn't come to our next date, no."

"Boys and their moms," she said, and kissed him on the lips. "So, lunch again tomorrow?"

Theo looked at her and thought, for the first time in his entire life, that he might actually be in the right place.

"Customer satisfaction is Lindbergh's number-one goal," he said. "It's right there in the ads."

WHEN LINDBERGH'S REOPENED AND THEO TOOK OVER, HE'D EXTENDED THE pharmacy's hours to 6:00 p.m., partly because they needed to recoup all sorts of lost revenue and mostly because Theo usually sent the staff home at five and just worked the last hour, usually a slow one, by himself. He worked for free—after all, he owned the place. He walked to the front cashier stand, put up a PLEASE GO TO THE BACK FOR CHECKOUT sign, and opened that big black door, which creaked a little too loudly—he'd always hated it anyway, he should replace that thing, it scared little kids. He began to count inventory for the day as a smattering of customers milled around. He hadn't had an Opana since before lunch and was starting to click his tongue against the top of his mouth and squish up his toes. He'd cut back in recent weeks. But not that much. Not enough.

He was going to be all right, though. He looked out upon the store, the pharmacy, his grandfather's pharmacy, his father's pharmacy, the Athens institution. It didn't belong to them anymore, just like it didn't belong to the neighborhood or any of the ghosts that haunted it. It was his. What happened next with it was entirely up to him. He could modernize the place. Or maybe he'd just blow the place up and turn it into the world's last Blockbuster Video. He could do whatever he pleased. This place was *his*.

He was gonna get rid of that door, though. He was sure of that. His phone buzzed. It was a text from his friend Karson.

yo how bout those hawks! trae's the real deal! hes a bad man!

The Atlanta Hawks, his Atlanta Hawks, had just beaten the Philadelphia 76ers to reach the Eastern Conference finals for just the second time in fifty years, and it was *fantastic*. He'd gone to State Farm Arena in Atlanta to watch game 4 of the previous series with Karson, and it had been glorious: a full-on whupping of those New York assholes, with a riotous twenty-five thousand cheering people who'd been locked inside for a year finally getting to scream and rejoice. He'd known Karson since high school—they'd actually played quiz bowl against each other, if you can believe that—and he considered him a friend, though in your thirties that basically meant planning on making plans to get together but never actually doing so. (Karson, unlike Theo, had a family, which put him in an entirely different plane of reality as well.) But that game had been incredible, the most fun Theo had had in . . . my god, when *had* been the last time he'd had that much fun? They'd been texting regularly since then and had plans next week to catch a conference finals game against the Bucks at the pub down the street from Lindbergh's.

Bucks are scary, man, Theo texted back. Giannis is a freaking dragon. But we're hot!

He wished he hung out with Karson more. Karson was the sort of person Theo wanted to be more like, if only he could get his act together. Karson didn't live his entire life under another man's shadow, cursing the hand that fate dealt him. Karson went out and dedicated his life to making a difference, to trying to change a world that didn't want to change. He didn't grouse about what he wanted his life to be; he went out and *did* something. He went out and started a group called Athens Youth Active, and every day he touched people's lives, gave them food, kept them out of trouble, assisted with their math homework, did real shit for real people. He made the world better.

What had Theo done to help? How was he trying to change the world? He hadn't been. He'd been too caught up in his own dramas, his issues with his dad and this store and everything that was expected of him and everything that he didn't want to be. He had it good, he thought, so much better than so many other people, and still he had just sat there in self-pity, bemoaning his ill fortune when so many had it so much worse. He could help. He would help. He could do some good.

Karson was always looking for more help. Why hadn't Theo helped? Maybe it wasn't too late.

Maybe, even, he could use this place for good—maybe use its institutional power to support the organizations he cared about, to fight for social justice, to help people who needed it.

He looked at his phone again. Karson. Good dude. It wasn't too late.

BTW, would love to talk about AYA and how Lindbergh's can be a part. Happy to meet for a drink or whatever you want. Shoot, come by the store! Free milkshakes!

He could do some good here. And he could do it on his own terms.

That was what Betty had meant about the monster. It wasn't that Jack was himself a monster, though he probably was, or at least as much as a nattily dressed philandering college town pharmacist could be. It was that wherever Theo had gone, Jack had loomed over him—had decided what the world would look like for Theo without Theo ever having a say in it, without ever realizing it. That was still happening, for sure: Theo was indeed running Jack's old place, just like Jack had always wanted. But it was Theo's place now. He could do whatever he wanted to do with it. Maybe it would work. Maybe it wouldn't. But it was *his*. It was his life, and his only, for the first time in his entire life. He didn't have to be Jack's son. He didn't have to be a Lindbergh. He could just be Theo.

What did that mean? He didn't know. He didn't even really want to know. Whatever happened in his life was because of what lay ahead of him, not what came before him. It was thrilling. Maybe it was his mom. Maybe it was Alexis. Maybe it was the two Opana he'd just popped. But it all spread out before him, this world, and it felt new and right, a vessel just waiting for him to fill it. All that had happened was the journey to this point. This was where he'd ended up. It was his now. It was finally his.

His phone buzzed again.

Hells yeah. lets chat. actually. im in your hood now. you at the store?

Theo texted back.

Yo! Definitely. We're closing up in an hour, but definitely come by, it's super slow. I'm even up for a beer afterward if you are. Up for the Pub?

The three dots came up immediately.

on my way dawg.

He smiled. He smiled real wide. He saw an older woman shopping and caught her eye.

"Hello, ma'am," he said. "Can I help you with anything?"

"I'm fine, thank you," she said. She looked around. "The old place looks great. Your father would be very proud."

Would he? Theo realized, at last, that he didn't care—it didn't matter to him one bit.

But he didn't say that. He just said, "I sure hope so. Let me know if you need any help." She smiled back and nodded.

Theo went back to his inventory. He had a few more receipts to sign off on before he could relieve the pharmacist, who was staying an extra twenty minutes to take care of the last few straggling customers. He nodded to her—*Just a sec, thanks for staying*—and remembered that he'd left his solar calculator on his desk, so he turned around to get it. As he passed by, he saw a bag of trash by the side door, the one that led out to the alley where the dumpster was. He grabbed the trash with his left hand, holding his calculator with his right, and kicked open the door with his foot.

He heard an *oooooooph*. A voice, a groan. He'd just smacked someone with the door. He put his calculator in his pocket, lightly pushed the door open, and peered around the corner, a little embarrassed.

A woman was standing there. That was odd—he never saw anybody standing in that alley.

"Oh, shoot, sorry," he said.

DOROTHY

5:21 p.m.

Dorothy thought the little place mat was nice. It was a math place mat, to put under the dinner trays of little kids so they didn't spill their food all over the nice table. It had all sorts of facts and figures on it, little multiplication tables, tips and tricks to help them get the basic mathematical fundamentals while stuffing their faces with macaroni and cheese.

She would get one of these for those gorgeous granddaughters of hers. That was the nice thing about a little place like Lindbergh's. You could come here for stamps, or a sandwich, or a prescription, and there were all sorts of little tchotchkes and curios you'd end up taking home with you. She'd once bought a ceramic dog bowl here, with the G Georgia logo and a cute little pawprint on it, though she didn't have a dog and neither did anyone in her family. Lindbergh's was a place you bought stuff sometimes just because it was there.

She loved this place mat. She grabbed two, one for Wynn's little girls and one for Jeff's great-grandchild. She'd just slide this right into the package. All it would cost was one more stamp.

DENNIS NEVER KNEW ABOUT JEFF. HE'D BEEN CURIOUS ABOUT THE MEN IN Dorothy's life before him, as any man would be, but he was reasonably curious, Dorothy thought, not *too* curious. He wasn't invasive or possessive, and he'd asked with a mischievous twinkle in his eye, likely to assure her he wasn't going to be a lunatic about it. She told him about Jimmy, a two-bit hustler who'd tried to get her sister and her best friend before settling for Dorothy (he'd end up busted trying to break open an ATM with an aluminum bat, the moron), and she'd told him about Harold, a polite Christian man who was so nervous around her that when she'd once started to un-buckle his belt in the car at the end of a date, he squealed, opened the passenger door, and sprinted away. (She'd eventually get him to come around, repeatedly, though she left that part out of the story.) But telling him about Jeff, even playfully, was asking for trouble.

Apparently Jeff went to the same grade school Dorothy did in Brunswick, though Dorothy doesn't remember him at all and has never quite entirely believed his insistence that this is true. *I sat two chairs behind you from third grade to sixth grade, and you never looked back at me once,* he'd written in one of his letters last fall. *You always paid so much attention to those books. I could not believe how smart you were.*

Dorothy sure did remember meeting Jeff, though. It was a rainy afternoon their junior year of high school, and she was sitting in Mrs. Burton's biology class trying to get her tweezers around the liver of a frog. She'd failed: the liver dissolved into mush. It amused Dorothy to no end that dissecting dead animals was so commonplace when she was in high school. She had never dissected any animals at any other time in her life and really didn't know anyone who had—she was pretty sure she wouldn't want to know anyone who had, all told. That the one time in your life when someone gives you a scalpel and commands you to cut into the flesh of an animal would be in *high school* grew more hilarious the more she thought about it. One kid in her class actually ate the formaldehyde-filled frog's head on a dare and ended up having to go to the hospital to have his stomach pumped. All his friends thought it was cool.

She cursed her clumsiness with the liver and asked Mrs. Burton to use the restroom to wash her sticky, disgusting hands. "Take the frog with you," Mrs. Burton said. "We'll get you a new one after you throw that one away." Dorothy grabbed a napkin, picked the frog up by its left leg, and carefully balanced him in her hand so that the rest of his guts did not fall on the floor.

Dorothy slowly turned the corner out of the classroom and ran straight into Jeff. He was wearing an old tank top—a wife-beater, they called it back then—and had his hair all greased back, like it wanted to be an Afro but he didn't know how to spackle it down without looking like he was being rained on. He was tall and rail-skinny—she could see his ribs through his shirt, almost distended, like he wasn't just thin, he was starving. And he had a wispy little mustache that made him look like the numbers runner for a series of amusingly inept criminals. He also had the most incredible blue eyes. She thought he was one of the most ridiculous people she'd ever seen, and she could not stop looking at him.

"Hello?" Jeff said. He was holding a ruler in his left hand, for some reason.

"Hi," Dorothy said.

Jeff was a good foot taller than Dorothy, and he leaned down to her. "Hello there," he said, composed now—prepared. He was smiling at her like they had known each other for forty thousand years. "I'm Jeff. I've been waiting to talk to you for a long time, Doe. You're Doe, right?"

"Dorothy," she said. "But I like Doe." She felt her tongue go back in her throat. She did not remember a time in her life that those eyes had not been looking at her.

"I, uh . . ." Then Jeff kissed her, right then and there in the hallway. Before she knew what she was doing, she was kissing him back, lost in all of it, somehow feeling stronger than she had ever felt before.

Then she brought her hands up to his face, and he jumped

back about five feet and began gagging. "Damn, woman, why you got a frog in your hand?"

She dropped it on the hallway floor, grabbed him by the shirt, pulled him to her, and kissed him again. They ended up squishing the frog.

They saw each other every day for the next forty-three days. The thing that blew her away the most about Jeff was something so simple and straightforward that she couldn't have possibly known at the age of sixteen how rare it truly was: she always knew what Jeff was thinking, and he always knew what she was thinking. Neither of them had to guess, or wonder, or was ever worried that the other's feelings about them were in danger of changing or altering in any way. She never fretted about whether she'd say the wrong thing around Jeff because whatever she said *was* the right thing, no matter what it was. Even then, Dorothy didn't believe in past lives or reincarnation or anything like that, but there was absolutely no way, she thought, both then and now, that they hadn't known each other long before they met. It was as if every moment before they got together was some sort of pointless exercise—like up until then, they'd been just kidding.

Sure, they'd have disagreements—they were high school kids, Dorothy knew they were fundamentally idiots, she had no illusions about that. But they fit together in some cosmic way, not like puzzle pieces, but like they'd worn grooves in a bed that the other one nestled into perfectly. They loved each other, instantly, but that seemed to understate it. He was unlike her in so many ways: dull, first off, or at least quiet—maybe that was it, just quiet. She wanted to move to the city and see the world; he didn't really want to do much of anything other than be with her. "I don't even like to leave the house, let alone leave Brunswick," he'd said, and she'd frowned, but only for a split second. It's obvious now that these would have all become big problems down the line, but they didn't matter then. They didn't talk about the future because no high school kid ever talks about the future, especially not when they're in love. They were just together, every day, all of the time.

And then his mom died. Heart attack—came out of nowhere, found her dead on the toilet, a wretched and stupid way for anyone's mom to die. The next day was the forty-fourth. Then they buried her, and it was obvious that Jeff's dad was in no position to take care of Jeff and his sister, so in came their grandmother, and a week later the whole family was in Brooklyn, wherever that was. They'd had one day to say goodbye. They were both so stunned and shell-shocked, not just by his mother's death but by the sudden introduction of conflict and trouble in the blissful cloud-floating of the first forty-three days. Once you threw a cog in the machine, the whole thing jammed up and broke down. Their last meeting featured him mumbling that he was moving, her hugging him awkwardly and telling him to call her, and him getting in his dad's old Ford and driving away. She cried for a second, and then stopped. At the time she moved right along because she was young and stupid and because if she stopped and looked down, she might realize there was no ground beneath her and perish.

She did not talk to him again for fifty-five years.

She'd heard stories from some classmates, but who knew which ones were true. He'd gone to the army. He'd become a drug addict. He'd joined a gang. He was a priest. He'd gone gay. He was married to two women at once. No one knew, and Dorothy was too scared to look. Besides: she had her own life to live. She wanted to see the big city. Athens was a big enough city for her, with the university and all the different kinds of people a university introduced you to, so she moved there right out of high school and grabbed the first waitressing job she could find. Life would find her next path. She knew she was in the right place to find it.

The ache of Jeff's loss was always there, though. It caught up with her even before she knew it was chasing her. There were trillions upon trillions of molecules in the cosmos, and they had somehow collided in a way that had led those two humans to instantly feel like no one had ever existed on the planet other than the two of them—and boom, like that, he was gone. Dorothy was not old enough to put any of that in any sort of perspective, but she knew there was something wrong about it, just as she knew there was nothing she could do about it but try to keep herself busy and distracted.

And then a handsome man who was going places drew her some dogs on a check, and then fifty-five years had passed, and he was dead. Dorothy knew no one—and certainly not her younger self—would believe her on this, but it was true. It happened just like that, just that quickly, all of it.

The letter arrived exactly forty-three days after Dennis died. Dorothy didn't notice that, and Jeff surely didn't either, but nevertheless it was true. It was scrawled in shaky, barely legible handwriting, which Dorothy would later learn was because Jeff had started getting slight hand tremors in his seventies; his kids had thought it was Parkinson's, but he didn't really like doctors, and besides, *I can still clean the gutters and change the oil on the car so it ain't really no thing*. It was April when she received the letter, still just an unholy terror inside her house and out, and she'd almost thrown it out with the junk mail. But she'd noticed a return address from Plainsboro, New Jersey, so she opened it. It took her a while to decipher it, but this is what it said:

Doe—

    I was so sorry to hear about your husband. Sounded like a good man. Lost my wife four years back. You are really going to be in for it for a while. But you gonna be OK, dont you worry.

    I just wanted to say how sorry I was. The sad part is the part of them that is left, the part of them you still have. Hang onto that. I always have. You have had a great life and Im happy for you Doe. I am sorry to reach out like this but it gets real quiet these Covid days and I thought maybe this was the time to say hello. So hello.

Jeff

She wrote him back that day, and he wrote her as soon as he got her letter, and then she did the same, and now she had a fridge full of photos of Jeff and his late wife and his kids and his grandchildren and new great-grandchild on the wall of her kitchen. Those eyes were the first thing she saw in that kitchen in the morning and the last thing she saw before she went to bed. The letters had been the world outside this one—they'd saved her life, and she was sure they had saved Jeff's as well, she knew that because she just knew it, just like she knew he knew it.

Dorothy didn't think Dennis would have much liked Jeff. Jeff was too laid-back, too passive, too, as he put it, just-lyin'-around. A driven man like Dennis would have found him lazy, which was about as serious a crime as Judge Johnson could accuse a man of. But Dorothy didn't think Jeff was lazy. Jeff was just *content*. That was what Dorothy needed—that was what she always needed. She wanted to be able to take a deep breath and feel like it was all going to be OK—that she'd done enough. Those letters did that. Those letters made her feel like she could start living again. Jeff wasn't Dennis; she didn't feel like she was betraying him, any more than Jeff was betraying his late wife by writing to her. The letters— and their meeting, that's what this was about, that's what all the letters were leading up to—were just something for two old folks from the Deep South to look forward to. That was enough, she thought. She believed Dennis would approve. She even thought he'd be a little proud of her.

Those letters were also the reason for the first time she'd ventured out into the world the summer before: she had to buy stamps. She'd headed out to Lindbergh's, wearing a mask, and a shield, and the gloves you cleaned the toilet with because she didn't have any other gloves but didn't want to take any chances, and bought a hundred of them. She had smiled as she looked at the roll of stamps on the kitchen counter this morning. There was only one left.

That's why she was here. She was out of stamps. They were going to meet over the Fourth of July. She held the place mat to her side and tapped her leg. She realized she was excited, and this made her happy. She was feeling happy a lot lately.

DOROTHY PICKED UP SOME GAUZE, SOME FIBER PILLS, AND A MANILA envelope, and walked to the back of Lindbergh's. She took a place in line behind a tall man and his even taller son, who was leaning on crutches and holding his arm in a sling.

"What happened?" she asked.

"He fell off the roof," his dad said.

The kid grinned. "Roofs are always higher up than you think they are."

Dorothy laughed. "Well, I never thought of it that way, but I suppose that's true."

The man looked at his phone for a second, and they all turned back to face the register and continued to wait in line.

7. PAIN (INFLICTED AND ENDURED)

I've never hurt anyone in my life. But I have thought about it.

It's clarifying, pain. They say the worst pain is childbirth. I can't speak to that. But a kidney stone has to be close. I passed a kidney stone about three years ago, and it was so painful that the pain became a tangible, palpable object. You could almost touch the pain. It was its own living, breathing thing.

That experience was so awful, three days alone in my room, screaming and crying, that I think I haven't quite experienced life the same since. That feeling was so unbearable that everything that *isn't* that feeling is comparatively wonderful. Colors are brighter, food tastes better: sleeping through the night is a gift rather than an expectation. Pain strips away all that isn't real, anything that's artificial. There is something so honest about pain. No one is fake about pain. No one tells you one thing when they are in pain but secretly believes something else. Pain is pure.

Pain is simply the body telling you that something is wrong. If we did not feel pain, we could be on fire and not have any idea until we were already dead. We have been trained to believe pain is bad, that it's something that must be avoided, but that's misunderstanding what pain is meant to do—why it's here in the first place. To shield yourself from pain is to doom yourself to death.

Mom was like this. She was in such pain that she numbed

herself to it so much that she could no longer feel it at all, which is to say, she could no longer feel anything. Once she walled herself off from pain, there was no real reason to do much living at all anymore. When she shut off the pain, that's when I lost her.

Sometimes people have to feel pain to see things the way they really are.

Pain is the world working the way it is supposed to. Pain is a warning. Pain is a sign. Pain is an alert. Pain means you need to start doing something different. Pain is your body and your mind telling you that the status quo is no longer acceptable. You find out what truly matters to you when you are in pain. Pain leads to transformation. Colors can be brighter. Food can taste better. You can be purified. And you can be reborn.

JASON

5:21 p.m.

The hardest thing about being a parent, in Jason's view, was that your children weren't nearly as special, as *protected*, as you thought they were. To you, the person who stayed up all night that first week just staring at them to make sure they were still breathing, who saw their eyes light up in infinite wonder when they unwrapped that toy car from Santa, who held their hand when you crossed the street to school, who looked at them and thought they were definitive proof of an altruistic force in the universe that was good and just and kind . . . to you, they were everything. But to the rest of the world, they are just another lump of flesh—one more tick on the tote board, one more person you're stuck behind in traffic. His children were the center of everything that had ever mattered to him in the world—it struck him, still, today, how much he had loved them, *instantly*, the very second he first saw them—but to everyone else, they were just another dope walking the earth. If he ever lost any of them, he would crumple into a heap on the floor and never get up. But the rest of the world wouldn't do anything. Everyone would just walk around like nothing had happened.

That indifference was impossible for Jason to square. If the world knew his children the way he did, it would understand how much they needed to be safeguarded from all the damage it could do to them. It would never let Jace lie there like that. It would never let him feel pain.

"I'm all right, Dad," he said, there on the emergency room cot, arm in a sling, ankle in an air cast. But Jace didn't look all right. He looked like he was in pain. And there was nothing that could possibly be worse than Jason seeing his son in pain.

It made him want to . . . well, it made him want to do something that Jason made a point to never do.

Jason figured a man was allowed two good cries in his life, so you better use them wisely. He'd used one of his, a big one, and it bothered him a little that when he thought back about it today, the primary emotion he felt was shame.

It was six years earlier, just outside the First Baptist Church in Moweaqua, Illinois. Helen's father Troy had initially been a huge pain in the ass about Jason's courtship of his daughter. Helen had a lot more dating experience than Jason had when they met, and having a lot of dating experience meant she'd come across clown car after clown car of assholes, including, infamously, a drunk cop who'd gotten mouthy with Troy and ended up missing two teeth. You could see how Troy might have been a little skeptical of Jason, who was big and burly and bearded and worked construction and had a southern drawl so thick that Troy, who was already hard of hearing and rather irritable about it, on the night Helen brought him back to Illinois to meet her parents, threw his hands in the air and said, "I can't tell what the hell that kid's saying, can any of you?" But Troy had also mentioned at that first dinner that he was heading out to Stonington first thing tomorrow to go chop down some trees for firewood, and when he went out to his truck the next morning, he found Jason, in his overalls and work gloves, waiting for him. He nodded at Jason, Jason nodded back, and nine hours later, the Thompson family had enough wood for the whole next winter and the two men were bonded for life.

That next fall, the two men were out hunting together, sitting silently in a tree drinking Busch Lights and looking for any movement in the bushes below, when Jason turned to Troy.

"Troy, I'd like to marry your daughter," Jason said.

"You gonna keep that job of yours?" Troy said.

"Yes, sir," Jason said. "I'll make us a good home."

"You better." Troy lifted his beer to Jason's, and Jason tapped his can to Troy's, and then they sat there in silence for two hours until Jason spotted a buck and bang he got him right in the rib cage. They did that trip together every year from then on out. That first time was the only buck Jason ever got.

Troy had smoked, like, seriously smoked, three packs of unfiltered Pall Malls "every day since I got hair on my lip," he told Jason. The lung cancer still came and got him faster than anyone could have seen coming. He'd had a persistent enough cough that Marisa finally made him go to the doctor—he'd fought her for weeks, saying "They'll always find something wrong with you if they look hard enough," Jason always remembered him saying that—and by the time they got the scans back, it was too late. "We're looking at six months," the doctor said, and Troy only made it four.

Jason was a pallbearer at the funeral—he'd volunteered for it, so he wouldn't have to stand in that line by the coffin, shaking everybody's hand, saying the same shit over and over—and he'd carried the casket into the hearse with Troy's brother and an old drinking buddy and some stray cousins. He returned to his car for the funeral procession with Abby and Jace, who were both just barely old enough to understand any of this, in the back seat. He pulled into his spot behind his brother-in-law's minivan, which carried Helen and Marisa and Helen's three sisters, and he thought about the hunting trips, and the Busch Lights, and that time that Troy was grilling steaks and asked Jason how he liked his, and Jason said "Well done," and Troy said, "That ain't how we do it here" and served it to him bloody and Jason smiled and ate up every bite and he had eaten his steaks like that ever since and then, "Ohhhhhhhhhh awwwwwww," Jason just convulsed and burst into tears right then and there. Jason hadn't thought about crying, hadn't thought it was particularly close, wasn't fighting it, and then, as if a bomb had gone off, he just started wailing. In front of his kids and everything.

It lasted roughly five seconds. He pulled himself together, wiped his nose with his suit jacket, coughed to his armpit, and let out a small *Woooo*. He looked in his rearview mirror and saw his children staring at him in shock. He looked back at the road.

"Underwear must have been too tight there." He followed his place in the procession and never talked to anyone about it ever again.

Jason hadn't thought about that moment in years either. It came rushing back to him as he had watched Jace lying there, holding his arm, trying to look tough for his father but clearly in immense pain.

Jason didn't cry. He was lucky to feel this one coming on, so he had time to fight it off. But he wanted to. He really wanted to cry.

JACE HADN'T BROKEN HIS WRIST, OR HIS ANKLE. THANK GOD. HELEN, WHO had been much kinder to Jason about what had happened than he had expected her to be, had called in a favor to a doctor she knew at St. Mary's, so Jace got right into the ER. He had some scrapes up and down his arm and a scratch across his left cheek, but he didn't have a concussion, mostly because he broke his fall by thrusting out his left wrist just as he landed. He had also fallen on his ankle and twisted it badly; there were bruises up and down that leg, like all his muscles and tendons had been pulled apart like yarn. It wasn't quite a sprain, Dr. Meyers said, but it was "almost" a sprain. Jason didn't understand that part. What was *almost* a sprain? Was it a sprain, or wasn't it? Doctors were never as clear as you wanted them to be.

Jace, for his part, was proud that it was his left wrist. "See, didn't hurt my throwing hand," he said in the truck on the way to St. Mary's. "Even my subconscious told me to land on my left side." Jason grunted and tried not to look at him. He still wanted to cry and was afraid, if he made eye contact with his son, he might.

Dr. Meyers gently held Jace's left arm in her palm and lifted it slightly. Jace winced, and Jason caught him glancing at his father to make sure he hadn't seen him show any sign of pain. Jason worried sometimes that maybe he'd toughened his son up *too* much.

"I do not think it is broken," Dr. Meyers said. "We won't know for sure until we get the X-rays back. And there is of course your ankle. We are going to have to get you some crutches, at least for the next week or so." She looked at Jace. "You're quite lucky. You said you fell ten feet?"

"More like fifteen, right, Dad?" Jace said. Jason mumbled something and looked at the tile floor of the intake room. He hated hospitals. It wasn't the sickness or the pain or even the death that bothered him. It was that hospitals were so *bureaucratic*. There were constantly people coming in and out of the room, asking him to sign this form, to initial this one, to check on his insurance, to confirm that he was willing to pay for this or that test. It was a whole sham industry run by people like Derek Peters—who, it should be noted, was weirdly helpful and considerate after Jace fell; he was the only one there who thought to get some ice to put on Jace's ankle, and Jason had to admit that he was appreciative—soaking every penny out of you at the very moment you were most desperate and confused. You could spend your life savings in a place like this before anyone even told you what was wrong with you.

"Well, you're very fortunate, but I'm afraid you're going to be missing some baseball for a while," Dr. Meyers said. It had disturbed Jason that the main thing Jace seemed to be worried about all the way to the hospital was that he wouldn't be able to play in the game that night. Jason loved baseball and Little League, obviously; he did think about sixteen-year-old boys in the shower all the time, after all. But after he saw his boy, *his boy*, lying there in the grass, having fallen fifteen feet, from the sky, while working on his site, all Jason could think about was how he couldn't protect him. How Jace was hurt, and how it was his fault.

"Aw, sh—" Jace eyed his father and caught himself. "Crap. Aw crap. That stinks." He turned to his father. "I'm sorry, Dad," he said. "I should have been more careful."

There were so many things Jason could have said to his son in that moment, things he should have said. But he didn't. Or he couldn't. Or he wouldn't. He wasn't sure. How could Jace possibly understand? How could Jason possibly express it? How could he express that Jace was the best thing he'd ever been a part of in his whole stupid life, how he and his sister and his brother and his mom were the only reason he did anything, that if it hadn't been for them, he'd probably be just another screwup like White Harold, or, worse, like his brother? How he had no idea how such a brilliant thunderbolt of a son had been raised in his house, how he felt like his life's mission was just to put a roof over his head and stay the hell out of his way, and how his biggest fear was that he—not Jace, him, Jason, the oaf—was going to mess him up somehow? How Jace was going to be gone from his house soon, out in the world, lighting up the planet, seeing things Jason could never imagine, being the person Jason knew he should be, the person Jason knew he never would be? How he hoped Jace wouldn't be ashamed of his dad? How Jason *wanted to fucking cry*?

He didn't say any of that. He just put his arm out awkwardly and patted his son on his right arm while looking intently at a spot on the wall. "It's fine," he said. "You did just fine." He coughed and scratched the back of his neck. Helen told him he always did this when he was anxious.

"OK, I'm gonna go call your mom," he said.

Dr. Meyers nodded at him. "We're almost done here," she said. "I'll write you a prescription for some pain medication, and you might want to pick up some extra dressing and splints at the drugstore."

Jace smiled and threw his arms in the air. "Milkshakes at Lindbergh's!" he said. "Bonus!" Jason looked at Jace and saw the ten-year-old boy who, to his parents, Jace would always be.

Then he stepped out into the hallway.

"Yeah, the wrist isn't broken, but it's not a sprain, it's almost a sprain," he told Helen. "It's very confusing."

"Oh," she said. "And his ankle?"

"That's a sprain," he said. He thought he had that right? Maybe he had it backward? He hated hospitals. "He's going to be hobbling around on crutches for a week or so. But he's still very lucky."

"Thank God," Helen said. Jason could hear a cat screeching and shrieking somewhere behind her. Jason could not understand why people spent so much money just to keep a cat alive. "So how is he doing?"

"Fine," Jason said. "Trying to look tough for his dad, I think."

"He comes by it honestly," she said. "How are you holding up? You sound . . . well, you sound a little rattled."

"I do?"

"Yes," she said. "Are you OK? How'd the rest of the job go?"

Jason had completely forgotten about both Derek Peters and his stupid shit-for-brains brother. He hadn't had a second to even think how he was going to handle that mess. Before he could even respond, Helen spoke again.

"Oh, by the way, this was weird," she said. "Rick called my office."

"What? My brother?"

"Yeah," she said. "He left a message with the receptionist saying he was trying to get a hold of you but he'd lost your number. I guess he must have found our office number online and called it. What in the world does he want, do you think?"

Jason had an idea of what Rick might want. "Did he leave a number?"

"He did, but maybe now is not—"

"What's the number?" Jason growled.

Helen sighed. "Well, excuse me," she said. The cat screamed again.

Jason scratched the back of his neck again. "I'm sorry," he said. "It's been a long day."

"It's OK," she said. "I don't really want to be dealing with your brother either."

He hung up the phone and ducked back into the room. Jace was there by himself, with his wrist in a sling, trying to figure out how to use the crutches.

"When do we get to get out of here?" he said.

"Soon, I hope," Jason said. "You need anything? I gotta make one more call."

Jace still looked like that ten-year-old boy. "As long as I get my milkshake, I'm happy," he said. "Though I guess I'm wearing the mascot costume tonight. I'll be the one-armed cheerleader. Did we pack me a skirt?"

Jason smiled at him. The kid was gonna be all right. "We'll grab one of your sister's at home."

Jason went back out into the hallway. Helen had texted him Rick's number, and Jason scrolled to Rick's name in his contact list to add it. Somehow, there were *nine* different numbers next to Rick's name. Three 706 numbers here in Athens, an 843 for a year he spent in Charleston, a 217 from a two-year farming stint in Illinois, and a bunch Jason didn't even recognize. It used to be, if you really needed to get a hold of Rick, the only reliable way was to call their mom, the only person who would go through much trouble to find him. But there was really no reason to get a hold of Rick, not anymore.

He dialed the Jacksonville number and caught himself praying that it would go straight to voice mail. He caught a break.

"This is Rick. Leave a message or not, I don't care."

Jason sighed deeply and waited for the beep.

"Hey," he said. "Got your message. You're causing me some trouble around here. Anyway, Jace had a little accident, he's all right, we're fixing him up, but I'm gonna be running around. We're gonna hit Lindbergh's, grab a sandwich before the ball game tonight. Just text me with whatever you need, I'll call you back when we're done." Anything else? That was probably too much already. "Bye."

Jason hung up the phone and put it in his pocket. Goddammit.

JACE STOOD IN LINE WITH JASON, WAITING FOR HIS PRESCRIPTION AND their food, leaning on his left crutch and sucking down his milkshake like it was water.

Jason had calmed down enough that he was starting to think about the lineup again. With Jace out of commission, he was in a clear bind. Not only was Jace the team's best-fielding shortstop, he was the cleanup hitter. As a player, in this game tonight, he was irreplaceable. A sprain, or whatever, would put him out a week, at least—the rest of this tournament, no question. But if they could somehow make it through this tourney, if they could win it, Jace could reasonably be back for sectionals in three weeks, assuming the ankle healed all right. How could he cobble together a lineup? He could switch Denny Stallings from center to short, no problem, and maybe put that Kuhns kid in center. Kuhns couldn't hit a lick, but he could field the position enough to save a run or two. But then it came back to the mound. Allen Bishop was still the safe pick, but the safe pick might not be enough without Jace, the big hitter, in the middle of the lineup.

"You need upside," Jace said, as if reading Jason's mind. "Matt might walk ten guys. But he also might strike everybody out. If he's on his game, you don't need me at cleanup. Scratch out one or two runs, and that'll be enough."

Jason grinned and nodded at him. Jace was right. He always was.

A woman behind them, an older Black woman who Jason found striking in a way that disoriented him, tapped him on the shoulder. "What happened?"

"He fell off the roof," Jason said.

Jace grinned a toothy grin. "Roofs are always higher up than you think they are."

The woman laughed. "Well, I never thought of it that way, but I suppose that's true."

Jason's phone buzzed a text alert. It was from the Jacksonville number. Rick.

Call me after the game. Usual shit, no big deal. Need some help.
Hope Jace is all right. Good luck, kick their asses at the game.

Jason didn't expect the news from Rick would be good, but all told, he was sort of touched that Rick even remembered Jace's name, let alone was worried about him. Maybe the arrest is gonna scare that old dumbass straight, he thought. At least it was a start.

He took a sip of Jace's milkshake, and then they turned back to face the register and continued to wait in line.

KARSON

5:21 p.m.

It had not taken long to get Kyla and Asa home. Kyla said it was Asa's fault, that Asa had always wanted to see Murray, where Kyla went to school, back when she got to go to school—"Asa didn't believe that Murray was a real school!" Kyla had run off from her house to show Asa her school, and gotten lost. Karson had avoided Five Points for years, but once he realized she'd only been gone about five minutes, and that her house was on Pinecrest, a main road, it wasn't difficult to find it and walk Kyla and Asa there, particularly since the house had a terrified, weeping woman on its front porch. The woman, poor haggard Hannah Goldschmidt, actually jumped over her white picket fence and grabbed her daughter so energetically that Asa landed at Karson's feet. Karson picked Asa up, lifted the puppet to his own eye level, and felt a powerful urge to put him on his own hand. Would Asa magically come to life? Would he have wisdom for Karson? Did this turtle have all the answers? Would he be able to light the path forward?

Hannah Goldschmidt had thanked Karson, he'd said it was no big deal, she'd asked him if he wanted any money for his troubles, he tried to hide a frown and probably wasn't successful and said please it was his pleasure, and she tried again, and he said he had to go. Karson bent down on one knee and said goodbye to Kyla, who said thank you, and Asa, who licked him again. It was always something when Karson was in Five Points.

Karson walked back to where he had parked on University Drive, took one last little lap around the pole and the fire hydrant, whistled to himself, and got back in his car. He sighed and looked at the calendar app on his phone. The rest of the afternoon was filled with the usual errands and busy work. "Ugh," he snorted. He put the phone on the passenger seat and admitted to himself that he didn't really care about picking up the meat-and-cheese plate for the mixer anymore.

He started the engine, turned on the air conditioner, and decided to just sit there for a bit. The radio came on. He'd been listening to sports radio, Atlanta sports radio, which was on fire for the Hawks, his Hawks. They'd just won game 1 of the Eastern Conference finals the night before, putting them three wins away from their first NBA Finals ever. It was incredibly exciting. He'd been at one of their playoff games last month, when they crushed those lame-ass Knicks, with his buddy Theo, the guy who owned Lindbergh's, the famous Athens pharmacy, a guy he'd known for years because he grew up in Athens and everybody who grew up in Athens knew all the Lindberghs. Karson found Theo good-hearted and well-meaning, but he was also pretty sure he was Theo's only Black friend, and Theo had a way of unwittingly confirming that hypothesis every time he saw him. He'd be cool at first, studiously, carefully cool, but inevitably something in the politics or culture would come up, and Theo would take the opportunity to let Karson know that he was one of the good guys, that he was on Karson's side, the whole "I voted for Obama" *Get Out* shit. Theo was a gentle person, but a sheltered one. He wouldn't have liked the Elysian real estate dudes, would have thought them too cutthroat, but there was always a moment with Theo that felt a little like those guys inviting Karson into a room and making sure he knew how progressive they were. Theo meant well, though, and Karson liked him. Even more, though, Karson did love his Hawks, and so did Theo. More to the point, Theo had access to courtside seats for the both of them. That had truly been an incredible night: the place was roaring, Trae Young was unstoppable. Karson smiled thinking of it. He had whooped like a little boy.

Karson picked up his phone and texted Theo.

yo how bout those hawks! trae's the real deal! hes a bad man!

Theo had invited Karson to the game at an event for a charity, one of the fancy ones he was always awkward at—he was almost always the only Black person there, other than the poor people shown in the videos meant to pull at the rich folks' heartstrings and yank their wallets right out of their pants, and he usually stood in the corner, near the bar, by himself. So he was grateful to see Theo. Theo was tall and handsome and looked the part of an Athens elite, but he was obviously uncomfortable with any attention (of which there was plenty; Karson counted four different people who told him how much he looked like his father), and really with the fact that he was there at all. Karson had always thought of him as vaguely haunted, as if he were short a couple pints of blood. Karson felt for him, and they ended up hiding in the same corner.

Theo had just moved from Atlanta and was hoping to get more involved politically. Karson was happy to make the pitch for Athens Youth Active and the Athens Anti-Discrimination Movement—that's why he was there, after all. Theo did what rich, earnest, liberal white people always did to make themselves feel better: he gave a little money, he signed up for all the mailing lists, he posted his support for all the right issues on social media, he put up one of those lawn signs that listed all the issues This

House Stands For. Some of his fellow organizers were frustrated by this sort of suburban hashtag nonactivism, but Karson took it for what it was: mostly empty gestures, but well-intentioned ones, ones that came from a good place. With as many outright villains as there were out there, having someone like Theo who was doing the least they could, even if it was in fact the absolute least they could do, was important. As bad as the bad guys were now, simply standing up and saying to the world, "I'm not bad like those guys," even in the most meek, ineffectual voice, meant something. It was a start. It truly was better than nothing. And the money didn't hurt either.

Theo was a good guy, Karson thought, as good as he could be. And he was always up for texting about the Hawks.

Karson's phone buzzed.

Bucks are scary, man, Giannis is a freaking dragon. But we're hot!

The man on the radio droned on. Karson scrolled through his texts. A few from Annette, including a couple with nothing but gibberish and emojis, clearly Vanessa just pressing buttons on the iPad screen. A check-in from Michael: The guys loved you, man! And we could use a hooper for the real estate league too! Coldwell Banker pricks have won three years in a row! But it was mostly people wanting something from him. Althea from the church, wondering when the meat and cheese platter was coming. His friend Trent from the Chess & Community group, asking if he could pick up a couple of middle schoolers after school and take them by the chess event at the Bethel Homes that night. Someone from the school board, wondering if he had the password for the Zoom event the next night. The vice president of the Athens Anti-Discrimination Movement, asking him to come speak at their first in-person event next month. A banker at BB&T who wanted to contribute money to Athens Youth Active because he knew what it had done for his nephew and wanted to pay it forward. One of the seventh graders he'd been mentoring, simply texting to ask if Karson could come by and play NBA2K with him next week, he was feeling lonely and sad, and Karson had told him that any time he felt lonely and sad, he was supposed to text Karson, so here he was, he was texting Karson.

Karson smiled to himself. He dug that kid. He was gonna smoke him in 2K too.

He scrolled, and scrolled, and he saw person after person with one thing in common: they needed help. They needed something from him: favors, money, time, attention, love, little pieces of Karson distributed out to whoever requested some. These texts came one after another throughout a day, *ding ding*, each text another item on Karson's to-do list. Usually it ate at Karson, wore him down. The fact that the chirping never stopped made him wonder whether anything he was doing was making any difference at all.

But looking at them like this, as one never-ending scroll of contacts and friends and colleagues and kids and strangers, as the sprawling web that was Karson's life, it didn't feel exhausting or overwhelming or draining. These weren't nagging irritations, or constant stressors. This was his life. These were just people who had an empty space, and they needed Karson to fill it. Their lives were not fulfilled, in some cases not even *capable*, without Karson. These were not birds flapping about desperately: *This was his flock.* Every single one of their lives was different because Karson was in it. The chirps, the dings, each was evidence that Karson was a part of this world, that there was a problem to solve, and he was the only one who could solve it. They were not tasks, or annoyances, or burdens. They were connections. They were little moments where he was there for someone. What could be more important than that? What more could he do for this world than be there for people?

Could he do that and still work at Elysian Fields? Maybe he could. He wasn't sure. He knew those people were his North Star, though. Maybe that's what all this was: bundling your individual connections into something larger, having the powerful people aid the needy people . . . via *him*. He was only a conduit. He could help. He just had to figure out the right way. But there was a right way. He knew it.

His phone dinged once more. Theo, again.

Hey, man, would love to talk about AYA and how Lindbergh's can be a part. Happy to meet for a drink or whatever you want. Shoot, come by the store! Free milkshakes!

Was Theo reaching out about AYA because he felt bad, or because he really wanted to help? Did it matter? The man on the radio screamed that Trae Young was a legend like Atlanta sports had not seen since Dominique Wilkins—maybe an even bigger one. Karson grinned. Go Hawks.

Hells yeah. lets chat. actually. im in your hood now. you at the store?

The three dots popped up immediately. The response read:

Yo! Definitely. We're closing up in an hour, but definitely come by, it's super slow. I'm even up for a beer afterward if you are. Up for the Pub?

Karson really could use a drink, now that he thought about it.

on my way dawg.

He looked back at the pole and the fire hydrant at University. Then he put the car in gear and drove to Lindbergh's. He turned the radio to an oldies station and sang along to a Gladys Knight song. It was an extremely lovely day outside.

8. THE BLUEPRINT

I've got the plans. I know what it looks like in there. I think I even know where the boxes are.

It's all thanks to Kathy. Kathy is an old teacher friend of mine from Fox Mountain I chat with on Facebook all the time. She's a very kind woman who is going to be a grandmother in a couple of months. Her son's wife looks beautiful in the pictures she showed me. She grew up in Athens too, and I brought up Lindbergh's because I'm always looking for anyone who has been around this town forever and might know something. We were chatting about the big black door—she was terrified of it as a child too—and I mentioned that I'd always wondered what it was like back there, back behind that door. Was there a trapdoor somewhere? A secret passageway from the alley to some sort of closet? Was there a special place, say, where they might stash documents?

Kathy responded with a series of lightbulb emojis. MY HUBBBY!!!!!! It turned out that she was married to a man who works in the mayor's office here in Athens as the City Hall handyman. He basically runs the entire building and has free run of the place. Kathy said sometimes they sneak up there and drink wine on the roof and look at the silent, empty downtown. It's spooooooky!!!

Kathy also told me that City Hall also has decades of public records, including building schematics for every major business in the entire county. For taxes, I guess? There's a room, just off the mayor's office, that has the blueprints of every building, from Sanford Stadium to the post office to the Rook & Pawn, all mapped out and bound up in a series of huge books. You want to know the floor plan for any business in Athens? You can find it right there. I bet Lindbergh's is in there!!!

It was. I asked her if she could get it for me.

Why??? You gonna rob the place? [SMILEY FACE EMOJI]

I'm just curious, I wrote. I don't like lying to friends, but I wasn't sure Kathy would understand. My grandfather built houses, and he taught me how to read blueprints. It's sort of a hobby of mine. (My grandfather did not build houses.)

OK! she typed. I'll just take some pictures when we're there next week! Bringing a bottle of wine! Date night!

Kathy is nothing if not reliable, and sure enough, that next week, she sneaked into that room, found the Lindbergh's blueprint, and took pictures of it for me. She sent it to me right there in the office, along with a selfie with her tongue out. I could not Like her message often enough.

So I've been poring over the blueprints for a few days. Kathy's photos were not perfect. There are blurry sections, words I can't make out, and considerable visual evidence that she was eating some sort of cheesy snack before taking the picture. But we've got some answers.

1. There are several cubbyholes and side closets that are unaccounted for and seem to offer no obvious purpose. Why does there have to be a small closet next to the bathroom? Could that be where the boxes are?

2. The big black door isn't accounted for in the plans, which appear to have been initially drawn in the 1940s. They may not have had big black doors back then. But what's behind that door is the same as it was back then: a small hall that leads to a fork. If you head right, you will go into the actual room where all the medicine is found. If you head left . . . I can't tell. It isn't labeled, but there's a small room that, as far as I can tell, has no water line leading into it, so it's not a bathroom. Maybe that's it?

3. One of the rooms in the blueprint is clearly, and unmistakably, labeled "Bedroom." It's right there in the plan. Now, you tell me: Why does a pharmacy need a bedroom?

4. This is the big one. There is a secret door. *There is a secret door.* I almost missed it at first. There's a tight alleyway just off to the side of Lindbergh's. I've been there myself: it's the best way to get from Lumpkin Street to Milledge Avenue without getting stuck at the five-way Five Points intersection and sitting there forever waiting for the light to change. I've walked through hundreds of times in my life and never thought one second about it. But it turns out there's a door there. It only opens from the inside. There's no handle on the door outside, which is surely why I never knew it was there. But it is. It goes directly into yet *another* unmarked room, on the entirely opposite end of the building from where customers eat and the checkout girls ring you up and the Lindbergh family has been dispensing various drugs throughout the Athens community for decades now. There's no reason for that room to be there. It's larger than it needs to be, and it doesn't seem to serve any purpose toward the actual function of Lindbergh's. It doesn't even connect to any other part of the building; there's a

door across from the alley door, but it just takes you into another hallway. It's just a fifteen-by-fifteen-foot room that leads nowhere, with a secret door, a door you could walk by for years and never once realize is there.

Why's that there? I wonder.

But now I know how to get to it. And I think I know where those boxes are.

DAVID

5:21 p.m.

Apparently Allie smoked now. Wasn't she a little too old to start smoking?

"Aren't you a bit too old to start smoking?" he asked her, the California sunlight so clear and lovely on her face that his computer screen seemed to light up the whole dank, empty club by itself.

"Oh, relax, Dave, I just have one every once in a while," she said, calling him Dave like she always had. She'd called him Dad once, years ago, when she was first trying to reconnect, but awkwardly, like she didn't really quite buy it. He noticed—he'd been clean for about four years then, the time he'd felt the most confident and assured—and took the pressure off her immediately, telling her, "You don't have to call me that." She'd protested, briefly, but had called him Dave ever since. He'd come to love it. It made him feel like her friend, like she'd chosen to spend time with him, like she actually *liked* him. He also legitimately enjoyed listening to her talk. As she grew older, she'd become even more at ease with herself, and as her band got more popular, she'd taken on a clear rock-star energy that David knew all too well. That she wanted to talk to him didn't make him feel like a good dad. Honestly? It just made him feel sort of cool.

Particularly because—and this was a secret he'd always tried to keep from Allie, the only one he allowed himself—he knew how good she was. He'd always listened to the band's music, back when they were called Dog Bark, back when they had some dipshit lead singer who could barely fit into his vinyl pants. Allie only played drums back then, and you could tell, already, how much more she brought to the band than she was allowed to show. David went to one of the first Dog Bark shows and noticed immediately how the rest of the band looked more at her than the lead singer or even the audience. The spotlight was always on her even when it wasn't. They ditched the Candlebox guy and started a new band, first called the Gravitating Hoes (named after a misremembered Nirvana lyric), then the Doogie Howsers. They were a little too jam-bandy for David's taste, but with every incarnation, Allie stepped more and more to the forefront, from the drums to bass to lead guitar to eventually the lead singer.

She started writing all the songs too. She used to send lyrics to David on crinkled steno pad sheets. He didn't always understand them—there was one song that seemed to just be about napkins—but he was always moved by them. They were always so sincere and straightforward in a way that he appreciated. She wasn't trying to be hip or part of any sort of trend. Her words always made David's heart ache. They were about longing, about wanting something and not getting it, and ultimately being fine with that—even feeling blessed because of it.

But it was "Magic" that broke through. She had emailed the lyrics and they knocked him over so much that he avoided the phone the next three times she called.

I know you're out there.
I know you still want me.
But it cannot be.

It can never be.
You know I'm out here.
You know you still want me.
But it cannot be.
It can never be.
We are still here, though.
Both here and there.
There and here.
That's always me.
And that's always you.
It's magic.
It's magic.
It's always magic.
It's always us.
And it's always magic.

Allie sent him the demos of "Magic" a month later. David wasn't a musician. He'd played a little guitar with Allie when she was a kid, but he wasn't good at it; the most rhythmic sound he'd ever made was falling down the stairs. But he'd been around music his whole life, and he knew a hit when he heard one. By that time, the band was called Hotel Arizona, which at last stuck. Most important: the band was now Allie's. The rest of Hotel Arizona revolved around her, as it always was going to. Her voice, once so small and meek and unsure, once begging him for an ice cream cone on her visits to Athens, was now sly and confident and *searching*. Her voice had wisdom and fear and power and could sound both sarcastic and hopeful at the same time. It was the voice of a star. David knew it. It was only a matter of time until Allie did—and the rest of the world followed.

He'd called her. "This is fantastic," he said.

"Thank you, Dave," she said. "I think we might be onto something."

Before you knew it, "Magic" started to make its way around

the scene—David heard a band playing it over the speakers before they went onstage within a matter of weeks of it landing on Spotify—and then Hotel Arizona had an agent and then Allie had her own, *different* agent, and then she started to become a lot more difficult to get a hold of. She opened for Black Joe Lewis & the Honeybears on a West Coast tour, and then "Magic" made it into heavy rotation on Sirius XM's Spectrum station, and then there was an album, and my god the songs were *so good*. Then Black Joe Lewis & the Honeybears were opening for *them*. Then they were on tour with the Jayhawks, then the Black Crowes, and then Wilco. Then they were headlining their own shows. Allie had buzzed all her hair off—she'd told David she wanted to "desexualize the performance"—and she looked incredible. She fucking killed it. She was a rock star.

And now she was here, smoking a cigarette in the Los Angeles sun, probably at the Chateau Marmont or something, as Dave soaked his right hand in a bowl of ice.

"What happened to your hand?" she asked.

He used to be able to hit a guy square without tearing up his knuckles, but he was out of practice, and also he was just old now.

"Aw, I cut it chopping up some carrots," he said, in a way that let Allie know he was lying but that she shouldn't give him any guff about it, it's all good.

"Are you OK?" she said. One of the many things he loved about Allie was that when she asked him questions like "Are you OK?" there was no accusation in her voice. Everyone else in his life, when they asked him that, it was always with a tone of wary suspicion. The subtext to the question was always, "You're not about to fuck it all up again, are you?" Allie, somehow, never spoke to him that way. She just wanted to know if he was OK. That the one person who had the most right to be furious at him and skeptical of every move he ever made—the one person he'd screwed up the most with—was the one person who constantly believed in him was a miracle that David would never stop marveling at.

"I'm fine," he said. "I promise." He waved the hand in front of his camera to show it was fine, as if she could tell over Zoom anyway. "I'm more concerned about your sudden nicotine habit."

Allie laughed. "Life on the road, Dave," she said. "We're recording the new record, and the rest of the band smokes, so now I smoke."

"I thought everybody just vaped now," David said.

Allie nodded and waved at someone just offscreen. "All those vapors and chemicals will destroy your lungs."

"That's what it has come to." David laughed. "Smoking is now the healthy option. It's all natural! Comes from the earth!"

"Free-range tobacco, grown locally, farm-raised," Allie snorted, and they had a good laugh about that for a while. God he loved her so much.

Over Allie's shoulder, Hotel Arizona's guitarist, a shaggy reedy fellow named Harry who always wore ripped blue jeans, a bow tie, and a handlebar mustache onstage, popped up in the corner of the screen. "Hey, Mr. Gallagher," he said, smiling. "How's Athens?" Allie waved him off, whispered "Gimme a couple more minutes" to him, and turned back to David.

"Hey, so I wanted to ask you something before I let you go."

"Anything."

"So, we're all about to do our first tour since all this happened," she said. "We're co-billing with Big Thief, it's pretty exciting. And we're going to be coming down your way. So I was wondering . . ."

She paused and looked away. David thought she almost looked . . . nervous?

"Well, we thought we might see if we could play the Red Rocket," she said. "I don't know if you could talk to Theresa, or you could make that happen, but we had an opening in the schedule, and I tossed it out to the guys, and they were down with it. We could, maybe, even have Mom come?" She looked away again. Her profile was that little girl, begging for an ice cream cone.

David wasn't involved in booking—that was above his pay grade—but he knew Theresa would flip her wig to have a Hotel Arizona/Big Thief double bill at the Red Rocket. Who wouldn't? It was way too big a show for a small club like the Red Rocket; two hot up-and-comers like them could sell out the Fox Theatre in Atlanta in a second, particularly with everyone so desperate after a year without shows. Allie's band was too good for the Red Rocket. She had to know that, right?

"Wait, you want to play the Red Rocket?" he said, a little stunned.

Allie fumbled for a second, then lit another cigarette.

"Well, if you don't want us to, we don't have to," she said, and something in her face seemed to harden.

"No, no, no," David said. He suddenly felt like the conversation was getting away from him. "God, Allie, of course we'd love to have you. Are you kidding?"

Allie took another drag off her cigarette and began to scratch the inside of her ear. "I've never played there before," she said. "And you and Mom sort of, you know, ran the place back in the day." She rubbed out the cigarette after only a couple of puffs. "I thought maybe it might be time, I don't know."

"Oh, Allie."

"I've always wanted to play the Red Rocket," she said, and she smiled a smile that looked nothing like a rock star but looked exactly like her.

David wiped something out of his eye. Probably a speck of dust.

AFTER DAVID SIGNED OUT OF ZOOM, HE'D LOOKED AT HIS KNUCKLES. THEY were pretty gnarly, all told, and the one on his ring finger was black and still bleeding. There were also little pieces of pebble and dirt on there, probably from when he picked dumbass Joe off the ground. He called his doctor friend, Jake: he'd met him in group,

Jake had had his chip for eleven years. He told Jake he'd scraped up his hand pretty good and probably could use an antibiotic, and Jake agreed to call him in a prescription.

Dave hopped in his truck. He was hungry. It occurred to him that, between all the rocking and dumbass Joe punching, he hadn't eaten all day. The National, his favorite restaurant, was right across the street from Lindbergh's. He wanted to pick up his scrip, eat all the tagliatelle they could feed him, and get his fat ass to bed.

He pulled the truck out onto the street.

"Siri," he said to the air. "Play Hotel Arizona playlist."

He turned up the volume as his daughter's voice came on. He rolled down his window and let his left arm hang out. There wasn't anything wrong with the world, he thought, that music couldn't heal. There wasn't anything that hurt so much that music couldn't, at least for a little bit, make it right.

DAPHNE

5:21 p.m.

Daphne had an uncle, Gary, Uncle Gary, her mom's older brother, a big burly trucker who smoked unfiltered cigarettes and gave the warmest hugs. Uncle Gary told her that life was so much simpler than people made it.

"Either it is, or it isn't," he said. "All the things you're worried about, they either are, or they aren't, and there ain't nothin' you can do about it. You're either going to be eaten by a tiger tomorrow, or you're not. Either there's a tiger around the corner, or there isn't. You won't know until you turn the corner, and you can't do anything about it anyway. Fifty percent chance. Either way. You are, or you aren't."

She thought about Uncle Gary every time she waited with family like this. Somewhere outside this room, people she didn't know and would likely never meet, people who were highly competent and highly paid and highly specialized in this sort of thing, were working their fingers to the bone to save the life of a little boy. Daphne didn't know what they were doing, or how they were doing it, and neither did Becky. They couldn't control it. They couldn't affect it. They couldn't do anything but sit there and wait to find out if there was a tiger around the corner or not. Fifty percent chance. Either way. You are, or you aren't.

You could pray, and they did, and Daphne truly did believe that prayer mattered, that it could make a difference. Not always, not immediately. But enough, and eventually. God would provide, in one way or another, on this day or the next. Did it always pan out? Did it always make sense to Daphne? It did not. Uncle Gary died of prostate cancer at the age of forty-seven. It ate him so fast Daphne never even saw him sick. He was just gone. Tiger got him. But you had to try.

They looked at the door, again, and knew at some point they'd know. All those doctors, all that medicine, all that technology, it all came down to that one answer: it is, or it isn't. Every time someone walked past the door, each of them took a quick inward breath.

"So how does your insurance work around here anyway?" Becky asked.

"I'm sorry?" Daphne said. She was a little confused by the question but also wasn't sure she'd heard Becky right.

"Insurance. How's your insurance pay for all this?"

Daphne had learned in her very first week on the job that talking about insurance was the quickest, most efficient way to make patients want to throw you through a window. The labyrinth that was the American medical insurance industry was baffling to the people who worked in it—the people doing all the work that insurance was ostensibly supposed to pay for—and hieroglyphics to those who didn't. Nurses were taught to refer all billing and insurance questions to the clerical and accounting people, and Daphne was eager to oblige. She didn't understand it, she didn't want to understand it, she hadn't gotten into the field to understand it, she truthfully wanted nothing to do with it. And yet patients asked her questions about it all day, every day—more questions, really, than they did about their own physical care. And in her three years here, she had yet to meet a patient who was satisfied with a single answer they got. Insurance was this massive industry that drove nearly every aspect of the American economy, one that affected the lives of each human being, and not one of her patients—not one—had ever said "My insurance is great and I'm not worried about it at all." It was the central pain for people already suffering. She didn't understand it. But Lord, who would want to?

"Well, I don't really deal with—"

"Yeah, but I don't know, this is gonna be a lot, isn't it?" Becky said, and she was already up off the bed and starting to pace around the room. Daphne had never held a boy's heart in her hands before. But this, this she saw all the time. "Who's paying for that doctor? Who's paying for this room? Who's paying for this orange juice? His asshead father sure ain't, that I do know. How do people pay for any of this?" Becky was now fired back up again. This had happened often enough today that Daphne could now tell when a Becky outburst was coming.

"And what if he has to stay overnight?" Becky said, her voice rising enough that Daphne could hear stirring coming from the nurses' station again. "Or a week? Who pays for that? Are you? 'Cause I know I can't, and his fuckwit dad can't. You know who should pay for all of it? That idiot kid Jacob's mom, for having her gun out and unlocked in the first place. I always thought that kid was a moron, so I guess I shouldn't be surprised that his mom's an idiot too. Who leaves their gun out like that? Yeah, yeah, yeah"— Becky was now actively shouting—"She can pay for this, that bitch, that stupid motherfucker, she'll pay for this if she has to sell everything in that whole shithole house." She smacked an empty plastic water pitcher off the room's sink. It flew across the sheet vinyl floor, clacking and clanging with each bounce, and skittered out into the hallway.

"Becky, I don't think you should—"

"Oh, you don't think, do you!" Becky roared. It occurred to

Daphne that Becky was looking at her like she had never seen her before in her life. "Well, honey, you've been sitting around here all day, and it doesn't look like you've done a goddamned thing other than wipe my snot. Who's paying *your* salary? It sure as hell isn't gonna be me."

Daphne moved slowly toward her and realized she was holding her palms up as if she had a gun on her. "Becky—"

"What's going on in here?"

Deborah appeared in the doorway. She entered with an icy authority that made her look a foot taller than she was, and she changed the energy in the room so instantly that Becky took a small step backward. Before Becky could get her composure back and start barking at Deborah the way she wanted to, Deborah had pulled a mask out of her pocket and was handing it to her.

"Here. You need to be wearing a mask to be on hospital grounds," Deborah said. "It is our policy, and federal law." She turned to Daphne, who realized that her own mask was dangling from her left ear. When had she done that? Deborah stared at her. "Do you need one too, Nurse Preston?" Daphne pulled her mask up so fast she almost poked herself in the eye.

Becky looked at Deborah and snarled. But this snarl had fewer teeth in it. "My kid's in the operating room, and you're worried about my mask?"

"Yes, I am," Deborah said. "Please put it on." To Daphne's surprise, Becky did. Deborah smoothed out the bedsheets, sat down, and motioned Becky to join her. She did this too.

"So why are you yelling at my nurse?"

Becky's eyebrows flared, but she stayed seated. "Well, she's a nice lady, but I don't think she, or any of you people, are helping. Y'all are just running up our bill, and I still don't know what's going on with my son." She had unquestionably calmed when Deborah came in the room. Daphne supposed that being able to do that to patients was how you became nursing supervisor.

"Nurse Preston is an excellent nurse who, I must point out, is not technically on her shift right now," Deborah said, and Daphne prepared for a sideways glance her way that never came. "She is here on her own time. Is there any other way she, or any of the rest of us, can help you?"

Becky snorted. "Well, all she really does is make me pray with her, so it's probably better that y'all ain't paying her for this." This time the sideways glance did come.

Deborah put a hand on Becky's shoulder. Daphne didn't think she'd ever seen Deborah touch anyone before.

"I cannot fathom what you are going through right now," she said, a tenderness in her voice that seemed to come from another human entirely. "But you are making it more difficult on yourself, and more difficult on the people who are trying to help you. Please, miss: let us help you."

Becky looked down at the floor, then back up, then to Daphne, then to Deborah.

"Thank you," she said, so softly. "I'm sorry. I'm . . . I'm very sorry."

Then there was a figure at the door. Daphne didn't recognize him, had never seen him on this floor before, which meant that this was the person they had all been waiting for. She froze in place, then looked to Becky, whose shoulders had instantly tensed. Her body seemed to be contracting in upon itself.

Daphne's eyes met Becky's.

I do not know if I can do this.
I am here for you.
Will you come with me?
I will.

Daphne walked over to the bed, took Becky's wrist, stood her up, wiped her eyes, and put a hand on each of her shoulders.

"He is here with us," Daphne said. "And I am here with you."

Then they turned to the door and walked, together, toward the man no one knew, toward the man who knew the answer, toward the tiger around the corner.

"THIS IS PRESTON."

This was how SFC Bill Preston had always answered the telephone, the same landline, with the same number he'd had his entire life. "The phone is all the technology I need," Bill Preston had always said, but when his daughter—his whole life, what it had all been about—was deployed to Germany, he'd bought a cell phone and an iPad and she'd shown him how to use them. They still mostly sat unused in his house, particularly since Daphne had come home. Bill Preston believed there should be boundaries in a man's life, and the phone was one of them. If he was home, you could call his house: he would answer and talk to you about whatever you needed to talk to him about. If he wasn't home, you could leave a message and he would call you back when he was home. That was enough. If you needed Bill Preston, you could wait until he was home. That's how he answered the phone, "This is Preston," and it filled Daphne with warmth every time she heard it. He answered every phone call the same way he'd answer a superior officer's request, or a neighbor's knock on the door. You got Bill Preston. What do you need?

She collected herself. She was not going to cry on the phone with SFC Bill Preston.

"Hey, Dad," she said.

"Hello, Daphne," he said. Daphne always appreciated that her father did not give her little pet names, no *darlin'* or *li'l munchkin*. She liked her name. He'd given it to her. It wasn't a family name. It was only hers. "Are you finally off work?"

"I am," she said. "It was a long one today."

"That Kennedy kid come by for more drugs?" he said, lightly chuckling. Bill Preston had gone to high school with a man

225

named Nathan Kennedy who had a son who was always coming by the ER claiming some sort of ache or pain that needed narcotics. They were required to give out Vicodin—the job of the ER staff was to treat pain, not to diagnose addiction—so Nathan Kennedy's son was a regular presence in Daphne's life. Daphne wasn't supposed to talk about specific patients, but you couldn't visit the ER as often as Bill Preston did without running into him regularly. *He should just get on the payroll, make himself useful*, Bill Preston had said. Daphne didn't always like that joke.

"Naw, not today, Dad," she said. She started to say something else, coughed a little, and started over. "Just a rough one, Dad. It was just a rough one."

Bill Preston's voice softened. "Well, get home then," he said. "I've got some pot roast on the stove. You'll be home in time for *Jeopardy!*"

"I've gotta pick up your meds," she said. "I was going to get them earlier, but I didn't get out until just now."

"Oh, don't worry about that," he said. "It can wait until tomorrow."

"It can't," she said. Bill Preston hated taking his Coumadin, the medication he'd been on since his stroke. He said it made his food taste bland, which may or may not have been true but was his way of trying to get out of taking it. She really wasn't in the mood, after her day, after all that had happened, after the thinness of the boy's heart, after Becky's screams, to go by Lindbergh's, which was entirely out of her way, and grab her father's scrip. Making a stop before coming home was the opposite of what she wanted to do. What she wanted to do was crawl into bed and sleep. She would sleep as long as she could, she would sleep until it was time to go back to work and take care of someone else, someone who could take her mind off what had happened today: someone she could help. It was days like today that turned you into Deborah, or Sally, why you had to make that shift from being the person who would stay up for days on end with a disabled patient who had been beaten or the mother of a boy who'd been goofing around with his friend and gotten shot in the chest to being the person who kept yourself at a remove, who left a little part of yourself at the door when you clocked in at the hospital. She understood why it had to happen. She knew today had made it a little bit closer to happening to her. She knew it was coming. But she wasn't ready for that yet. She wasn't ready to let go. She wasn't ready for it not to hurt.

She just wanted to go home and sleep until it hurt a little less.

"It can't, Dad," she said. "You ran out on Sunday. You need to take it with dinner tonight."

"Not if I want to actually taste dinner tonight," he said, but he was gentle about it. He knew to take it easy on his daughter right now. "Well, the pot roast will be ready for you when you get here."

"Got it," she said, certain that, even though she hadn't had a bite to eat in about ten hours, she wasn't going to touch that pot roast. She wished there was a technology, maybe a drone, that she could program to lift her and the Coumadin and carry them both the seventeen miles out to Danielsville.

"Hey," he said after a moment of tired silence. "It'll be all right. Just come home."

"Thanks, Dad," she said. "I'm on my way."

When she'd first moved back in, she was so worried about her father after his stroke that she tried to savor every conversation she had with him, every bit of wisdom he could provide, every time he was there when she needed him in the exact way that she needed him. Seeing her indestructible father, the rock center of her universe, weakened, even just a little, kept implanting an involuntary thought in her brain each time she spoke with him: What if this is the last time? What if another stroke takes him away from me forever? That had only become more intense in the last year of the pandemic, when she was constantly worried she was going to bring something home from the hospital that might kill him. She tried to put it out of her mind, but she couldn't: she didn't know what she'd do without him. He was all she could rely on. He was the only one who could always make her feel like it was going to be OK. And she really needed to feel like it was all going to be OK today.

But—it should be noted—this time she didn't have that thought. There was no *What if this is the last time?* whisper in the back of her brain. She didn't notice that it didn't pop in there. It just didn't. She only said "I'm on my way," and then hung up. She was very tired. It had been a very long day.

At the Five Points intersection, Daphne turned right onto Lumpkin, waited for a man and his son to cross the street in front of her, and then turned left into the parking lot behind Lindbergh's. She pulled into her spot, shut off the car, and caught a glimpse of herself in the rearview mirror. *Huh*, she thought, *after all that, I don't look half bad.* She sat and stared at her reflection for what might have been a full minute. Her eyes were a little saggy, her hair was crusty and reeked of all sorts of chemicals, her cheeks were pretty sunken, but you know what, she was hanging in. Get a full night's sleep, she might just be right as rain.

She locked her car and walked through the lot toward Lindbergh's. *You know what I could use?* she thought. *Some chocolate.* She could use a milkshake. She deserved a freaking milkshake. Lindbergh's was out of her way. There wasn't a drive-through where she could just sit in her car and then go straight home. She wasn't really in the mood for any friendly, face-to-face neighborhood conversation today either. But she could order a milkshake and, while waiting for her father's Coumadin, drink it down in big, huge gulps. Wow, it occurred to her, she *really* wanted a milkshake right now.

She turned the corner toward Lindbergh's front door, looking up at that dopey sign they'd had up forever, the old guy, his son, his grandson, and their dog. When she was in high school she had once made out with Cindy, an undergrad sorority girl a couple years older than her, right under that sign when she'd sneaked onto campus one night. It was just bright enough so they could see each other but dark enough after closing that no one else could. She smiled at the memory. She should grab Bill Preston a milkshake too.

And then there was a pop, a loud pop—like someone had slammed a heavy book against a wooden table as hard as they could. Then there was another one, and a crash, and a flash of light.

Daphne felt a sharp, quick pain just below her left eye, and she bent down to one knee to get her bearings. She heard a scream, and then someone yelled, "Help! Help!"

She touched her face and looked at her hand. There was a driblet of blood and two small shards of glass that had come from the Lindbergh's window, which had just exploded.

"Help! Oh my god!" a voice shrieked from inside.

Daphne stood up straight—she was proud of her posture; Bill Preston had made her work hard on it. She rubbed the glass off her hand, pushed her hair back out of her eyes, and squinted through a puff of smoke slowly emanating from inside the pharmacy.

She ran inside.

9. COUNTDOWN

So here we are.

I have what I need. I have the gun, I bought it legally, I've even taken it out to the shooting range. There's a place on the edge of Athens, right out off Route 316, Clyde Armory—it's owned by that guy who's in Congress now, if you can believe that. I walked right in there, told them I wanted two guns, didn't care which ones. I thought that would scare them a little bit, but that's exactly what they wanted to hear. They sold me two Smith & Wesson M&P22 Compact pistols. I've gotten pretty good at shooting them; they've got a range right there in the store. Well, "pretty good" is probably pushing it, but I will say that I hit the target more often than I don't.

I should say, straight up: I'm not planning on shooting anyone. Hopefully everyone's going to do what they're supposed to. They're going to see the guns, and they're going to take me back there, through that black door, and they're going to show me where the boxes are. I don't want to shoot anybody. I don't think I could if I wanted to. But they have to know that I'm serious. Sad to say, the only way anyone ever thinks you're serious is if you have a gun. The gun means you're serious. And I am serious.

I'm gonna go in the side door, the one we know about from the blueprints. That should get me in the safe area right there:

only the people who work there will see me. We don't have to run into any customers, though just in case, I'll make sure to show up late in the day, right before they close, when there's less foot traffic, fewer people. With any luck, it'll just be me and the staff. I assume the boy will be there, *his* boy. He runs the place now. I'm sure he had to. If anybody else ran Lindbergh's, they'd be in danger of giving up the whole enterprise. Maybe they'd be on board and maybe they wouldn't be, but you'd never truly know if you could trust them. That's why places like Lindbergh's have to keep it in the family. Only family can know where all the bodies are buried. Only family can keep them protected for so long.

That's why he's the key. That's why I have to find him first. That's why I'm going through that door. I think that's his office, right off that little hallway. That's where I'll have to go first.

I wonder what he'll think when he sees me. He'll know, I bet. He'll have known this day was coming for a long, long time. I wonder if he will be relieved. I bet the truth will feel like a burden being lifted.

This is not a complicated situation. The person with a gun tells the person who doesn't have a gun to give them what they want. And then they give it to them. Happens all the time. Happens thousands of times a day. It could go sideways. But we can just keep it simple. Walk in the door. Find the kid. Tell him to show me the boxes. When he gives them to me, I take the ones I need, and I leave. It doesn't have to be difficult. It doesn't even have to be scary. It can be over in ten minutes.

Is that how it will go? I do not know. But I know when I am there, I will not be alone. Mom will be with me. Sue will be with me. Aunt Mandy will be with me. Every moment of my life that has made me the person I am will be there. I am not meek. I am not sitting idly by. I am strong, because they are with me. I am taking control. I am making change. I am helping people. This is what I was put here to do. This is where it was always going.

June 24
5:22 p.m.

LINDBERGH'S PHARMACY
1633 Lumpkin Avenue
Athens, GA 30605

I

"Sorry, grill's closed," the older woman behind the counter told Karson as she pulled off her hairnet and washed her hands. "Pharmacy's open until six, but we close up the food at five on Thursdays. New policy."

"Oh, I'm not hungry," Karson said, moving out of the way of a burly man holding ice on his right hand. "I'm just looking for Theo. He still here?"

The woman, who had the impatient look of someone who had been asked to account for the whereabouts of Lindbergh men for several decades, rolled her eyes. "He's in the back," she said. "He makes a lousy grilled cheese, though, I wouldn't press your luck."

"No, really, I'm not—" Karson realized he was talking to the back of her head as she grabbed her purse and swept out the front door. He looked around the pharmacy. There was a short line of people waiting for their prescriptions. He thought he saw Theo pass behind that weird old black door they had back there, but he didn't make eye contact with him. They were closing soon. He'd hang around until Theo was done back there.

He picked up an old copy of *Bulldog Illustrated*, a society rag with pictures of all the pretty white people of Five Points who had shown up wearing pretty white-people clothes at G-Day, the Georgia Bulldogs football team's spring practice a couple of months earlier. He was just about to place the magazine back on the waiting desk and walk to the front door, marveling at just how blinding some people's teeth could get, when he heard a loud pop from behind the pharmacy counter, behind that door. Just to his right, on the other side of the counter, one random sprinkler started going off, splashing him with water.

Huh. He looked behind the counter and saw a thin plume of smoke wafting from the back. Was there a fire?

And then there was a scream.

Karson looked up to see a woman in a pharmacist's apron leaping over the back counter, slipping and landing on her right shoulder with a dull thud. She jumped up, grabbed her shoulder, shook her head briefly, and then began to run again . . . before slipping again. Karson ran over to her.

"Are you OK?"

"She's got a gun!" she screamed, and sprinted toward the front door.

There were two more *pop*s. Karson now had no illusions about what was happening. He was nine years old when he was shooting horse with his friend Carlos at the pickup hoop at Nellie B and saw a man get shot. It wasn't a drive-by or anything dramatic like that. He was sitting on a stoop with some guys from the neighborhood, and there was a disagreement. There was some yelling, and next thing Karson knew the guy was lying on the ground, grabbing his left arm and groaning. He turned out all right. Karson saw him out with the same crew, on the same stoop, a couple of weeks later, arm in a sling, like nothing had happened. Maybe this would be like that. A sudden spasm of violence and chaos, something that feels like the end of the world, but in a couple of weeks it's all fine, everything has returned to normal, back to the regular course of business.

Karson ducked behind a shelf that featured all sorts of absorbent pads and girdles and peered around the corner. He heard the pharmacist shove open the front door to the comforting *ding-dong* that rang every time Lindbergh's welcomed a new customer and saw two patrons, along with the hairnet woman, follow behind her. He saw that Lindbergh's front window had been blown out. He was about to stand up and follow them when he saw, out of the corner of his right eye, a figure emerge behind the counter. It was a round woman with her hair pulled tightly behind her, bouldering into the frame like she was chasing Indiana Jones.

"Stop!" she yelled. "Please stop!" Karson saw her point her gun, not at anyone in particular, just in the air in front of her. That was what it looked like: like she was aiming it at air. She didn't seem to have much experience with handguns, or at least not the sort of real-world experience you might need to navigate whatever this was. Karson instinctively ducked, even though she was facing the opposite way from where he was, then turned his head back to the front of the pharmacy. The place seemed mostly empty now, and the woman didn't seem to have hit anything other than the window. There was nothing but smoke and water and the woman's arrhythmic panting.

Suddenly she turned her head to him. They made eye contact. She was no longer pointing the gun at air. She was pointing at him. Karson just stared at her, motionless.

Karson heard another groan. "Oh, fuck me," he heard a man's voice say. The woman heard it too, her eyes darting to the sound's source, a few feet in front of Karson. She let out a small gasp and, to Karson's relief, lowered her gun. She turned around and went toward the back of the pharmacy.

Karson looked down. There was a puddle of water in the middle of the floor, and a stream of blood had started to flow through it. He followed its trail to a spot about ten feet ahead of him, just below the pharmacist's counter at the back. A man was crouching there, the same man he'd seen when he'd walked in, a bigger man, middle-aged, sturdy, wearing a rock band T-shirt that didn't fit him particularly well; he could see the man's hairy belly poking out from under it, like it had been trying to escape but eventually just gave up and lay down. The man was holding his right hand, which was sending spurts of blood down into the water below. His face was a howl of pain and confusion. His eyes met Karson's.

"Fuck, what the fuck, I think I just got fucking shot!" he said to Karson like they'd known each other their entire lives. "I think I got shot in my hand!"

Karson looked to his right, where the woman had been standing, but she was gone. He crouched lower. "Stay there!" he said. "I think she's gone! I'll be right over there!"

Karson had no idea what he was going to do when he got over there, what the point of going over there, potentially in the line of more fire, was supposed to be. He wasn't a doctor. He wasn't good at things like this. Vanessa had once cut her hand pretty bad on her toothbrush—Karson would have thought that impossible, but somehow she'd done it—and Karson had spent five minutes just trying to figure out how to get the Band-Aid packaging open. They make it so hard if you don't have fingernails—Annette had made fun of him for weeks for that one. He had no expertise, no ability to help this man at all. But he was going to get over there anyway. He'd figure out what was next when he got there.

The man nodded at him and stayed crouched on one knee. The blood's spurting had slowed, but even from across the room, through all the smoke and water, Karson could see he looked pale and weak. He took one look back at where the woman had been, decided it was now or never, and prepared to make his dead-ass run toward this man, where he'd do something, probably, whatever it was.

Karson paused and happened to glance at the shelf next to him. He saw two packages of incontinence pads, Tranquility Premium brand, and grabbed them. You never know.

He looked back toward the guy, and just as he was about to take off, he saw a flash of movement out of the corner of his left eye, near the front door. After hairnet lady and pharmacy woman and all the people that followed them had scrambled out of there, there was someone, amazingly, sprinting in. There was a *whoosh* of movement, a blue streak across the lunch counter, with long dark hair flowing behind it. He thought of a proud, valiant mare, galloping to the rescue.

The woman—it was a woman, Karson realized, a small young woman, nothing like a horse at all—slid next to the man and, all in one motion, swooped him behind the counter and out of the way of any bullets that may or may not have been coming. She was wearing scrubs, Karson realized. This mare was a medical professional.

She guided the man to the floor and had him lie down, his head cradled in her arms.

"Sir," she said to him, lightly tapping his face. "Sir? My name's Daphne. I'm a nurse. Can you look me in the eye, please?"

The man opened his eyes and looked into hers.

"Good job," she said. "Great job. Can you tell me your name?"

He grimaced and wiped water—Karson thought it was water—out of his eyes with his good hand.

"David," he said. "My name is David."

"Hello, David. Can you tell me what happened? Can you tell me what hurts?"

David's eyes began to roll back in his head, and she tapped him with the back of her hand again.

"It's his hand," Karson yelled to Daphne.

Daphne nodded at him. "OK, I need something to stanch his bleeding." Her eyes turned downward, to the pads that Karson was still clutching as hard as he could.

"Yes, those are perfect, good idea," she said. "Toss those over if you could." Karson looked back to the counter. The woman had not returned. "Here goes," he said, and gave the pads a basketball chest pass toward Daphne.

She caught them and flashed him a smile. "Nice toss!"

Karson chuckled. Something about this woman complimenting his passing ability right now struck him as hilarious.

She ripped open the package and put David's face in her hands.

"OK, so you've got a wound on your hand. I'm going to stop the bleeding, and you're gonna be fine, you just gotta work with me, OK, David?"

David's eyes returned, and met hers. "Yep," he said, and

Karson did think he looked a little more alert, and a little less scared, which made one of them.

She covered his hand in the pads, found some masking tape next to the pharmacy's post office station, and tightened it around his wrist. Then she propped him up, back against the wall, so he was facing the front door with his legs stretched forward on the floor. She took another pad, soaked it in a puddle by the cash register, and placed it on his forehead.

"There, that'll hold us for now," Daphne told him. "You're going to be fine." She pulled a rubber band out of the pocket of her scrubs, tightened her long black hair into a ponytail, and tightened the band around it. She looked at Karson, who was pretty sure he'd follow this woman into hell.

"Whew!" she said. "Hi, I'm Daphne. What's your name?"

THEO COULDN'T FIGURE OUT WHY HE WAS ON THE FLOOR. HAD HE DROPPED something? Maybe that's what had happened. He was always a bit of a klutz. He must have dropped something and went to pick it up, slammed the top of his head on the lab table, and knocked himself out. That's why he was on the floor. He must have really knocked his head hard—he was awfully woozy. Also, why was he wet? He wiped his eyes with his hands, but when he opened them, everything was still fuzzy. Also, his stomach clawed at him. Was he hungry? It had been a while since lunch. He'd grabbed a bite with Alexis—*Ah, Alexis*, he thought idly, briefly getting lost, *I like her*—but that had been hours and hours ago. He must be hungry. He made a mental note to Door-Dash a burger from Grindhouse once he closed up. He could use something hearty and filling.

He angled his left arm down on the floor to push himself up. He'd probably been on the floor long enough.

The second he put weight on that arm, he screamed. The pain he felt in his midsection was unbearable. He collapsed back on the ground and realized that his white shirt was covered in blood. Was it his blood? It couldn't be. But the pain was overwhelming. He crumpled into a mound and laid his head on the linoleum. It felt so cool and wet. He wanted to lie there forever.

"I'm . . . oh, wow, I didn't . . ." A woman's voice, both halting and forceful, echoed above him. "I was just . . . you surprised me with the door."

Theo began to remember.

He'd been holding that door with his left hand and the trash bag with his right when he saw her. She was small and compact, a stout, sturdy woman who, for just a second, looked vaguely familiar to him in a way he couldn't quite place. Something in his mind had flickered when he saw her face, maybe? He'd noticed that she seemed to be wearing two, maybe three different coats. It was the middle of June—that was two, maybe three coats too many. It made her look faintly ridiculous, like she was twice as wide as she needed to be, like she was trying to sneak in a BarcaLounger behind her back. It had been very odd.

Theo had stood before her, holding that door and that bag. "I'm sorry, I didn't see you there," he'd said. "I should be more careful—it's hard to see this door from the outside."

He'd made eye contact with her to let her know this was his fault, he was sorry, I was just taking out my trash and you happened to be standing here, we're all good here, yes? But he couldn't get her to focus on him. She appeared to be looking behind him, or perhaps through him. She didn't seem to be there at all.

"Ma'am?" he said. "Ma'am, are you OK?"

And then her eyes came back into focus, and sharpened, suddenly honing in precisely on him. Her brow had narrowed. Her back arched and then straightened; she appeared to have grown about three inches taller. Whatever had been gone a couple of seconds before had returned. Her lips pursed. Theo saw a bit of white spittle settle on the left side of her mouth.

She pulled her head back, and her body locked into place.

"You," she said calmly. "It's you."

Theo remembered cocking his head slightly to his left. "Me?"

Then the woman had put her hand in her coat, pulled out a gun, and pointed it at Theo. Her hand shook, but for just a second. "You," she said.

Theo had been calm, calmer than he would have imagined himself to be. "Ma'am, can I help you?"

She coughed, a small cough, and then a louder one. "You need to show me," she said to him. "I need to see it. People need to know. You need to show me. You need to show me—"

And then she had coughed again, harder, and the gun went off. And then Theo fell.

And now he was here.

The woman bent down and put her face up next to his. She had foul breath and a hair growing out of her chin, but Theo still found her face oddly pleasant. He caught himself staring at her and felt embarrassed. "I was the one who was supposed to surprise *you* at the door," she said.

Theo put his head back in the puddle and, groaning, rolled over on his side to look at the woman. "What . . . happened? Why am I on the floor?"

The woman appeared to be the scared one, even though she wasn't the one lying in a pool of her own blood.

"I think . . . I think I shot you," she said. Something about saying it out loud seemed to solidify the thought in her mind, make it more concrete and real. "Then I heard a sound and just . . . shot at it? I think I shot twice. Three times? They really do come out very fast."

She looked down at the gun like it was a small animal that had just bitten her, like it needed to be scolded. Theo watched as her eyes began to harden on him.

"You're the son, right?" she said. "The Lindbergh son?"

There wasn't much Theo disliked more than being referred to as "the son," but he wasn't in much of a position to complain at the moment. "Theo." His words seemed to evaporate the second they left his lips. "I'm Theo."

Something gray and shiny flashed in Theo's face. It was the gun. This woman was pointing a gun at him again. *Oh*, he thought, *this must be the gun she shot me with*. Because he'd been shot, apparently. That's why he was on the floor. Unless he was clumsy. He was very wet. He laid his head back down and tried to go to sleep.

The woman slapped him on each side of his face with the back of her hand, not violently, actually—a lot more gently than Theo might have expected. "Wake up, Theo," she said, with a calm that surprised him. Maybe if he told her what she wanted, whatever that was, she might let him go back to sleep? "Wake up. I'm sorry, I didn't mean to shoot you. I just want to see the boxes."

Theo had a difficult time hearing her. What had she said? Did she want to see his socks? Lox?

"What?" he exhaled. He was beginning to feel a sharp twinge in his gut every time he breathed.

"The *boxes*," she said, more annoyed than angry, as he drifted off to sleep. "Where are the papers? The boxes. Where are they?"

"DAD, *OFF*," JACE SAID. "GET *OFF* ME."

At the first pop, Jason—who knew what the pop of a gun sounded like—grabbed his son and threw him to the ground. He'd hadn't thought about the ankle, or the wrist, or the crutches. He hadn't thought about anything at all. He just needed to get Jace *down*. Jace started to say something, but Jason put his large, meaty palm over his mouth and squeezed. "Shut up, Jace," he hissed in his son's ear. They lay there for a few seconds as muffled sounds and squeaks rattled around the store, and just as Jason started to take his hand off his son's mouth and peek his head up, he heard the second and third pops. He pushed his son down again and crawled on top of him, making himself as big as he possibly could. If he could expand himself, maybe spread out his arms and legs and shirt and pants and boots, he would dwarf his son entirely, and whoever was firing that gun wouldn't know Jace was there at all. The person could shoot Jason all they wanted. They would not get to his son.

They both lay there silent after the third shot, trying not to breathe. They heard some whispers over to their left, and some moans, which made Jason try to expand himself even further. He could feel his son start to fortify himself underneath him, the boy blanching under the weight of his father. But you'd have to pry Jason off his son with a crowbar.

Jason saw smoke coming out from behind the counter, as well as a slow stream of water from the ceiling. He found himself keenly aware of the hum of the pharmacy's drab overhead lights above him, honing in on them, listening for any break in the pattern. There had only been three shots. Was that all there would be? When could they make the run for the front door?

Jason shifted his weight from his left leg to his right leg, and he heard his son groan beneath him.

"Ohhhhhh," Jace groaned, as quietly as he could. "My ankle. Watch it, Dad."

Jason looked down and saw the crutches his son had just been using scattered in opposite directions behind them—too far away to be reached without turning around and crawling. Jason thought it over. He could scamper over there and get the crutches, but surely the shooter would hear him, and even if they didn't, how was he going to get Jace propped up on them in time anyway? Jace had tried to be tough, but it was obvious, just on the walk from the car to Lindbergh's, that he could barely put any weight on his ankle at all, let alone run on it. Could Jason pick him up? He could still carry his boy, absolutely, but he'd certainly be slower: Jace's workouts had put twenty-five pounds on his already-muscular frame just in the last six months. Could he get off him, roll over, lift him, sprint toward the door, and make it out without the shooter seeing them and firing?

He doubted it. He couldn't chance it.

What else? Jason lay on top of his son and thought some more. Maybe he could wait until he heard the shooter's footsteps draw closer, turn over, get into a crouched position, and then leap up and make a dead sprint at them. If he was lucky, the shooter would be looking in the opposite direction and not see him coming. If he wasn't lucky, he could just charge forward anyway, taking all the bullets, *bring them on, you motherfucker*, be just enough of an obstacle to give time for Jace to crawl out of there. Jason was a big guy. He figured, as long as he kept running at the shooter, as long as he hollered and yelled and fussed, as long as he *kept moving*, he could absorb enough shots to get his son out.

Would that work? He wasn't sure. But if Jace couldn't get to the door quickly, and he couldn't, Jason would have no choice. Because Jace had to get out. Whatever happened: *Jace had to get out.*

Jason craned his ear to try to hear any steps. If he did, he decided, he was gonna go for it.

He turned his head to his right, in the opposite direction from where the shots had come. For the first time, he noticed the older Black woman, the woman he'd just talked to in line, sitting about seven feet away from him. That's what she was doing: she was sitting, her knees up, leaning forward. And she was making eye contact with his son. She put a finger over her mouth, and Jace nodded. Then she looked up at Jason.

"*Shhhhhh*," she said.

Jace wanted to save this woman, this scared old woman who had seemed very nice. She looked like she needed saving. But he could only take the bullets once.

He tried to mouth her his plan, such as it was, but she couldn't understand him and kept telling him to shush anyway. Then Jason shifted his weight again, adjusting his bum right knee, which always barked at him when it rained, and his son let out an audible yelp.

"Dad, *off*," Jace said. "Get *off* me."

But he would not move. They'd have to kill him five times before they'd get to Jace. He was goddamned sure of that.

DOROTHY FIGURED THEY'D BEEN DOWN THERE ABOUT FIVE MINUTES, WHICH was her best guess between the two most likely answers, "Four or five seconds" and "Their entire lives." She found it comforting, weirdly, to see two other people that she had no association with talking about the very situation she was herself in. Hearing them try to make sense of it assured her that she hadn't imagined it, that it was really happening, that someone else was living through it too. She was confused, but she was not panicked. She was calm. She was once again in a movie theater, watching a character that looked like her go through the experience. It made her feel strong.

She found herself looking around the pharmacy, trying to piece together what had gone down, what was still going down, where all the key players were, how this all might end up shaking out. How many people were in here? Where had the shots come from? Where was the shooter now?

The father and son were mumbling to each other—too loudly, Dorothy thought. She put a finger over her lips and tried to shush them again. The father seemed to get it, but kept trying to mouth something to her. He's in shock, Dorothy thought. He needs to stay right there.

A sound. Not footsteps, not gunshots—a groan. Then whispers. She craned her head around a corner and saw a woman in nursing scrubs tending to a man whose hand was bleeding as a young Black man, a man Dorothy thought looked faintly familiar, leaned next to her. She tried to get their attention, waving her right hand wildly, but they didn't see her.

She looked back at the father and his son, who had somehow

gotten his father off of him. What had the boy said? *Roofs are always higher up than you think they are.* His ankle looked busted. That young man would have to be dragged out of here.

She made eye contact with the father again. He put his palms in the air and mouthed, "OK."

Then, in an exaggerated pantomime, he pointed two thumbs at himself and moved them upward, as if to say, *I'm going up.* Then he pulled his arms back and made a wild running motion with them, like he was in a race. Then he pointed toward where the sounds of the shots had come from.

He repeated this twice: Thumbs pointed at himself. Thumbs moving up. A running motion. Toward the shooter.

Dorothy gasped. *This man's about to get himself killed.*

Dorothy did not know what to do, what the right course of action was, what even was going on. But she knew that she could not let this man get gunned down in front of his boy. And that's exactly what was going to happen. This man, this big dumb man, was trying to make himself the hero, but he was just going to make himself—and god knows who else—dead. Now was not the time to be stupid.

Which meant Dorothy would have to take care of this.

Stay there, Dennis would have told her. Let the whole thing play out, trust the people who handle these situations all the time, don't stick your nose in. Had Dennis been there when Teddy Crosby's brother had come into their house, he would have attempted to calmly talk the man down, to find a mutual understanding as two rational, reasonable human beings who have found themselves on opposite sides of a conflict. Dennis would have tried to fix it.

And Teddy Crosby's brother probably would have shot him right square in his beautiful face.

Dorothy had lived a good long life. She'd helped people, she'd made the world better by being smart and capable and trying to do her very best. Whatever happened here, she would be all right—they would all be all right—if she took charge. Not this fool who might just get them both killed.

She took a deep breath. *I'm the one who has to do this.*

Dorothy looked at the man, put her hands out in front of her, and mouthed, as violently as she could, *NO!* He frowned at her. She mouthed again: *Wait.*

She took one quick peek above the countertop to make sure that whoever had fired the gun was not currently pointing it in her direction, and saw nothing and no one. She glanced to her right. The threesome on the other side of the pharmacy was still whispering to each other without noticing her. If she crouched low enough, she could get to the man and his son without being seen. She'd have to go flat. She could go flat.

She mouthed "Stay" to them, got down on her belly, and, slowly, began to crawl, keeping eye contact with the man. His eyes went wide, but he stayed silent and waited for her.

She reached them and put her mouth between the father's left ear and the son's right.

"Stay here," she said. "You need to stay here. I think it's happening in the back. There haven't been any shots in a couple of minutes. So I'm going to go check it out. If the shooter sees me, well, then you need to get your ass out of here when they do."

The man opened his mouth to protest. She shot him a steely look, the look that William and Wynn always knew meant that the time for debate was over.

"Be with your son," she hissed. "Stay down. And be ready to grab him and *run.*"

The son lightly groaned and caressed his ankle gently.

"Yes, ma'am," he said.

The father pushed his son back down closer to the ground, and he pulled himself down there as well. "Yes, ma'am."

Dorothy poked her head up again. There was still no sign of anyone beyond the counter, though she could hear some faint squeaks coming from *something* back there. She heard a cough, and a loud moan that sounded less like a human than like air being expelled from a dying animal.

It was time to move. If she could get around that corner, she could be at the black door in a matter of seconds. What would happen then? Perhaps it would be nothing; perhaps this was all a misunderstanding; perhaps everything was actually fine. Or maybe behind that door there was a big man with a big gun who would unload it the second he saw Dorothy.

She did not know. She just knew it was time to move. She was going to be fine, she knew, whatever was waiting for her. She did not feel brave. She just felt like she had purpose and direction— and therefore power. She did not know what was going to happen. But she knew that whatever happened, it would be because she made it happen. She would not sit around waiting for someone to tell her what to do. She would be in charge. It'd all be on her terms.

She began a slow, careful, labored shuffle toward the counter, toward the sound of that moan.

Deep into their eighth decade, her bones creaked and popped and snapped. But she liked the shake and rattle of her body coming back to life, finding its purpose.

As she reached the big black door, she put her ear to it. She heard . . . nothing. No talking, no moaning, no sounds at all. She pushed on the door lightly and found that it was unlocked. She edged it open, carefully, keeping as low to the ground as she could. She scanned the floor. There was a trash bag leaking banana peels and old napkins. A few feet away, a soiled prescription for Xanax for a Mr. Cetera of Hardeman Road.

Then she saw two pairs of shoes. One—white athletic shoes, running shoes, maybe, Asics brand—was pointed upward, attached to a person lying down. The other pair was, Dorothy thought, surprisingly stylish: little green pumps, striking but still practical, the sort of shoes you can walk in all day and still get compliments about when you wear them out to a nice dinner that evening. Dorothy made a note to find out where the woman wearing them had bought them. If she had the opportunity. Maybe not just yet.

She looked up and saw the face of the owner of the shoes. It was puffy and scattered, Dorothy thought, the face of a woman who had been pretty once but had stopped caring about being pretty anymore—something, too, that Dorothy could appreciate. She had a bewildered, slack expression, and she was holding a gun. It was a bigger gun than the one Teddy Crosby's brother had pointed at Dorothy's face, and in the hands of this tiny woman it looked like a bazooka. The gun was pointed at the ground.

Dorothy glanced at the man on the ground, and it dawned on her: That's Jack Lindbergh's son. She had known Jack Lindbergh, of course she had. He'd once propositioned her at the country club when Dennis was out of town. "You ever touch me again, *Jack*," she'd told him, "I'll put you through that plate glass window." She never told Dennis that: the two men played golf together. She'd been fond of his wife, though, and her son, this boy. They'd been through so much. And this was him, right there. His white shirt was covered in blood, as were his pleated khaki pants. His chest appeared to still be moving up and down, though it was hard to tell. You didn't need to be to a doctor to know he was in serious trouble.

She took a long, deep breath. *Now.* Rising from her crouch, she put her hands out in front of her, palms out, and stared directly at the side of the woman's head. Sensing movement, the woman almost as slowly turned her head toward Dorothy. Her eyes widened, then twitched, then narrowed. Dorothy kept her arms stretched out, her hands open and empty.

"Hello," Dorothy said. "My name is Dorothy. I need to help that man. Did you shoot that man?"

Eyes still narrowed, the woman, standing behind that black door and peering over it as if looking upon a steep cliff, put her left hand on the gun and lifted it toward Dorothy with both hands. Her arms were shaking, like she was having some sort of minor spasm, and she was hopping up and down lightly on her ankles. But she looked Dorothy dead in the eye.

"Stop," she said, her voice clear. "I don't want to shoot anyone else."

Dorothy's voice was clear too—clearer. "And I don't want to get shot." She gestured toward Theo with her right hand. "I just need to help that man. Will you let me help that man?"

The woman kept the gun pointed at Dorothy, but her face softened. "I did not mean to shoot him," she said. "I just needed some information."

Dorothy angled her head slightly to the left, originally an involuntary movement but one she adjusted to give the woman the impression of sympathy, and even usefulness—she could help her get what she needed. For someone who had apparently just broken into a pharmacy and shot the owner, the woman looked almost . . . approachable? Dorothy felt she could talk to her without getting shot, anyway. At least not on purpose.

"OK, so let me help him, so he can tell you what you need to know," Dorothy said. "He sure can't tell you right now." Dorothy's heartbeat was normal, but she felt a weird exhilaration. She was in her element.

The woman looked to Dorothy like she wanted to go home. "Yes," she said. "Maybe you can help him." She lowered the gun and turned slightly away from Dorothy. "I . . . I really did not mean to shoot him. Please. Help him if you can."

Satisfied that this woman would not be shooting her in the next five seconds, anyway, Dorothy put her hands down and walked over to Theo. She bent down. He was ghastly pale, soaked with sweat and blood, water still beading across his forehead. His breath was halting, but he was definitely breathing. Dorothy looked at his now-beet-red shirt and realized, now that she was here, that she had no idea what to do.

"Uh . . . ," she said out loud, without realizing she was saying it out loud.

From the other side of the pharmacy came a woman's voice. "Hello! I'm a nurse! Do you need me to help you?"

The voice startled the woman in the green shoes, who grabbed her gun with both hands again. "Who said that?"

"I did," Daphne said. "My name is Daphne. I'm a nurse. If someone is hurt, I can help them. I'm helping another man who has been shot as well. He needs medicine and bandages." She cleared her throat, as if it were important that she be heard. "Will you let me come back there?"

The woman with the gun pointed it over the door, in the direction of the sound, and Dorothy saw her eyes widen and focus again. She had pretty eyes, Dorothy decided.

"Who else is out there?" There was more fear in her voice than menace. "Is anyone with you?"

And then Dorothy realized just how many people were still here.

Daphne stood up from where she had been crouching with David and Karson. "There's me, and two men with me," she said. "One of them is shot in the hand, and the other is helping me help him."

The woman looked confused. "Wait, who shot that man?" she said.

David, with an arm on Karson's shoulder, stood up next to Daphne. Karson rose with him. David had gotten most of his color back and was starting to feel ornery. "I'm pretty sure you did, lady," he said. "You see anybody else here with a gun?"

"Oh," the woman said.

Karson looked at the woman. To him, she looked angry, almost snarling. Though everyone was starting to look like that to him these days. He shrugged a little, put up his left hand, and gave a light little wave. "Hey," he said.

He looked over the black door and saw his friend Theo, his Atlanta Hawks buddy, trying not to die. "Oh, shit, Theo," he said, not very loud, and put his hand over his mouth. "Oh shit."

The woman pointed the gun at a spot above the heads of all three of them. David, next to Karson, couldn't believe this woman had just shot him. She probably couldn't hit the ceiling shooting straight up. "If you can get him standing, you three should probably come back here," the woman said.

She looked at Dorothy. Sirens began to blare outside Lindbergh's, and Dorothy saw the woman shuffle in place for a moment as she glanced over Dorothy's shoulder, trying to see out the window. Then, her face oddly slack again, she looked back to Dorothy.

"Can they get back here?" she said, as if asking for extra ketchup on her fries. Dorothy found her absolutely mystifying.

"I did, didn't I?" Dorothy said. She looked up and raised her voice to carry over the threshold. "Just come through the black door, it's unlocked," she said. "Be careful, it's very wet and slippery."

David put his left arm on Karson's shoulder, and Daphne held his right wrist, keeping the hand elevated and stable. They inched toward the big black door, each small step somehow tinier and tighter than the last. Karson had known Daphne and David for roughly 180 seconds, and he felt closer to them right now than he'd ever felt to anyone, other than his wife and daughter, in his entire life.

Just as they made it to the threshold, there was a rustling behind them, and a crash. The woman thrust the gun toward the sound. Dorothy cursed under her breath. They'd almost gotten out. But the kid was too big to carry.

Beneath her, the father began to rise.

Jason stood up with his hands in the air. "Don't shoot," he said slowly, trying not to set off a bomb. "My name is Jason. I'm here with my son, who injured himself and cannot walk. May I pick him up?"

Daphne cautiously opened the black door, walked over to Jason, and with the gun still trained on them, helped Jason pick up his son, and they carted him across the threshold of the big black door. Karson held the door for them. It was a very heavy door.

As he crossed the threshold himself, Karson looked across the pharmacy. His friend was on the floor of his family store, dying. The rest of Lindbergh's was empty. They were the only ones here. They were the people who stayed.

II

Alexis hovered above Theo, her body pressed against his, her hair hanging over her eye and into his mouth, rubbing her cheek gently against his, her hands holding his face, staring right at him with a wry, sympathetic smile.

I'm so happy we met today . . . It is going to be all right . . . I can stay here forever if you want me to . . .

Theo felt flushed, almost embarrassed to have her so close to him. But she didn't run away. She just lay there, on top of him, telling him it was all going to be all right, not a salvation but a fellow traveler, wherever he was going, she'd be right there beside him, on her own journey but also there for his. He was excited to see where she was going to go too. He couldn't believe they'd get to go there together. Her skin was so soft.

Somewhere he heard a scream. He was pretty sure it wasn't his. Maybe it was.

KARSON COULDN'T BELIEVE THAT LUMP OF BLOODY FLESH, THAT PALE, FADING face, was his friend Theo. He wasn't dead, but it was obvious that something that had been inside him a few minutes ago—a soul, a kind spirit, several pints of blood—was gone. It was as if his body had gone flat, like a cartoon animal run over by a road roller; Karson saw a face, some clothes, and otherwise everything was just wet. It was like he'd been liquefied.

Daphne was kneeling beside Theo, checking his pulse, doing all sorts of medical things Karson didn't understand, when she did something strange: she flipped him over. Karson feared all Theo's internal organs were going to come tumbling out.

She grabbed some of the pads that Karson had brought with him and began to soak up as much of the blood around his wound as possible. There was still blood spurting out of the hole in his stomach. He didn't have that much more time. She met Karson's gawping stare.

"You!" she said. "Come here!" Karson glanced at the woman with the gun to make sure it wasn't on him. She was still pointing it, shakily, at the man and his son as she stared at them blankly. His hands in the air just in case, he bent down and ran to Daphne like an eager student called to the front of the class.

"Take these pads and hold them on his stomach." She checked Theo's pulse and made a worried face. His eyes had started to roll back in his head. She slapped his face. "Hey," she said, "hey, we need you up here."

Karson held the pads on a wound that was so deep he saw nothing but black. His heart was beating so fast, it sounded like a bass line. Theo looked even more like liquid up close.

"What else can I do," he said, "to help you with . . . whatever you are doing?"

"I'm trying to find an exit wound. I'm hoping the bullet came out. Here, lift up his shoulders."

His right hand still covering the wound, Karson cupped his left arm under Theo's neck and lifted. Theo was asleep, and so white he was almost translucent.

"It looks like it entered his abdomen just below his left rib cage," Daphne said. "It obviously missed his heart, or he'd be dead already. He's not gushing blood, so it missed his spleen—he'd be dead already if that got hit as well. Missed the pancreas too."

A rush of wooziness came over Karson, and he feared he might pass out. "There's a lot of blood, though."

"That there is," Daphne said as she pulled up the back of Theo's shirt. "Please let this bullet be through," she said, and Karson knew she wasn't talking to him.

"Is an exit wound good?" he asked. Annette would have been smart enough not to ask all these dumb questions, he thought. She watched *CSI* all the time.

"Yes," Daphne said, frantically scrubbing Theo's back with a wet towel she'd found behind the counter. "We can help him here if the bullet went through. But I can't get a bullet out of his stomach in the back of this room."

Karson really hoped the bullet had gone through.

There was grime and blood soaked through everywhere, so she cupped her hands around a puddle of water on the floor and splashed it across Theo's back, then began wiping away the area with a wet paper napkin, a little sandwich napkin, probably meant to get mustard off your kid's face.

"Whew," she said, almost whistled. "There's the hole." The bullet had passed through. "It might be in his stomach, I don't know. But we don't have to get it out."

"Thank you, Jesus," she said.

"Yeah," Karson said, finding his footing a little bit. "Thanks, Jesus." He then rolled Theo on his back again, where Theo continued to sleep.

THE WOMAN HAD BEEN STARING AT DOROTHY AND THE WALLER MEN FOR A full minute, pointing a gun at them, without saying a word. The nurse and the other man were working on Theo, the man with the busted hand was moaning and cursing, and Jason was standing in front of his son, glaring at the woman, daring her to shoot him. Momentum was building, and it was not building toward anything good.

Dorothy thought the only thing to do was talk.

"We need to help that man on the ground," she said to the woman. "Theo. That man on the floor, the man you shot, his name is Theo."

The woman, looking angrier than Dorothy had seen her, furrowed her brow and stared back at Dorothy. "I know who he is," she said, with a hint of a hiss that alarmed Dorothy. "I have some questions for him to answer." That alarmed Dorothy too.

"Then you need to let us help him," the nurse said forcefully over her shoulder, her hands deep into Theo's wounds. Dorothy immediately recognized her as someone who could maybe get everyone through this.

The woman turned back to Daphne, and her eyes began to soften once more. "Yes, please," she said. "Don't let him die."

Dorothy watched the woman closely, and slowly—imperceptibly, she hoped—began to inch toward her. She had seen something in Jason's body, an ominous shift of weight, that made it look like he was about to do something foolish. She had to stop it.

She had moved about six inches when a loud electric screech came from the front of the pharmacy. Dorothy thought it sounded like microphone feedback. The sound filled the room.

"Hello?" The voice was booming, very male, but a little uncertain. "Is there anybody in there? This is the police, the Athens Police Department. We're all, uh, out here. There's no exits available. Anyone holding a weapon needs to drop it and come out with their hands in the air." The mic cut out with a snap, then returned. "Out here. Come out here with your hands up. Without your weapons." A cough. "Do so immediately."

There was another screech, and a thud. Then silence.

Dorothy immediately looked at the woman, whose eyes began darting around the room in panic. "Oh my god," she said, as if she were surprised that the police would show up.

This woman doesn't know what she's doing, Dorothy thought. That wasn't good. She saw Jason slowly pull his son's head down to the floor.

Dorothy stepped forward and spoke directly to the woman. "It's OK, it's OK, he's outside, we're all in here," she said in her best calming grandmother voice. "It's OK, there's nothing to worry about." The woman began to pace back and forth and mutter to herself.

"Not yet, not yet, not yet, we don't know anything yet," she seemed to be saying, though Dorothy couldn't quite hear her over the faint alarm and the clanging about of a billion different noises from inside her own brain.

DAVID FELT LIKE THE FEW HAIRS HE HAD LEFT ON HIS BIG DUMB SKULL WERE all standing straight up. His hand hurt, hurt like a motherfucker, but that wasn't it. He knew that voice outside the door. He knew that cop.

The bullet had gone through his hand right next to his ring finger, where he used to wear his wedding ring—he'd only stopped wearing it a few years ago, after Allie told him her mother had asked him to take it off, it was honestly a little embarrassing. A couple inches up, the bullet would have only knocked off the tip of a finger; a couple inches down, it would have shattered his whole arm. Of course, he thought, a couple *more* inches up, and it would be in his brain. He was trying not to think about that.

The cop, David was certain, was Lt. Anderson, his buddy on the force, the guy he'd just dropped Joe off with a few hours earlier. He'd been the first officer on the scene, and that made sense too: David had had coffee with Anderson at the Jittery Joe's just around the corner many times, and he knew it was the officer's favorite haunt. He was a smart kid, but green. David was actually sort of proud of him for being the one they gave the bullhorn.

David knew they'd be in here soon. And he knew, as he looked at her, the woman who had just shot him in his fucking hand and might well have just killed the poor kid who ran this place, he knew he had to slow them down for a second, or there was no telling what she would do. She had a gun on the dad and his kid and the old woman. She didn't have a plan. She was scared as shit. If they could calm this down, she'd probably just hand them the gun. Rushing in was gonna get more people shot.

With his left hand, the one that didn't have a huge fucking hole in it, he reached into his right pocket, his eyes locked on the woman. She had sat down in a chair. It had all gone so wrong, so quickly. He pulled out his phone and sneaked a quick glance at it. Holding it, and barely balancing it, in that left hand, he typed as quietly and carefully as he could.

i . . . m . . . n . . . l . . .

He was almost finished when the woman, for no reason at all, happened to turn her head and look directly at him. She saw the concentration in his eyes, the way he was staring at her like he was doing something that he wanted to make sure she didn't notice. She was no dummy, he thought.

She turned to him. David instinctively ducked, a cacophony of pain sprinting up his right arm as he did so, and sent the message to Lt. Anderson with his phone before dropping it again and rolling over onto the floor.

What a maroon, he thought as he lay on his back, staring at the ceiling, the torture of his fucked-up hand to his right and an almost obsolete iPhone with a probably unintelligible text message lying to his left. He smiled. *What a dumbass way to go.*

The woman's face was quickly over his. There was no way she was relaxed and serene and warm. That was impossible. But that's how David saw her. He had no clue why he saw her that way. But he did. That's how he saw her.

He closed his eyes.

imnlndbrgs now stay out hold off gun lady gun stayou

THE WOMAN WAS NOW CLOSER TO DOROTHY THAN SHE'D EVER BEEN, AND Dorothy got her best look at her. You could see the contours of her face, her widow's peak, her crow's feet. Dorothy thought she was probably younger than she looked. She still looked pretty, but she also looked like a stiff wind would shatter her into a million little pieces. She was holding David's phone in her hands.

To her right, lower, Dorothy heard Jason and his son murmuring about something. She was about to turn to them and tell them to be quiet when the boy, Jace, stood up.

He turned to face the woman, his back arched. The woman turned to him and lifted the gun, with both hands, toward him. Jason leaped up and attempted to throw himself in front of his son, but the son, smaller than his father but firm, tall, *certain*, shoved him off with his right arm.

"No, Dad," he said, gun still on him. "I know now." His mouth opened slightly, softly, and he put his hands out in front of him, cupped, like he was trying to get an old dog to come to him and drink. His eyes were wide but clear and sharp. Dorothy felt a powerful surge of pride for this boy she had just met. This boy was like her boys—strong, sturdy, and kind.

"Sit down, goddammit!" the father said, but the boy did not sit down.

The boy's eyes met the woman's. He smiled. He really did smile.

"Miss Lamm?" he said. "Is that you, Miss Lamm?" He paused. "Mommy Mario?"

III.

The last thing Jace wanted was to be different. There hadn't been a moment growing up that he didn't walk in a classroom to a hush, a *There he is, the gifted kid, the genius.* Watkinsville was a good enough school district, but it was still Oconee County. Everybody wore camo to school, everybody's dads drove big-ass pickup trucks, most people's moms didn't work. It was conservative, upscale-redneck country, where everybody watched football every Friday night and all day Saturday, went to church every Sunday morning, and listened to Rush Limbaugh all day every day in between. It was a good place to raise a family. But it was not a good place to be different. And Jace knew, from the get-go, that being known as the gifted kid was a great way to get your ass beat.

So he looked to his father, his massive, hulking, work-your-sweaty-ass-out-in-the-heat-all-day father, for every cue as to how to act. He wore camo shirts too. He pretended he enjoyed going hunting, though he never once fired a weapon and always claimed he hadn't seen any bucks, even though he clearly had. He leaned into his dad's drawl. He even had learned to love work like his father did; Oconee County might not love the intellectuals, but it respected a man who worked, and the Wallers always, always worked. But mostly: it was baseball. Jace loved baseball like his father loved baseball. He loved the way the sport had clear rules and set lines of play, immutable numbers—sixty feet, six inches; ninety feet; four balls; three strikes; three outs—that everyone involved had to follow, no matter who they were. Baseball was a place where Jace could be himself—where he could obsess over numbers and figures and strategies and geometry and even philosophy and poetry—while still fitting in with everyone else, including his father. Nobody cared how smart you were on the baseball field. It was the only thing Jace could pour his whole self into and not stand out in the slightest. It sometimes felt like the sport was created specifically for him.

He had spent every day at school, really since he'd been in kindergarten, bored, before he'd learned how to mix in with the other kids, before he knew how to get people not to look at the big GIFTED sign on his forehead. So he got through the days by becoming friends with his teachers. Every teacher loves the smart kids, not because they're more likely to follow all the rules but because teachers want to feel like *someone* cares about their work, and because they'd like to someday be rewarded. Someday, when that kid in their second-grade class is accepting her Nobel Prize for building a rocket that helped colonize Mars, they want her to say, "Thanks to Mr. Coleman for inspiring me when I was seven. I wouldn't be here without him." They want to be vindicated. They want it all to matter. So they loved Jace, saw him as a peer, really.

And in fourth grade, his teacher at Fox Mountain Elementary School in Watkinsville, Georgia, was Miss Lamm. Though nobody called her Miss Lamm. They called her Mommy Mario.

Jace had a different relationship with Miss Lamm than he did with most of his teachers. He wanted to protect Miss Lamm. She was a fine teacher; she had this game she'd play where she'd give you five facts every Monday morning and whoever remembered the most facts at the end of the week got to stay after school with her and play Mario Kart. Jace always won that game—Jace had been born to win games like that. But what all her students noticed about her, even in the fourth grade, and what made something in Jace's chest throb and ache back then, even when he was just ten years old, was how sad she was. She was so sad. There was one morning Jace never forgot. A kid in class would not stop pestering this girl in front of him, even after Miss Lamm had asked him multiple times to knock it off. She finally hit her breaking point, but rather than scream at him, punch the wall, send him to the principal's office, like most teachers would do, she walked over to him, bent down on one knee, and burst into tears.

"Why won't you stop?" she said, just a few feet away from Jace. "I don't know how to make you stop. I'm sorry. I'm sorry

I can't make you stop. I'm sorry to both of you." She put her head in her hands and continued to weep. Everyone sat there in silence until the bell rang for recess. When they returned to class, Miss Lamm acted as if it had never happened. The funny thing was, after that, the kid never acted up again, and the class never misbehaved. It was as if they were afraid if they did not do what they were supposed to, Miss Lamm would shatter. She was as fragile as they knew, deep down, they were too. They would have never articulated it that way; they were ten, after all. But looking back at it, Jace knew this was what it was. She was one of them. Other teachers marveled at Miss Lamm's fourth-grade class that year. *Such gentle children. How does she do it?*

Jace always won the factoid game, so every Friday, he and whatever student had finished second that week played Mario Kart with Miss Lamm. He was terrible at Mario Kart, terrible at all video games, and he always finished last. But she was always so happy when she played the game, so joyous and grateful to hang out with the kids. The other teachers felt like adults, but being with Miss Lamm, to Jace, was like having an actual friend—another child he could act, at last, like a child around. Miss Lamm was the first teacher Jace had who didn't care that he was gifted, that he was The Special Boy. She was just happy to be around children. And he was happy to finally get to be one. By the end of the year he'd stay at school on Fridays after Mario Kart was over and the other kids had gone home, and they'd play checkers, or talk about Harry Potter, or ask each other Trivial Pursuit questions. Fourth-grade Jace would never have admitted it, but teenage Jace could: in fourth grade, Miss Lamm might have been his best friend. Fox Mountain had a big graduation for the fifth graders, before they all went off to the horrors of middle school, and the top five students in the class got to walk across the stage with their favorite teacher. Jace of course chose Miss Lamm. They locked arms, turned to the audience, and waved. Jace walked her to the other side and released his arm from hers with a big theatrical bow. He was delighted by how much she giggled.

He lost touch with Miss Lamm in middle school and high school, because who wouldn't? It would be weird for a teenager to hang out with his fourth-grade teacher. He hadn't thought about her, really, in years. But she occupied a warm place in his heart, even if he'd had no recent reason to visit that place. Had he thought about it, he would have figured he probably occupied the same thing in her heart. Had they met in any other context but this one—maybe at the Wal-Mart, maybe at dinner at the Expat in Five Points, when he was an adult with a full life of his own and she was an old favorite teacher remembering one of her most beloved students—he would have hugged her, and she would have told him she couldn't believe how big he had gotten, how long it had been, isn't life so funny? They'd have walked their separate ways in a slightly better mood than they'd been in previously. It would have been nice.

But that was not the context in which they had met again. They had met in an increasingly bloody back room of Lindbergh's pharmacy, as sirens and alarms blared all around them. They had met right here.

"Mommy Mario?" said Jace, feeling much dumber about the world right then than he usually felt about the world.

Next to him, his father was equally agog. "What the fuck?" Jason said. Dads never knew who their fourth grader's teachers were.

The woman—Tina: her name was Tina—wiped some water out of her left eye with the hand that didn't have a gun in it. "Jace?"

The whole group seemed to be staring at each other.

Jace, Jason noticed, had a weird grin on his face, like he had been dosed with some sort of drug and his face had frozen that way.

He didn't look happy, or amused. He just looked slack-jawed—slap-happy. Jason figured he probably looked that way too.

Dorothy stood up a little taller. She felt the small, sharp twinge behind her ears she always got when something confusing was starting to come into focus—like it was involuntarily lifting her left eyebrow.

Tina stared at Jace.

"You're a teacher," Dorothy said to Tina. "You were his teacher."

Tina turned her head to Dorothy. Dorothy didn't think she looked puffy or scattered or like someone who used to be pretty and didn't care anymore. She was no longer a vague outline of a person. She was now Tina, a woman with wet hair and a gun and wide eyes, a woman who looked absolutely terrified.

"I was a lot of kids' teacher," she said, lowering her weapon and stepping backward.

"She was Mommy Mario," Jace said, almost in a whisper. Jason watched him, thought Jace was somehow making himself smaller, like he was trying to look to her the way he looked to her in the fourth grade. "What is happening here, Miss Lamm? Or . . . Tina?"

Tina looked at him as if she were struggling to resolve several alternate realities at once. "Oh, Jace," she said. "I was just trying to understand what has been going on."

"Where?" Jace asked.

"Here," Tina said. "This store. And this family."

Jace looked down at Theo's limp body and was about to say something when, with everyone staring at Jace, David's phone buzzed so loudly that it fell out of his hand and landed on Theo's chest, which elicited a small, sad moan. This caused Tina to jump back up and point the weapon back at David, and at the phone, and at Theo, then back at David again.

"Who is that?" she said. "Who are you texting with?"

David, busted and in the principal's office, tried to figure out a way to tell her that wouldn't upset her more than she was already upset and decided it was impossible.

"It's a police officer," he said, trying not to audibly gulp or cartoonishly tug at his collar, *zoinks*. The mental image almost made him laugh. He choked it down as Tina glared at him. "He's right outside. I told him to stay outside."

There was a sharp second of silence as everyone processed this new information. Karson decided to fill it. He worked with people in periods of intense distress all the time; most of the people he helped *lived* in periods of intense distress. His eyes went to the floor. His friend was fading a little more with each glance. They were running out of time.

"So, Tina," he said. It was strange—funny, really—how quickly they all adapted to calling her Tina, as if her name and her profession and her general mood had been information they'd possessed all along. The human brain adapted so quickly that Karson sometimes wondered if there were really any such thing as "the present," or if we were all merely constantly reacting to whatever it was that just happened five seconds ago. In the forty-five seconds or so that he'd known Tina's name and her profession and her general mood, he'd come to believe he could talk to her.

"So what do you want?" Karson said. "How can we help you? Because I do not think this is what you want."

"Yeah," Dorothy said, trained on Tina like a hawk about to dart toward its prey. In her peripheral vision, she noticed Jason looking at her and briefly locked eyes with him.

Don't.

I won't. Not yet. But I will if I have to.

But not yet.

Dorothy turned her attention back to Tina. "I think you need to tell us what you are trying to do. Are we hostages? Are you going to shoot all of us? What is your plan here? Why are you doing this?"

Tina took a deep breath, which appeared to fortify her some-how. "It's him," she said, pointing to Theo on the floor. "I wanted to talk to him."

DOROTHY NOTICED, AS TINA SAT DOWN ON A CHAIR AND TOOK A SERIES OF deep, labored breaths, that she had put her gun on a counter next to the sink. The gun was a little farther away from Tina than she probably would have wanted it to be if she had been thinking correctly. But Dorothy no longer believed there was much chance of Tina thinking correctly.

Could she get to the gun before Tina did? Dorothy was quicker than people thought she was, but she was still a woman in her seventies. If she could get to the gun, though, this whole thing would be over, just like that. All she had to do was get the gun. Once she had it, Tina would wither—she had mostly wilted already anyway. Just get that gun, and we can all go home.

Dorothy eyed the gun, and Tina.

"Miss Lamm," Jace was saying, "I think you need to talk slower. Nothing you are saying makes any sense." Tina had been talking about her mom, and her sister, and Theo, and Theo's dad, and boxes of papers, and something about forced pregnancies, or something like that, and none of them could make heads or tails of it. She seemed to lose steam as she went on about it, like the looks everyone was giving her were making her question herself. Which ended up making her angrier—and more unstable.

"You didn't see what I've seen!" she said. "You don't know, you didn't know him, his dad, what he did, who he was." Her voice was starting to rise to an uncomfortable pitch. "They've been doing this for YEARS. For decades! And he kept records on all of it. And it's here . . . somewhere!" She flung her hands wildly in front of her as she yelled, and Jason stepped up to his son's side and then in front of him, in something resembling a wrestler's crouch. *This is escalating*, Dorothy thought, *and he is preparing himself.*

268

Dorothy did the math. If she made her move, Jason would be right with her, a fullback plowing in to send defenders flying in all directions, if he had to. The woman on the ground, the nurse, Deborah, something like that, she was also speaking to Tina, also calmly and carefully, a pilot on the ground trying to explain to a civilian in the cockpit how to land the plane. She looked to Karson, who was furiously typing into David's phone, probably to that police officer, probably telling him to stay away. But who knew how long the police would, and who knew what would happen when they finally did bum-rush the place? Dorothy could hear the clock ticking. This would have to go down soon. It might just have to go down right now.

She thought of Dennis, how he would tell her to park her Black ass right here, how he was always wrong about stuff like this, how she loved him so much, how he'd always thought she'd collapse without him and how wrong he was about stuff like that too. She thought of Jeff, and what a story it would be to tell him, if she made it through this, of all the stories they'd have to tell each other, of all they'd missed, of all that might have been, of all that was wonderful because it hadn't. And she thought of her boys, William and Wynn, and how they'd turned out so much better than she even could have hoped for, it had all been worth it, it had all been just incredible, even the bad parts, sometimes even especially the bad parts, because everything she'd ever done had changed the world in even the tiniest ways, just like everything everyone else had ever done, and that was beautiful too. She'd done her part. If this was how it ended, she was all right with that.

But it ain't gonna end like this. She almost smiled.

She glanced again at Tina, and at Jace, still muttering urgently to her, and at Deborah or whatever, at these scared people, all trapped in a room together at the end of the world.

It was time.

Dorothy stepped to her left about two inches, hopefully imperceptibly, to stay out of Tina's peripheral vision. If she began her run sideways and then pivoted to her sprint, she could have the gun in her hands—or at least away from Tina—before anyone understood what she'd done. She lowered her head to her chest, whispered a silent prayer, bent her knees slightly, and took in a deep breath. She looked at Tina one last time.

And then there was a moan beneath her. Then another. Then, after a deep breath, all the scream a dying man could muster:

"STOP!" Theo wailed, spittle spraying all across his face, his chin quivering and red. "Stop it!"

Everyone in the room, including Dorothy, stopped what they were doing and looked down at Theo. Then, amazingly, he began to pull himself up, propping himself on his left elbow and twisting himself into a seated position on the floor.

He looked up at Tina.

"I know you," he said. "I know who you are. You're her daughter. I remember you."

He coughed and spit, and his tongue dropped out of his mouth for a split second. He reeled it back in and wiped his face with his right hand.

"I'm so sorry," he said, and slumped back down to the floor.

DAPHNE WAS ON THE GROUND WITH HIM BEFORE HE EVEN LANDED. SHE cradled Theo in her arms and laid him down gently. There was still blood spurting out of the hole in his stomach. His eyes were closed. She needed his eyes open.

She thought about the urgency with which he had just spoken, how he had pulled himself up like he was trying to keep the world from ending. "What were you saying?" she said to him as she smacked his cheek with the back of her hand. "What do you need to tell us?"

"What did he say?" Tina said. Her voice was soft, gentle—even calm. Daphne found herself strangely moved by how concerned for him this woman was. Tina turned to Daphne. "Can you help him?"

"I'm trying," Daphne said. "He has lost a lot of blood."

Tina bent down on the floor and put her face next to Theo's. "What did you say?" she said. "Did you say you knew me?" Theo made a gurgling sound, but he opened his eyes. He turned his head and spat again, then looked at Tina.

Theo spoke with great effort. "You're the girl. . . . the sister who died," he said. "I . . . remember you."

Tina's eyes got wide, and she doubled over as if she had just been punched in the stomach and burst into tears.

Theo looked at her. "We've . . . met, when . . . when . . . I was a kid," he said clearly, surprisingly forcefully. "My father . . . your mother. I remember."

Tina looked at him. Jace was watching, and for the first time he saw the teacher he had once loved.

"Oh my god, I remember," Tina said. "We sat on my front porch. We played your GameBoy until he left."

Theo got a lopsided smile on his face. As the only other person in the room who had just gotten shot, David was impressed by Theo's strength. David sure as shit wasn't smiling.

Theo was still smiling. This was where he was supposed to be. All of it. All of it. "Yeah . . . ," he said. "So . . . why did you shoot me again?" He had been wondering about this.

Daphne felt Theo's body go slack. He was getting weaker.

Jason, who was standing behind Jace, tugging on his shirt and slowly inching them both toward the door, saw Tina look around the room on the other side of the black door, this back room of the pharmacy, like she was seeing it for the first time. He also looked behind her and saw Dorothy, that titan, standing at the sink and, to Jason's shock, holding Tina's gun. She wasn't pointing it at Tina. She was just holding it close to her chest, like she was trying to keep it dry. Jason let go of Jace's shirt, turned, walked toward Dorothy, and held out his hand.

"Why don't you let me take this?" he said.

"Thank you," Dorothy said. "I hate these things."

Jason clicked on the safety, detached the magazine, and released all the bullets into his palm. He put them in his pocket. He had a feeling someone would want to see these, when this was all over. Dorothy took his hand.

Jason watched his son bend down on one knee, next to Daphne, Karson, and the prone Theo, and take Tina's hand in his own. His teenage son's hand dwarfed hers. Jason thought he looked like an older brother caring for a younger sibling. He looked like a protector.

"Miss Lamm," he said. "I know you're scared. But this isn't what you think it is. It's just a drugstore. This is just the guy who owns it. And we need to make sure he's OK."

Tina looked at him, lip quivering, hands shaking, crumpling.

"And then," Jace said to her, so kindly that it could keep the whole world safe, "we can all go home."

Theo closed his eyes and went to sleep.

The situation was under control. Jason had the gun, which was now unloaded and neutralized. Jace was holding Tina's head in his hands while she wept. They were a few keystrokes on David's phone away from having the police in here to clean this mess up. They'd made it. Somehow, they'd made it out of this.

But when Theo closed his eyes, the only thing that mattered in the world, to every single one of them, was keeping him alive.

"What do we do?" asked Karson.

"He needs blood." Daphne looked at the IV tubes on the wall, near the blood-pressure machine. "Grab those," she barked, and Karson and David actually bumped into each other as they both darted for them. Karson got there first and brought them to Daphne. "I've got some needles," she said. "But we need blood."

Dorothy began looking around the pharmacy, but the silliness of her quest stopped her. If Lindbergh's really was the sort of place that kept bags of blood hanging on the walls, shoot, maybe Tina *had* been right.

Then Daphne spoke up. "Look . . . this is, fair to say, not proper procedure, but . . . what's everybody's blood type?"

Everyone blinked at once.

LT. ANDERSON CAREFULLY INCHED HIS WAY INTO LINDBERGH'S, STEPPING through the space where the front window used to be and around the broken glass spread across the linoleum floor. He loved this place, had been coming here since he was a kid. His grandfather used to buy him milkshakes here after his Little League games, would snag him a little Tootsie Pop on the way out to his truck. They didn't make places like this anymore, Anderson thought. You couldn't get a milkshake at a CVS.

His weapon was drawn, his two deputies were behind him, and he was on high alert. His buddy David from the Red Rocket was in here, and he'd told him the situation was under control, but no cop can ever assume any situation is under control. He waded through the water and the mist, wincing at the flashing strobe lights as an alarm continued to blare.

"This is the police," he grunted with as much authority as he could muster. It was convincing. His voice had gotten gruffer in the last couple years, and he found it made his job easier. People immediately respond to a scary-sounding cop. "We are coming back your way. Keep your hands in the air. We are coming in!"

"It's all good back here, boss." David's familiar voice came from the back room, beyond that big black door that had scared the officer when he was a small boy. Why did such a nice place have such a scary door? "I'd have your medics right and ready, though."

"Ten-four." Anderson opened that door.

He turned the corner and saw a big bearded man standing by the sink, behind an only slightly smaller teenager who was obviously his son. They both had their hands in the air. The dad nodded at him the way big bearded men like him always nodded at him—like they wanted to let you know that they were one of the good guys, that they were on your side. Next to him was an older Black woman who looked familiar. Maybe he'd seen her in court at some point? She had her hands in the air too, but not as high, and she gave him no such nod. Anderson was surprised to find himself a little scared of her.

Anderson turned to his right and saw David. His right hand was bandaged, and he looked to be in real pain. He knew David well enough to know he'd fight his way through it. One time Anderson had to respond to a fight at a club, and some guy had smashed a beer bottle against David's head. There was still a little piece of glass sticking out of David's head when Anderson got there. David just chuckled. "Close as I've gotten to having a drink in ten years," he'd said. "Don't look like I've missed much."

Next to David was a Black man Anderson instantly recognized as one of the players from the weekly basketball game he was in with a bunch of guys at his cousin's real estate firm. They always wanted Anderson to play because he was tall and wide, and having a tall and wide player meant you could just throw it inside to him and catch your breath for a second. He'd liked the way the guy standing next to David played. One time Anderson had gotten his legs kicked out from under him while trying to get a rebound, and he'd landed on his head, knocking himself out. When he opened his eyes, the man was standing above him.

"We got you, brother," he'd said, extending his hand. "We got you."

Anderson looked to the floor. To his surprise, one of the nurses from the ER was down there, Debbie, maybe, Denise, nice lady: the nurses out there always had coffee for the cops when they brought people in.

"Hello," she said, looking up at him. He thought she might have been elevating a foot above the ground. "I am glad to see you. We are only going to need a few more minutes."

Behind her, on separate cots, connected by a tube with red running through it, were two people. One was a man lying down, his shirt soaked with blood and gauze wrapped around his midsection. He seemed to notice Anderson looking at him, lifted his left arm in the air, and to the officer's amazement, gave a thumbs-up. Then he winked. The dude winked.

The other person was a woman. She was sitting up, her legs hanging off the side of the cot, clenching and unclenching her left fist as blood pumped from her body to his.

She turned her head toward Anderson and raised her right hand.

"Hello," she said.

Anderson lowered his weapon.

"Hello," he said.

after

Jace had lived in New Orleans for almost two years—a year and a semester, anyway—and he still hadn't figured out the most important lesson of living in New Orleans: how to get the bartender's attention at a loud music club. It was his generic face, he thought, exactly the sort of face that gets glossed over in a crowd. He wasn't handsome, but he wasn't ugly; he wasn't tall, but he wasn't short; he had no scars, he had no facial piercings, he didn't wear glasses. He was Replacement Level White Guy, the face bartenders forever passed by to notice someone who looked more interesting. Jace was not the sort of guy who snapped his fingers or raised his voice or waved his arms to be noticed—he saw those guys, he'd rather not get a drink at all than be one of those guys—so he just stood there, lightly hopping up and down, trying to make eye contact but also trying not to look irritated. It's a tough job, being a bartender. They'd have to see him at some point, right?

A voice came up behind him. "Here, I got you a beer," she said. "I seriously couldn't watch that any longer." He turned around and saw Allie, ducking by the bar while the opening band played.

"Ha, thank you," Jace said. "I'd have gotten one eventually."

"I'm not so sure about that," Allie said. "Fortunately you have connections."

Allie motioned him away from the bar and nodded to a security guy as they edged up to the door to backstage.

"So you didn't have any trouble getting the tickets?" she said, shouting into his ear. Her breath still smelled like cigarettes. She'd smoked the whole time that afternoon at the Labyrinth, the coffee shop on Tulane's campus, and it truly was repulsive: he realized that she was the only person he knew who smoked anymore.

This had been the first time he'd seen her since the week after Lindbergh's, but that first week had been more than enough to bond them forever. It was madness, a whirlwind of police stations and television crews and green rooms, "a full-blown media circus shitshow," Jace's dad had said, and the two people everyone wanted to talk to were the brave teenager who saved lives by talking down his mentally ill former teacher and the promising young rock star who suspended her world tour to come back to Athens and take care of her injured father. They were an instant hit on the circuit, the go-to feel-good storyline, two selfless young people who were able to make something uplifting out of tragedy—two kids who made you feel like maybe the next generation wasn't doomed after all. Neither one of them felt particularly overjoyed to be the public faces of the Lindbergh Seven—Jace would never forget how sweaty he'd get, how his heart would start throbbing, right before the red light of that camera came on—but they did consider it their responsibility, their way of letting everyone else who was there deal with it in private, on their own terms. The others needed the help. A photographer had shown up on the Waller family's front lawn, and Jace's dad had barged out the front door, shirtless, with a baseball bat, threatening to brain the guy if he didn't get off his property. That led to more reporters heading out there, not fewer, so Jace took it on himself to go outside and answer whatever questions anybody had while his father seethed inside. When Allie arrived from Los Angeles the next day, she immediately called Jace—she'd seen him being interviewed on television while flying back—and together they decided to handle all media questions moving forward. She was twenty-five and he was sixteen, but they both felt like the only real grown-ups in the room. It felt like the least they could do.

"Naw, they were right there like you said," Jace yelled back. "Will Call lady didn't even notice the fake ID."

Allie smiled at him. He had been absolutely in love with her on that media tour, the bald rock star with the kind eyes, beamed here from the outside world to stand alongside him during the scariest time of his life. Her hair had grown out since then—it was now all straight and shaggy and bounced all over the place when she was onstage—and she'd told Jace at lunch that it was a little depressing how the band hadn't *truly* exploded in popularity until "I dropped the bald thing." Jace didn't think that was it, though. The first track off Hotel Arizona's new album, "Lightning Strike," was a raging but upbeat light-punk little number that began with a peppy garage-rock guitar riff leading into a signature Allie scream, somehow anguished, fun, and cathartic all once, a *Yaaaaaaawwwwwwwlllllll* that, when Jace first heard it, made him want to leap up and throw himself against the wall. It was an instant four-quadrants hit, thanks largely to Apple using it in an advertisement for their newest Apple Watch, Allie's heart-and-soul soundtracking an impossibly gorgeous twenty-something FaceTiming with her even more impossibly gorgeous friends and flashing her Apple Watch to the camera. The song was everywhere. Jace had actually heard the Tulane band playing a version of it at a basketball game last week. It wasn't as wonderful a song as "Magic"—a song that nearly made Jace weep every time he heard it—but he knew, and she knew, that it was a hit that would outlive them all.

"I don't think they let people play on *Seth Meyers* just because they grew their hair out," he'd told her. That had been last month. Jon Hamm had been the guest. Jace had sat in his apartment with his girlfriend, not really his girlfriend, just a girl who he liked and who liked him but had no larger illusions about what this was, just kids, sharing a box of wine and watching the episode. Seth Meyers introduced the band, and there she was, *yaaaaaaawwwwwwwlllllll*, and he thought of how, right before the camera came on before every interview that week, she would briefly grasp his hand, lean over, and say, "You're so good at this. You're gonna do amazing."

And he did. He did amazing because he had to, and because she was there with him.

"So I, uh, gotta go?" Allie said now. A crowd of people bored with the opening act had noticed her and was gathering around the two of them in a contracting semicircle. Jace was sure this was a pain for Allie, but he didn't mind a bit; there were worse people to be than the last guy the big huge rock star everyone was there to see was talking to before going onstage. One girl was eyeing him curiously, intrigued, and he made a note to keep a look out for her the rest of the night.

Allie took Jace's hand. "It's really great to see you," she said. "I'm glad you're doing all right. Your dad's gonna get there." She looked him in the eye. "We're all gonna get there, OK?"

He nodded, lightly, not sure what to say, and she pulled him in for a hug. "Email me, OK?"

"I will," he said, and then the security guy opened the door and let her backstage and stared at Jace like she'd never been there in the first place, like if Jace tried to get past him to her, he'd break both his arms and not think twice about it.

Jace turned around and saw the bartender staring at him. Getting a drink would not be a problem the rest of the night.

Jace didn't really see most of the Lindbergh Seven anymore. That first week had been a rush, but then there was another mass shooting, and everyone moved on to that one, then the next one, then the next one. All told, it was surprising that they'd made such a big deal of this one. No one had been killed, after all, not even the shooter. That was probably it, Jace figured. People were so desperate for something to feel good about—or at least something not to feel miserable about—that it was simply heart-warming to hear about a mass shooting where nobody died. This was what passed for good news. It didn't last long, though. The next shooting's victims were not so fortunate. Neither were the next one's. Or the next one's.

Jace had always found his father indestructible—impervious

to pain, a slab of granite—but the Lindbergh's incident dispensed of that illusion. He thought his dad might have handled it worst of any of them. The nurse on the scene, famously, went back to work the next day like nothing had happened. She also organized the trip. The trip was the big pivot point. The group had been trading off shifts to sit with Theo at the hospital when she approached Jace. His dad was the one Lindbergh's victim who never visited Theo; he hated hospitals, wouldn't even step foot in one. "People just go in there looking for something wrong with them," Jason said, one of those little bits of Jason wisdom that Jace had once adored from his father and now just made him worry about him all the time.

"Hey," Daphne had said, sitting in the beaten-up wooden chair across from Jace. Theo hadn't woken up yet. They were all more concerned about it than anyone was willing to say out loud. "So Dorothy and I want to go see Tina. I wanted to know what you thought about that."

Jace had no anger toward Mommy Mario. He saw how lost she was—how scared. He just wanted to help her. Jace hated it when people called him "brave," or some sort of hero. He saw someone he cared about, who was in serious trouble, and he helped her. He did what anyone would have done. He believed this as truly and deeply as he had ever felt anything. Anyone would have helped.

"Yes," he said instantly. "I'm in. You won't get my father, though. I hope that's OK." Jace's dad had gone back to work the next day after the incident, but after he threw a screwdriver at White Harold for accidentally puncturing a gas line with a post-hole digger at Coach's house, Buck sent him home. "Don't come back until you're straight," Buck said, and Jace's dad told him to fuck off. After that, Jason would wake up, have a wordless, grunting breakfast, and go out to his garage. He'd come back in time for dinner, sweating, silent, brooding, and then he'd go back out to the garage and drink beer until the rest of the house was long asleep. It was like that for longer than it should have been.

His brother Rick, who had called Jason needing a lawyer, ended up staying with the Wallers for a month, sitting out in the garage with his brother, trying out different bourbons and watching baseball every night. Rick drove him all the way out to Virginia to serve his time, and all the way back a few months later when he was released.

It ultimately was just Daphne, Dorothy, Karson, and Jace who went to see Tina. (David skipped out; he was still pissed about his hand.) The guards at the jail let her, along with her lawyer, meet them in the visitors' room. She was small and frail and wouldn't look anyone in the eye. Dorothy took her left hand. Daphne took her right. Karson sat across from her, with Jace. It was Jace who spoke. He doesn't remember what he said. He was just thinking about that the other day, how weird it was that he doesn't remember what he said.

But then they FaceTimed in Theo. He'd woken up two days earlier, when Karson was on a shift, sitting with Theo's mother and some girl that Theo had been dating. He opened his eyes, looked around, and grinned. He actually did that—first thing. He grinned. The next day Daphne told him they were seeing Tina. "I want in," he said.

He lay there, blurry. "I'm all right," he said. "I'm all right, and so are you." Then they all held hands and Daphne led them all in prayer. And they left. At the sentencing, weeks later, the victims of the Lindbergh's shooting were the only people to stand up on Tina's behalf. Jace's father was in attendance, sitting in the back of the courtroom. He'd been talking to someone, a professional, after weeks of Jace and his mother begging him to. He was doing better. Jace thought he was going to be all right. He was back to coaching this year—said he's got a kid who can hit eighty-five on the speed gun.

At the end, Tina rose and spoke.

"I'm sorry," she said. "I'm sorry. I didn't know. I was so foolish."

She tried to say more, but she couldn't stop crying. The judge accepted the lawyer's guilty but mentally ill plea and sent Tina to the Central State Hospital in Milledgeville, Georgia. She's still there, two years later. Jace went to see her over his last Christmas break. She was very heavily medicated. They played checkers, and then he left. He thought she looked calm—better. Though he supposed he didn't really know her that well.

He was still glad he went.

The opening band finished up, and the crew tore down all their gear and began setting up Hotel Arizona's. Jace noticed that the gear had gotten a considerable upgrade since they were on Seth Meyers's show; the band now had a whole expanded back section for in-house violinists, surely to play that part of "Magic" that always wrecked him. He wondered if the next time he saw them, they'd be at the Superdome. He wondered if Allie would still be able to drop by the bar and talk to him before the show. He doubted it.

Jace ordered another vodka tonic from the bar—the bartender upgraded him from the well vodka and comped him; Jace made a note to wear a Hotel Arizona T-shirt every time he came here from now on, he'd never pay for a drink again—and elbowed his way to his preferred viewing spot, just in front of the sound guys in the middle of the pit. This was the best seat in the house: in the middle, far enough away that you could see the whole stage, buffeted by all the sound equipment behind you so no one jammed up next to you. As long as no one tall ended up right in front of him, it was the perfect music experience. He'd pop a gummy beforehand, lock into his favorite spot, and just let the music take him away. He always went to these shows alone. He found experiencing live music too important, too sacred, to share it with anyone else. He wanted to be able to dance without feeling awkward, or to shut his eyes and just soak it all in, or to just stand there and do nothing at all, without having to worry about whether or not the person he was with was having a good time. He could get lost in it, alone, just riding out wherever the song took him. He thought sometimes this might be his truest self.

The crowd thickened in front of him, and he felt grateful to have his spot secured. As the crew tuned the guitars with their discordant *twangs* and microphone feedback screeched from the speakers, he began to get in his zone. He looked up at the ceiling, then closed his eyes. They'd surely start with "Clamor Addiction," an upbeat number to get the crowd going, then probably "Adam's Apple," an Aerosmith cover that would seem out of character for the band but ended up sounding somehow both ironic and deeply earnest, the way Allie played and sang it, like she was both deconstructing cock rock and blasting it out in her dad's garage. That would have the crowd so riled up right from the get-go that the band could slow it down a bit with "The Plaintive One" and "Haunted Homeland," two slower songs from the first record that the most dedicated fans would revel in while everyone else hit the bar, the bathroom, or both. He'd studied the set lists online. They always planned out their shows so well.

God, he couldn't wait.

As the crew finished up, he noticed a clatter of activity about fifteen feet in front of him, halfway to the stage. A woman, a college girl it looked like, had fallen to the ground—overheated, drunk, or just sick, Jace couldn't tell which. She was awake and alert, but clearly stricken; her wide eyes darted around, confused, scared. Jace instinctively took a step forward—he was a little proud of that, when he thought about it later, proud that his body told him to help before his mind had a second to process anything—but then he stopped and just watched.

Instantly—quicker than Jace had taken his step forward—the sea of people, packed in shoulder to shoulder, cranky from heat and tired of waiting, surely well into an evening of drunken concert revelry . . . cleared out. People, creating space Jace hadn't realized was there, made an instantaneous protective semicircle around the girl. Strangers began waving their hands to the arena's staff. A man, identifying himself as a nurse, kneeled next to the girl, propped her up, cradled her head on his shoulder and wiped her head with a wet towel. Four bottles of water appeared in front of her. A group of burly frat dudes formed a makeshift security team, making sure the girl and those tending to her had enough space. From the back, two venue EMTs showed up with a stretcher, and they got her lifted up, strapped in, and carried off. Her friends followed behind as they whisked her out the exit.

Then everyone went right back to what they were doing. The nurse and the frat guys dispersed, the semicircle filled back with concertgoers, and maybe sixty seconds after the girl had fallen, all was back to normal. If you had looked away from those sixty seconds and then looked back, you wouldn't have thought anything happened at all. Collectively, dozens of people saw someone in need and instantly organized themselves to come to her aid, wordless, among a group of strangers, within a matter of seconds. And then, just as wordlessly, they went back to what they were doing. Jace didn't even see anybody all that put out by it. They simply looked ahead to the stage, ready for whatever came next.

The show was about to begin.

Allie walked onstage, her band in darkness behind her and a spotlight directly on her and her trusty Collings I-35 LC guitar. The crowd cheered, and then, as she waved her arms to shush them, went quiet.

"So, I have to tell you," she said as a few stray dudes whistled. "I am so happy to be here. Isn't it *fucking incredible* to be here?" The crowd roared.

Jace didn't know if she was looking at him. But it felt like she was. When you were listening to a great band, from this spot, it always felt like that.

"You gotta grab this while you can." She snapped her fingers as she said this into the microphone, and she was looking at him, something she knew, even if he didn't.

She tilted the head of her guitar down. She was ready to play. "Let's grab this night, New Orleans!"

The drummer went first, then Allie and her side guitarist jumped in, and the riff that launched a million Apple Watches roared into being, and Allie screamed "*Yaaaaaaawwwwwwwllllll*," and everybody went nuts. Jace felt as if he were being lifted up to the rafters, no longer alone, no longer afraid, bonded to this sound and these *people*—the world behind them, nothing real but what was happening right now, eight thousand total strangers suddenly in the same room, all suddenly each other's closest friends, all carried along together, all lifted, all soaring, all as one, I have to tell you, I mean it, everybody went nuts, everybody just lost their ever-loving minds.

ACKNOWLEDGMENTS

I know writers are supposed to be tortured, sullen types, as if the act of typing words is so unbearably painful that you should consider them heroes for just putting themselves through it. You should know—and hopefully, after reading this book, you can tell—that I am not that kind of writer. Writing is my favorite activity. It brings me active joy to get to do this with my life. So, first off, thank you for buying this book and allowing me to continue to do it. I'd be writing all the time even if no one read anything I wrote, but it's certainly easier to justify to strangers I meet at parties when people do. So thank you.

This book, just like the last one, and surely each one to come, does not exist without Noah Eaker, my editor and friend. He is so good at this, and I am so spoiled by working with him; my plan is to keep writing books for him until one of us dies. (Probably me.) My agent, David Gernert, has been my friend for nearly twenty years now, and the best person to have in your corner for just about anything: He's such a good guy that he almost makes you want to root for the Mets. (Almost.) Thanks as well to the whole Harper crew: Edie Astley, Elina Cohen, Chris Connolly, Kate D'Esmond, David Koral, Joanne O'Neill (what a cover, right?), and Miranda Ottewell.

One of my favorite things about writing books is that by the time the reader sees the finished version, a whole bunch of people much more intelligent than the author have read it and told the author all the stuff the author got wrong . . . so the author can then make it look like he had it perfect from the start. (Which the author absolutely did not.) Thank you, then, to my early readers, my friends who lent me their expertise and their time: Matt Adair, David Barbe, Amy Blair, Elizabeth Earl, Aileen Gallagher, Tim Grierson, Will Haraway, Carrie Kelly, and Tim Kelly.

Special thanks must also go to Chris Bergeron, Chris Bohjalian, Mike Bruno, Joan Cetera, Mike Cetera, Tommy Craggs, A. J. Daulerio, the David family, Joe DeLessio, Denny Dooley, Dave Eggers, Sam Fox, LZ Granderson, Benjamin Hart, David Hirshey, Jenny Jackson, Kim Keniley, Stephen King, Andy Kuhns, Jill Leitch, Mark Lisanti, Matt Meyers, Bernie Miklasz, Adam Moss, Matt Pitzer, Lindsay Robertson, Richard Russo, Trevor Stevenson, Wynne Stevenson, Susan Stoebner, David Wallace-Wells, Kevin Wiegert, Ben Williams, and Kevin Wilson. This book could only take place in Athens, so I also must thank my Georgia crew: Lindsey Adair, April Allen, David Allen, Lyric Bellotte, Hannah Betzel, Josh Brooks, Lillie Brooks, Hailey Campbell, Bertis Downs, Jennifer Duvall, Scott Duvall, Krystal Elliott, Seth Emerson, Kenny Esho, Kelly Girtz, Haley Graber, Bryan Harris, Todd High, Cristi Moore, Leandra Nessel, John Parker, Michael Ripps, Sallie Starrett, Chas Strong, Kingsley Strong, Tony Waller, and the Welter family.

It's an old saw that it's not until you get older and have children of your own that you realize just how much your parents sacrificed for you, and how much they put up with from you. So, uh, sorry about *all that*, Bryan and Sally Leitch. There are huge swaths of both of you all over this book: I would say I only included the good parts of you, but they're all good parts. And lastly, to my family: My wife, Alexa, and my sons, William and Wynn. Alexa is always the first person to read anything, and the voice I trust the most. She has also been extraordinarily patient with my constant fretting about this book, to say the least. It is also important that she know just how proud of her I am: Thank you, Alexa, for everything. And watching my sons get older has become the joy of my life. I'm so grateful for how wonderful they're becoming . . . because we're all going to need them and all their friends to fix everything we all have broken. Anytime I get too frightened, I look at the three of them and I know it's all going to be all right. I love you guys: Thank you for putting up with me.

ABOUT THE AUTHOR

WILL LEITCH is a contributing editor at *New York* magazine. He also writes regularly for the *New York Times*, the *Washington Post*, NBC News, *Medium*, and MLB.com, and is the founder of the late sports website Deadspin. He writes a free weekly newsletter that can be found at williamfleitch.substack.com. He lives in Athens, Georgia, with his wife and two sons.

Read More by Will Leitch

"*How Lucky* asserts that 'the world is a terrifying place these days' and the novel explores those terrors quite convincingly, yet I was heartened by the depth of Leitch's writing, his obvious love for the world and what it could be. He imbues his hero with a kind of hopefulness that comes from seeing the worst and finding some way to keep living."

—Kevin Wilson, *New York Times* bestselling author of *Nothing to See Here*

"If the truth is to be found in humor—and it is—then let Will Leitch lead our people's revolution. He's everything that's right and funny and true in American sports."

—Jeff MacGregor, *Sports Illustrated* special contributor and author of *Sunday Money*

HARPER PERENNIAL

HarperCollins*Publishers*
Discover great authors, exclusive offers, and more at HC.com.